A Home out of Ashes

Sisters of Stella Mare Book 3

Annie M. Ballard

Happy Reading!
All the best,
Annie M Ballard

Devon Station Books

Contents

Chapter 1

I t was Willie Martin's time.

The darkened hallway was quiet at eleven-thirty. Rett walked purposefully toward the one door with light under it. Pushing it open, she stepped into a puddle of warmth, soft music, and gentle lighting. Angelica sat beside the bed, holding Willie's hand. She looked up.

"Hey, Willie, Rett's here," she said clearly. The old man on the bed made no sound, no movement. He was wizened, bald, and his chest barely moved, but Rett smiled at him and patted his other hand.

"Hey, Willie," she said. "We're right here with you." Willie's body inhaled, making a loud, rough-sounding noise. Death was near.

"Audrey is here too," Angelica said, nodding toward the tablet angled toward the old man. Rett peered into it.

"Hi, Audrey," she said to the woman on the screen. "How you doing?"

Audrey sniffed. "I wish I could be there," she said. "But I'm so glad you and Angelica are with Dad."

"He knows you want to be here," Rett said comfortingly. "You were just here last week."

"But did he remember?" Audrey demanded tearfully. "Oh, I just wish..."

Willie took another torturous breath.

Audrey sobbed. "Is that it? Oh, Dad, I love you. I love you." She dissolved in tears.

Angelica stroked Willie's forehead with her free hand. She was humming. Willie's body exhaled and lay very still. Angelica, still stroking his forehead, rocked back and forth, eyes closed, still humming.

Rett reflexively checked the clock though, waiting for another breath, but there were no more. Willie Martin had died.

Angelica leaned over and kissed his forehead, then tucked the sheet up to his chin. Rett spoke to Audrey. "Do you want to stay here with him for a while?"

The woman on the screen wiped her eyes. "No, that's okay. There's probably stuff you guys have to do."

"Nothing that can't wait. This is your time, Audrey, if you want it."

"Yeah, okay," she said. "Yes. Thank you. I'll just stay here for a little while."

"I'm so sorry, Audrey," Angelica said to the screen. "He was such a dear man."

Audrey nodded. "Yes. Thanks, Angelica. You really took good care of him, I know."

"Bye, Audrey."

Down the hall at the nurses' station, Rett made the needed calls while Angelica typed notes into Willie's chart. Darcy, new to evening shift, returned from doing rounds.

"Anything going on?" Rett asked.

"Mrs. Mac is having nightmares again, but other than that I think most everyone is asleep. How's Mr. Martin?"

"He's gone," Angelica said. "It was a good one."

"Good? Dying is good?"

Rett looked at her. "Well, dying is inevitable. How you go, that's not as clear."

"What makes a death good? I don't get it."

Rett pushed her chair away from the desk. "Well, I guess it depends on who's talking. I'm thinking practical. No firetrucks in the middle of the night. No unnecessary drama. Angelica, what do you think?"

"Willie was ready," she said, her face glowing. "He told me so last week. And his daughter was with him, even on video, and we were there, and he could just step off into whatever is next. It was beautiful to be with him."

Darcy looked incredulous. "Beautiful? I'm scared of dying people. I don't get you."

"I used to be like you," Angelica said. "I didn't know that death was just like birth. Just part of life, you know, the whole circle thing."

"I don't want to have to be with somebody dying," Darcy said firmly. "That's not what I want."

"Well, you might be in the wrong place," Rett said. "People don't go home from here. They live here until they die, and hopefully they'll die here and not have to go to the hospital."

"I like the living part," Darcy said with a wry smile. "Maybe I should be working with children."

"You're really good with the old people," Rett said. "They love you. Don't let being afraid of death keep you from doing something you love."

"If you let them, they'll teach you how to be with death and dying," Angelica advised. "You can learn a lot about living from being with people at the end."

Darcy sighed. "Maybe I just have to try to be open. But I'm glad you guys will sit with them, 'cause I am not volunteering for that."

"Fellow travelers, check out the time," Rett said. "It's almost time for shift change. Let's make sure we've got everything in good shape for Darryl and Ellen."

A couple of nights later, things felt a lot more chaotic. The phone in the supervisor's office—cubicle, really—had been ringing for a long time when Rett was finally able to grab it. Nighttime meds were going out, their newest resident was struggling to settle in, and Mrs. Mac was having nightmares as usual. Helping Darcy and Angelica with residents was her priority, not some ringing phone. Her impatience showed as she answered.

"Streamside Residence. This is Rett."

"Loretta?" She recognized the voice.

"Hi, Mrs. Adamson," she said.

"This is Sherryl Adamson," the woman said, apparently not listening. "It took you long enough."

"Hi, Mrs. Adamson," Rett repeated, rolling her eyes at Angelica, who had returned to the nursing station. "Busy night."

"I need to talk to you. Is this a good time?"

Angelica grinned at her and grabbed a file folder. Rett leaned across the desk and shut the glass door. Maybe a little privacy, she thought, but like everything else here, not too much.

"As good as any, I guess," she said. She sat on the stool behind the little desk, admiring her neat stacks of papers and folders. Maybe they'd found someone new to add to the evening shift. That would be a welcome change. Rett juggled the schedule weekly and when someone was sick, things got very difficult.

"There's no good way to say this," Mrs. Adamson said. "Loretta, I'm putting you on administrative leave."

"What?" Rett was suddenly riveted. "Did you say you're putting me on leave?"

"That's right. We need you off site and on leave. At the end of your shift, please take your personal belongings, and leave your key cards in the safe."

"Wait, what? What's this about?" Rett's heart was racing. Administrative leave meant somebody had done something wrong, something terrible. "Did I do something? What's up?"

"I can't really say any more, Loretta. Just go home and don't come in until further notice."

Rett shook her head in frustration. "Go home? Now?"

"Well, no. At the end of your shift."

Rett's insides were boiling, a reminder to use her calm, measured tone, the one she used with recalcitrant residents. Her voice dropped as she said, "I don't think you can do that, Mrs. Adamson. I need to know why."

Mrs. Adamson's voice got a lot louder. "Actually, Rett, as your employer, I have discretion in this situation. You're on leave and you'll stay there until I tell you to return to work. It starts after your shift tonight."

"I'm off for the next four days anyway," she said, suddenly feeling weak. "Won't this get sorted out?"

"Rett, don't argue with me," Mrs. Adamson said firmly. "I don't like to do this, but I don't have a choice." Her voice softened. "You've always been a good employee. When there's more to tell you, I'll let you know. In the meantime, you're on leave with pay, and please don't discuss this with anyone else. Except Harry."

"Mrs. Adamson..." Rett said, but her boss hung up.

Rett slowly set the phone back into its cradle. Feeling a little sick, she went to the first floor kitchen and put on the kettle. She leaned out the doorway and gazed back toward the supervisor's cubby. The hallway was quiet, finally. Angelica and Darcy had returned to the nurses' station. The sound of their quiet chatting with an occasional giggle was muted.

Rett poured tea for herself and sipped at the cup. Her stomach settled slightly with the mundane activity and warm drink. She made tea for her co-workers and headed back down the hallway.

"Hey, you two," she mustered. "Good job tonight."

Darcy chuckled. "Yeah. Folks were a little restless, weren't they?" Darcy was new, or at least new to this shift. Rett didn't know her well. Angelica was another matter. Her dark brown curls were as familiar to Rett as her own children's locks. She and Angelica had been working together for almost eight years, since Rett's first child, Mason, was born. Angelica was younger, a single mom, and solid. She was exactly who Rett wanted around when things got a little rough, like tonight.

Part of her wanted to burst out with her news, but she could hear Mrs. Adamson's voice in her head: "Don't discuss this with anyone else." Rett was certain she meant other staff. Rumours and truth travelled quickly through the staff and the residents. Even the families knew what was going on with most people, and Rett treasured that aspect of her work. Streamside Residence was a family, no doubt, even though it was a peculiar and very extended family. Staff celebrated milestones with residents and their loved ones, helped families through the inevitable struggles of illness and end-of-life care, and made strong connections. Darcy had been on day shift, so she was already part of the family, but evenings had their own character.

"Anything unusual going on?" Rett asked.

Angelica gave her a sharp glance.

Darcy said, "Like what?"

Rett shrugged. "Like anything unusual."

"Sara's getting married." Darcy offered a bit of gossip about a day shift co-worker, and the conversation turned to chatting about staff.

"Well, I've got charting to do," Angelica said.

"Yeah and I guess I have rounds," Darcy added. "I hope it's a quiet night. I'm pulling a double."

"Really?" Rett was puzzled. "Did I schedule that?"

"No, Ellen from night shift asked me to pick up."

Rett looked at the younger woman. "Well, just remember to take care of yourself, too. You can't do everything anyone asks even if you want to."

Darcy laughed. "I'll be fine. But thanks."

"Also, I need you to let me know about schedule changes, okay?" The words came out automatically, but Rett wondered who'd be taking that responsibility now that she was officially off. *Not my problem.* She clenched her teeth.

A kerfuffle down the hall sent Angelica to see what was going on, and Rett went to the washroom. Closing and locking the door behind her, she perched against the sink. The only place where nobody was likely to hear her, she felt safe enough to call Harry despite the late hour. He'd be up packing anyway.

"Hey," he said.

Her chin quivered at the sound of his voice. She tightened her throat against tears.

"Rett?" he asked. "Are you there? Was this just a pocket dial?" His voice was warmly amused.

"Harry," she choked out.

"What? What is it?" She could imagine him folding his clothes and tucking them carefully into his suitcase, efficient and gentle. His hands were always busy at the house; cooking, soothing a fevered child, making art with the kids.

"They're sending me home," she said, and coughed.

"Are you sick? What's the matter, Baby?"

Almost undone, she shook her head to clear it. "No, not sick. Sherryl Adamson called and said I'm on admin leave."

She could imagine the look on his face. "What? What for?"

"Who knows? She wouldn't tell me, just told me not to discuss it."

"That's so weird," he said. "Why do people get put on admin leave?"

"For lots of reasons, I guess. If there's a clinical error. Maybe if you're cooking the books, or something like that. Something criminal. I do know that they use this a lot since the takeover."

"Since Briar Ventures bought Streamside from the Adamsons?"

"Yeah. I know a couple of people who were sent off for a week or so, then came back. Nobody knew why."

"I bet there was plenty of speculation."

"Oh, yes. If there's no obvious reason, people will make stuff up. We need something to talk about here, you know." Rett suddenly wondered what people would think when they found out. "Like now. I have to make stuff up about myself," she said. "There's some nasty irony there. I don't know what I did. She wouldn't tell me, just that I am officially sent home."

"So...are you coming home?"

She gave a harsh laugh. "At the end of my shift. Yes, she's sending me home, but I have to stay because there's nobody to cover my shift."

"Well, they must not think you're a danger to anyone."

"Harry!"

"Well, of course, I know you're not."

"Right."

They were silent for a moment.

"Do you want me to change my flight? I can go next week," Harry offered.

"No, absolutely not." She was firm. "I already took four days off to get us reorganized, and maybe this will all blow over. You've waited a really long time for this, Harry. We're not changing plans now."

Back at the nurses' station, the eleven o'clock news came on the TV. Angelica, behind the counter, grabbed the remote to un-mute it.

"...the untimely deaths of long-term care patients at Streamside Residence in the last six months. Maritime News Network has heard from family members who are concerned about an apparent pattern."

Rett and Angelica stood motionless, listening. Rett whispered, "Residents, not patients," but continued to listen.

The news item cut to video of a young woman holding a microphone out to a middle- aged white couple. "I don't know how Mum could have died so sudden," the man said. "She was fine and then she was gone."

The reporter commented, "Mr. Jones is only one of several family members who have questions." She turned to another person. "Ms. Shelly Smith, tell us about your loved one."

Ms. Smith was holding back tears. "My grandpa was old, sure, but he wasn't dying. And then he was dead. I want to know what Streamside is going to do about it!"

The reporter noted, "Briar Ventures, which owns the Streamside Residence in Saint Jacques, did not respond to our request for an interview. We'll keep following this up, and you can follow us to stay up to date with this breaking story."

Angelica clicked the mute as the screen went to an ad, and the two women gazed at each other. "Untimely? Come on," Rett said.

"Who were those people?" Angelica asked. "I think I know that man; Marielle Grant was his mother, right?"

Rett could feel her own frown lines. "Yes, I think so. He must be Elle's brother. I don't know if I met him. Did you?"

Angelica nodded. "Only once. Elle was in to see her mother almost every day. I didn't even know there was a son until a week before she died. When he showed up, he didn't seem to understand his mother was dying."

"That happens," Rett said, thinking about her own mother's death, four years ago. "You try hard to avoid thinking about it, as if that might keep it away."

"And Shelly, you know her, right?" Angelica asked.

Rett nodded. "She's grieving for sure. She was so close to her grandfather. I think he practically raised her, so it has to be hard to let go."

Angelica sat down behind the counter. "You know, we were both working when they died."

Rett shrugged. "Most people die at night. We work nights. Goes with the territory."

"Evenings," Angelica corrected. "Evening shift."

"Right. A lot of evening shift happens during the night."

"Death gets people all upset," Angelica noted. "I understand missing people when they're gone. I miss them too. But being with them while they pass feels so special. Like a privilege. It's like helping people find their way home, in a way."

"You do it well," Rett said. "Only now the Maritime News Network has decided there is something weird about it." Rett dropped into a chair beside Angelica. "This kind of scrutiny didn't happen before Briar Ventures took over."

Darcy came down the hallway. "Why so glum? Only another hour until you two get to go home."

Angelica sighed. "You're right. I guess I better get my work done." She left the nurses' station.

Rett wondered if she should tell Darcy what they'd just heard. Probably not, because she would hear soon enough. The night supervisor would be in shortly.

"Me, too," she said, and headed toward the medication room. "I mean I've got to get my work done."

"Okay. I'm charting," Darcy announced and sat in the chair recently vacated by Angelica.

Rett, counting and logging meds, had trouble paying attention. Did Mrs. Adamson put her on leave because she was at work when those people died?

That didn't make sense. Most residents were extremely old, ill, or both. People died. It had happened during her entire tenure with Streamside, though it happened less since the takeover. Policy had changed then. The corporate office wanted them to transport residents who were close to death, send them to the hospital. That way, the death was recorded as a hospital death, not a death at the care home. For some reason, that made a difference to Briar Ventures.

Another hour, Rett thought. Then I can focus on Harry and my kids. Suddenly reminded of her new status, she rummaged around for a plastic bag. Somehow she had to pack her personal items and get out of the building without other staff noticing. Yeah, right, she thought rudely. It's not my secret I'm on admin leave.

Chapter 2

I t was close to 2 a.m. when Rett tripped over Harry's loaded backpack in the garage. Nearly falling, she swore and the motion light
flicked on with a vicious glare.

Harry's laptop bag and coffee mug. The backpack was really a suitcase, just soft and with shoulder straps. Everything pointed to Harry's
imminent departure. Gut churning, she hoisted her own briefcase,
while tucking the stuffed plastic bag under her other arm. She shoul-
dered her way into the dark, quiet kitchen.

She dumped her armload on a chair, swiped at her eyes with her
sleeve, and reached for a bottle and one of the fine scotch glasses
she'd rescued from her father's house clean-out. She was sitting at the
kitchen table, pouring another, when Harry padded into the room.

"There you are," he said. Looking at the scotch and her piled up
belongings, he asked, "Rough night, eh?"

"I'm sorry I woke you," she said.

"No, you didn't, not really." He got himself a glass and sat across from her. She poured him a drink. "I was mostly awake. Too much to think about."

"Didn't you hear me swearing in the garage?"

"What? You were swearing?"

Her tears flowed again.

"This really has you upset, doesn't it?"

She sniffed loudly. "I don't seem to have any control over this. Sorry." She got up and buried her face in a tissue, blowing her nose. "It just keeps coming."

He went to her. "Oh, sweetie, it's okay." Cradling her shoulders, he led her to the sofa in the adjacent family room, pulled her down beside him. She carried the tissue box with her.

"Is this about administrative leave? Or about me going?" Harry asked, tucking her head onto his shoulder.

"I'm okay with you going," she sniffled. "I think I am."

"But..."

She sat up abruptly. "I can't believe she sent me home."

"Yeah, that's weird. What happened?"

Rett's tears were flowing freely now. "I don't know, Harry," she nearly wailed. "I don't know what's going on."

"It makes no sense," he said, thinking out loud. "You're in charge, yet they don't tell you what's going on."

With an effort, she settled her breathing and wiped her face again. "Did you see the news tonight? I don't know, but I wonder if it's related."

"I saw the blip about the deaths, yes. I wondered."

"We had another death this week, but honestly, that happens. Corporate management doesn't like it when residents die on site, but the residents would rather be in familiar surroundings than at the hospital."

"What about with a DNR? If you've been told Do Not Resuscitate, do you still transport them?"

"Well, obviously, if we have a DNR order on a person, we're not going to call an ambulance. They've made their wishes clear. But anyone who hasn't signed that paperwork, Briar wants transported. It's inhumane."

"What about these people on the news?"

"If the news is just looking at deaths, they aren't getting the whole picture. They don't know who had a DNR and who didn't. That's private information."

Harry patted her shoulder.

"Anyway, I don't even know for sure that being sent home is about the news story. It could be about something else. Except I can't imagine what that is. This whole thing just stinks."

"I'll say. Being sent home for something you don't even know about is hardly useful."

"It's almost like they think I'm a hazard at work." Her tears flowed anew. "Like I would do anything to hurt anyone."

"Of course you wouldn't."

"Or like I'm incapable of doing my job."

Harry said nothing, shoving his glasses up his nose.

She glared at him. "What, you think I'm incapable?"

He frowned. "You're the most capable person I ever met. You've also been pretty stressed out this last year."

She tossed off his comforting hand. "Stressed but not to the point of making mistakes at work." Her mind went to last week, when she'd forgotten to log in a shipment of linens and left it for night shift to handle. "Or no mistakes that endanger anyone."

Harry got up from the couch. "You haven't really been happy with work since the change in ownership."

She followed him to the kitchen. "Not happy with work didn't mean I was ready to get sent home. It doesn't make me a bad nurse. Or a bad supervisor."

"Of course not." He turned to her. "The big question is whether it's paid leave or unpaid." He waggled his eyebrows. "You know."

She snickered despite her tears. "Yeah, it's paid. That's the only decent part."

"Then maybe we just take it as a good thing," he suggested. "You'll be home for a few days with the kids. Then life goes back to normal."

"I guess." She sobered again. "It's going to be a different normal. I had already taken my days off to help the kids get adjusted. It's going to take time."

He leaned into her shoulder. "How about you getting adjusted? Aren't you going to miss me?"

She scoffed. "You know I'm going to miss you. I'm prepared to handle that. But the kids might need me around while we get used to not having Daddy."

He looked pained. "I'm just going out west to school for a little while. It's not like I'm leaving or dying or something."

She sighed. "You're pretty important around here, you know." Wrapping her arms around his waist, she leaned her forehead against his. He pulled back to look in her face.

"I'm fine, Harry," she said. "We're going to be fine. It's okay for you to go."

He sighed and leaned back toward her. "I know. I'm not really worried about you or the kids. I know you have things totally under control."

She smiled a little. "Good. I do. Let my previous display of erratic emotion be erased from your memory." She paused. "You're not worried about us here at home, but is there something else?"

"Me," he answered. "I've never been away from you and the kids. It's been years since I tried to do this kind of work. I'm going to be in the field with a bunch of young wunderkinder and I don't know how that's going to go."

"You are a wunderkind, too, aren't you?"

He scoffed. "The time for that is long past, I'm afraid. I'm the stay-at-home-parent with a big gap in their resume, remember? I just don't know if I've got the drive to do this work at the level that's expected."

"Sounds like you're suffering from second thoughts," she said. "Totally normal. Nurse Rett says so." She gave his shoulders a little shake. "I'm sure you'll be wonderful in Dr. McGinty's lab, and you don't have to worry about a thing back home. You've been the mainstay of the family for all these years, propping me up, and now it's your turn. Get that Ph.D. Make your career a priority."

"Leaving you to do it all. How are you going to do what it took two of us to do before?"

"It's not the same really. With all the kids in school, and Amrihta on tap for childcare in the evenings, we're all set. No babies anymore. Mason and the twins will be in school in a couple of months, and I got this. No worries."

Still, a question perched in Harry's eyes. "It is a lot to handle even with the kids in school. But now, I can see that a brief administrative leave might make the transition easier."

She winked at him. "Maybe the universe is providing. See, every little thing..."

He picked up the quote. "...gonna be alright." She started humming the old reggae tune.

"Rett." He rarely used her name. "You know, there's no shame in asking for help if you need it."

"Help." She scoffed. "What would I need help with? Kid stuff, home stuff, family...I got this. You're going to be the best researcher ever and we're all going to be fine."

The kids were sparkly eyed at 5 a.m., though Rett and Harry were not. Rett pulled the van out of the garage to let everyone get in. Harry carried his huge backpack and Mason took his laptop case, while the girls fought over who could hold his shoulder bag, what Rett called his man-purse.

The Saint Jacques airport was on the outskirts of the small city, and it was early, so traffic was light. Maggie was singing to herself in her car seat, and Callie was gazing out at the landscape. Mason suddenly called up to the front. "Did you say goodbye to Charlie?"

Harry, in the passenger seat, turned around. "I did, Mason. I don't think he understood what's happening, but I said goodbye."

"Yeah," Mason agreed. "A dog probably can't get it that you're going to be gone a long time."

"No, he probably thinks it's like every other day. Will you help Mum take care of him?"

"Sure," Mason said. "I can walk him myself already."

"Maybe you can be in charge of feeding him, too," Harry suggested.

"No, me!" Callie shouted. "I can do it!"

Rett glanced over at her husband, whose dark eyes and pale skin spoke of fatigue and worry. "We'll get it figured out," she said, in her best nurse-in-charge voice. "No worries. Hey, kids, why is Daddy going out West?"

There was a chorus from the back seat. "To save the planet from climate change."

"To go to school and learn new things."

"Daddy, will you bring us back a lynx?"

"Oh, no, remember? We study animals where they live," Harry reminded. He glanced at Rett. They had heard this question before. "We don't take things out of the forest, right? But we do take something...who remembers what?"

"Pictures!" The three voices were nearly in unison, though Mason's voice was lower and less enthusiastic.

"What's up, Mason?"

"I'm going to miss you, Dad," he said.

Harry sighed. "I'm going to miss you too, buddy. But remember we have a schedule for video chat, and you can call me on Mum's phone anytime."

"Anytime?" Mason perked up.

"I can't always answer, because I'll be in class or out in the woods or doing something, but if you call me, I promise I'll call you back."

"Okay." Satisfied, Mason relaxed into his car seat. The girls were chatty and busy with toys. Rett expertly slid the van into a drop-off spot on the Departures level.

Harry climbed in the back of the van to kiss the kids and retrieve his man-purse while Rett waited with his luggage on the sidewalk. He walked toward her, his crooked grin twisting her heart, as it always did. She hugged him tightly. "You're going to be wonderful."

He spoke into her neck. "I hope so. You guys will be fine."

They pulled apart. Rett said. "Got everything?"

He shrugged. "Hope so. I love you." Slinging the strap of his laptop bag over his shoulder, he picked up the handle of his backpack and turned toward the building.

Rett wanted to watch him leave, to even stay and watch his plane take off, make sure it made it off the ground safely, but her heart was squeezing already. Plus the squabbling was escalating in the van. So, instead of watching Harry get smaller and smaller, she threw herself into the driver's seat.

"Okay!" she said brightly. "Who wants french toast sticks?"

Five-thirty a.m. It was going to be a long day.

Chapter 3

"Helen, can you call me back?" Rett left her sister a voice mail message. "I'll be at home all night. Not at work." Her voice caught on the last word.

Harry had only been gone four hours but Rett felt like she'd been missing him for a month. The kids were cranky and so was she. Despite her inclination to let them sit in front of screens all day eating junk, she prevailed on them to go for a hike. She drove them to the harbour island that held the Nature Center Park.

Rett grabbed the backpack they always had ready for adventure. It contained Harry's homemade cookies from the freezer, water bottles, wipes, and jackets. She added Charlie's leash and started off down the path, but the kids didn't follow her.

"What? What's going on?"

"We don't go that way," Mason explained. "When we come with Daddy, we go this way."

Holding back her sigh of irritation, Rett said, "Okay, then, let's go Daddy's way." The path around the island was a loop, so it didn't much matter to her. But she wondered how much she'd be hearing about how Daddy did things over the next few months.

Maggie twittered at the chickadees and Callie ran down the path until she got tired and wanted to be carried. ("We can take a little rest, but you're going to have to walk, Cal.") Mason brought his rock collecting bag and was selective about his specimens, as he called them.

Maggie wore out before they made it halfway. Rett was peering at her phone, trying to decide if it was shorter to turn around or to finish the loop. Mason came over.

"Are you lost?" he asked, sounding so much like his father that Rett stared in astonishment.

"Are you?" she retorted, and they both giggled. "No, I'm just trying to see how fast we can get back to the car. Your sisters are tired." She gave him an appraising look. "Are you?"

He straightened up. "I'm okay. I can finish the hike."

"You probably know this place better than I do, so what do you think? Turn around or keep going? What's shorter?"

Mason looked thoughtful. "Turn around. We aren't even past the broken-down tree yet, and that's not even halfway. Do we really have to go back already?"

Rett looked at Maggie, languishing on the side of the path. "Yeah, I think so. We'll come again when everyone has more energy."

Getting back to the car was slow, but they finally arrived, and the kids piled in. As Rett closed the hatch on Charlie and the backpack, her phone rang.

She answered, looking in the windows at the children. She reached in to click the key over so the air conditioning could run.

"This is Rett," she said in her most professional tone.

"Loretta Madison?"

"That's right," she said, trying to place the voice.

"This is Constable MacLeod from the Saint Jacques detachment. I'd like to set up a time to meet with you."

She leaned against the dusty van. "Why? What's this about?"

She listened while her stomach clenched. The police were investigating a pattern of deaths, he told her. "Deaths happen in long term care."

He spoke calmly, quietly. "Of course they do. That's expected. But sometimes we need to investigate. When can you come in? Or I could come to see you at home."

She coughed. "No, that's okay. I'll come in." So much for her uninterrupted time at home with the kids. "Tomorrow?"

"Can you make it today at four?" he asked. "We'd like to get this wrapped up."

Wrapped up sounded good. "Maybe I can. I just have to get a sitter. Yes, I will be there."

She clicked off and sent her sitter a text.

Can you come over today? At three-thirty, just for a couple of hours? I've been called in.

She figured she didn't have to say what she'd been called in for. Hopefully it would be just as easy with the police. Maybe the police wrapping something up would get her back to work sooner. If their investigation and her leave were even related.

Well, she couldn't solve it now. Rett put it out of her mind and climbed into the van.

"Okay, guys," she said cheerily. What would a good mother do next? What would Harry do? "Who wants to go to the library?"

There was a chorus of sound from the children. The intent was unclear though, so she turned around to look at them. "What?"

Maggie was cuddled up with her stuffed puppy. Mason shook his head. "I want to go home," he said. "Can't we just go home?"

"Home!" Callie shouted. "I want to go home!"

Maggie, startled, began to cry.

"Okay, okay," Rett said. "Home it is. Maggie, you okay?"

The child stuck her thumb in her mouth and nodded, puppy in arm.

"Okay, then, the clan is going home. Hey, Mason, can you look at Charlie? Is everything okay back there?"

"He's good," Mason reported, after looking into the far back of the van. Charlie was silent, a dog of few complaints.

Tumbling out of the van at home, the kids were crabby, the dog was dragging, and Rett actively hallucinated another cup of coffee. She heated leftover coffee while the kitchen boiled with kid activity.

"You guys hungry?" she asked as she pulled out bread and peanut butter, and poured cups of milk.

"I want blueberries," Callie said plaintively.

"Of course you do," Rett said, digging the box out of the fridge. "Here, put some on your plate."

She took a long drink of her warmed-up coffee, feeling it hit her upset stomach and imagining the caffeine starting to circulate in her veins. "Ten minutes," she muttered to herself. "I'll feel better in ten minutes." She stopped Callie from taking all the blueberries, put some on Maggie's plate, and agreed when Mason asked if they could watch cartoons while eating lunch.

"Daddy never lets us," Mason said.

"Well, you've got Mum today," she said briskly. "So be grateful for that."

"What's grateful?" Maggie asked.

Rett's tired brain didn't have an answer, but Mason jumped in. "It's when you say thank you inside your mind."

Rett giggled. "That's a good description. It's like being thankful."

"Like when you say thank you to somebody?" Callie wanted to know.

"When you really mean it," Mason said.

Rett sighed and pulled at her coffee again. These children. These wonderful, irritating, precious children. Today she felt they were her responsibility in a way they never had been before. Harry had always been there, always been the main person for the kids, really, except for breastfeeding, and even then, he had taken parenting seriously. He'd get up with the babies, change them, bring them in to be fed, always (well, almost always) the first on scene when there was a kid need.

Now it's me, she thought. Well, it's just kids. Everyone manages their kids. It'll be fine. Harry needs to have this time to move his own career forward. She was grateful for Harry while she built her career and he held up the sky for the kids at home. Now she could be grateful for this time of being the main parent. It's a wonderful opportunity, she told herself, watching Maggie systematically smash her sandwich crusts into the carpeted floor, much to Charlie's delight. She grabbed up a damp cloth and took it to Maggie, pointing out where she should clean up the rug behind Charlie's busy tongue.

Chapter 4

The police station in Saint Jacques was a modern building, glass-fronted and made of stone. Little distinguished it from an office building, except the many black-and-white cruisers in the parking lot. She straightened her shoulders and reached for the door. Tired didn't matter right now. Let's get this wrapped up, she thought.

Constable Bryan MacLeod, ginger-haired, was young, maybe her sister Dorie's age, Rett noted with surprise. He was affable too, offering her tea and leaping up with alacrity when she suggested coffee. "I'm a nurse," she reminded him. "We live on this stuff." She sipped at the brew in the paper cup.

"We do too." He nodded at her. "It's almost always fresh."

"So," she said, setting down her cup. "What's this all about?"

He smiled at her but said nothing, just fingered the pen on the clipboard in front of him.

"Well? Constable?"

He smiled again. "Impatient?"

"Well, yes, I am. You said we could get this wrapped up. I have three kids at home. I'm looking forward to wrapping it up."

He nodded. "I'm sure you are. We're going to wait for Detective Gallant though. She'll ask the questions, and we'll be recording the whole process. I'm sure she'll be right here."

Rett sighed deeply. She had been on time; what was wrong with this detective that she couldn't be punctual?

The door opened to admit a tall brunette woman in a tailored suit and low heels. "Rett!" she said, smiling.

"Hello, Kathryn."

Constable MacLeod looked uncomfortable. "So, Detective Gallant, this is Rett Madison, shift supervisor from the Streamside Residence. It looks like you know each other."

"Rett and I were in university together," Kathryn said, looking at Rett. "Here we are."

Rett shifted in her seat. "Here we are."

Kathryn kept looking at her, smiling. "I'd like to catch up, but we have a job to do here."

"Yes," Rett agreed. "Let's get on with it."

"Okay." Kathryn tapped her stack of folders on the table and then opened the top one. "Constable MacLeod here is going to take notes, and I'm sure he already told you that we're recording this interview."

Rett shook her head and frowned. "Kathryn, what is this? Recording me? Why so formal? What's going on?"

Kathryn leaned forward. "This is formal, Rett. We've launched an investigation of a pattern of resident deaths at your facility. We need information."

Constable MacLeod asked, "Can you tell us your full name and your job?"

"Are you investigating me?" She scowled.

"Not necessarily. But you're the primary evening shift supervisor and you have been for a long time. We need to know what you know."

"Should I have a lawyer here or something like that?" Rett thought of Helen in Ottawa. Could she get her sister home in a hurry? Could her sister represent her anyway?

Kathryn leaned back again. "Do you think you need a lawyer?"

Rett sighed. "Of course not. Let's just get it done."

"Okay, then," Kathryn said. "Please state your name and employment."

Ninety minutes later, Rett was in her car calling Helen. This time her older sister answered.

"Nice to hear your voice," Rett said, acerbic. "I've just been interviewed by the police."

"Really? Why?"

"Apparently they think we're killing off our residents at Streamside," she said. "Like it isn't normal for old people to die in long term care. Where else would they die?"

"Wait, what's going on?"

Rett sighed. "My boss put me on admin leave last night, and today the cops interviewed me, picking my brain for any weird details, stuff I probably don't even really remember."

"Oh, Rett," Helen said. "Are you in trouble?"

"Well, it depends on what you mean," Rett said. "Nobody's accusing me of anything, but my manager sent me home from work."

"I saw that item on the news about deaths in care. You know I always read the news from home. It never occurred to me that you'd be implicated."

"Well, why would you?" Rett said practically.

"Right. I assumed it was grieving families who wanted to blame someone for something."

"That happens, and I understand it. But I don't know what they mean by a pattern."

"It does sound mysterious."

"There's no mystery, you know. Lucky people get to die with their families around them, like Mum. Some people don't have that situation, but we want them to have a good passing too."

"There's nothing wrong with that."

"The new corporate office prefers for us to send residents to hospital when they are dying. Something about their statistics, but most people want to die in their own beds. That includes their beds at Streamside if they've been living there for a while. It's their home."

"Of course it is. It's not Briar Ventures that's got issues though. It sounds like there's a public concern."

Rett felt her brow smooth out a little. "I'm starting to get a sense of this. Maybe some people are upset and calling the news, the news is poking around for a story, and Briar Ventures is doing damage control. A PR thing that unfortunately got the police interested."

"You're not too impressed by Streamside's new ownership, are you?"

"I don't think they know a lot about the work we do," Rett agreed. "I wouldn't be surprised that they want to deflect responsibility for people who die at the residence."

"Keeping up appearances?" Helen asked.

"Well, it could explain a lot," Rett said. "Annoying but not dire. The police want to wrap it up fast. I could be back at work in a few days."

"Didn't Harry leave today?" Helen asked. "Sorry, I forgot that this was the big day until just now."

"Yes, he did. Five-thirty this morning. I worked last night too. The kids and I have all been up since before dawn."

"Ugh! You must be exhausted."

"Not me. Caffeine gives me superpowers and nighttime is my best time," Rett asserted. "But I was pretty low a few hours ago."

"Listen, hopefully this whole thing will just go away. But keep in touch, sis, okay?"

"Yeah. And someday we can have a conversation about you, too, Helen, okay?"

Helen laughed. "My time will come. See you."

The rest of the week passed in a blur. She got used to going with the flow of the day, following the kids' energy, giving the girls nap time as needed, and drinking coffee and watching shows with Mason while they slept. They ate takeout every night. She knew Harry's principles would never have permitted so much screen time or fast food, but she wasn't Harry, was she?

She walked the dog late in the evening with the baby monitor on her hip, wandering around the yard and up and down the block, not going far but being outdoors. She took the kids on bike rides, to the swimming pool, and, one sunny day, they drove to Stella Mare to visit her father.

"How's it going without Harry?" her father, James, wanted to know.

"It's good," Rett said, pushing Maggie on the old swing set in the far backyard. "Not that I wouldn't rather have him at home, but I never had this much kid time on my own before. I kind of like it. I might make a good stay-at-home mom."

James chortled.

Stung, Rett glared at him. "Well, Dad, that was nice."

Smiling, he shook his head. "That was a little unkind, wasn't it? Sorry, Rett. I just can't quite see it. You're meant to be running the show. Getting everyone to do their best, work as a team, get the job done."

"Yeah," she said, uncomprehending. "You can do that being the home parent. Like Harry. He was the leader, plus all that thrifting, recycling, composting, and otherwise saving the planet."

"No disrespect to Harry. He's done a great job. But you–you're not Harry. Children are a little less predictable than employees. Or even patients."

"Residents. We call them residents."

"Right. Residents. As an almost-resident myself, I can say that having a firm hand on the tiller like yours would be a good thing. Maybe not so much at home though."

She folded her arms.

"Maybe you just haven't had a chance at the home stuff." James back-pedaled. "I could be entirely wrong."

"I think you'll see." She lifted her chin. "I can be as good as Harry at this stuff."

Patting her shoulder, he said, "Of course you can. I misspoke."

She didn't tell him she'd been put on administrative leave. When she'd be called back any moment, she saw no point in worrying him.

Chapter 5

Harry's apartment was tiny. He could stand up in the living room, holding his phone, and turn in a circle and show the whole place to the kids. It worked, but there wasn't much space for anything more than a pull-out couch, a tiny table for two, and a chair. His kitchen was a cooktop, air fryer, and a small refrigerator. But the price was right. For someone finishing his doctoral research and maintaining a family back home, cheap was most important.

Besides, he didn't expect to spend much time here. He'd be in the lab or out in the field a lot, but it hadn't happened yet. By the end of the week, he was tired of all the reading and bored being in his little place. His new supervisor was due back in the office from field camp today. Harry had an appointment at ten.

He was out of the apartment by six-thirty, walking the mile to the campus, eagle-eyed for a good coffee place. He tossed back an espresso and asked for an Americano to go. Rett's coffee habits had rubbed off on him.

The summer morning was warm, even this early, and at this latitude. He checked his watch, then headed to the library to hunker down until his appointment. It might be a good time to call the kids. They were always up early, and besides, there was a two-hour time difference.

"Good morning," he said, mindful of other people in the library. He popped his earbuds in quickly, before broadcasting the sound of childish excitement.

"It's Daddy!" Callie dropped her mother's phone in her excitement. Maggie apparently took advantage.

"Hi, Daddy. Are you saving the planet?"

He laughed "Hi, peanut. No, not yet. What are you guys doing?"

"Mum is hitting the washer, and me and Callie are having a snack."

He stifled a chuckle. "She's hitting the washer?" He could hear Rett in the background, talking to Callie.

"Where's Mason? And what's all over the floor?" He tried to see beyond his five-year-old's tousled head. She helpfully turned the phone so he could see. "Just some cereal, Daddy. Charlie's going to take care of it. No problem."

"Well, I'm glad it's no problem. What are you kids going to do today?"

"Mmm, well, Mum said we had to clean up. She's got some work stuff to take care of. I'm going to watch *Frozen*."

"Again?"

"Daddy, I'm trying to get to one hundred times. That's a lot."

"That is a lot. Don't you want to do one hundred push-ups or something?"

She giggled. "No way. That's too many."

"How about one hundred books to read?"

"Daddy! I already read a million books."

"Well, you're probably right about that. Is Mum coming to the phone?"

She dropped him on the kitchen counter and went running, shouting as she went. "Mum! Daddy's on FaceTime."

Waiting, he listened hard. The washer was running, the TV was on in the background, and dog toenails moved across the tile floor. Finally he heard Rett coming.

"Hey," she said warmly, as she entered the frame. "How are you?" She looked tired.

"I'm good," he said. "A little bored, if you can imagine that."

She laughed. That was a good sign. "No, I can't. I'm up to my elbows in stuff. Just like usual."

"I've got a meeting in half an hour with Dr. McGinty, my supervisor," he said. "I've never actually met her in person."

"That's right," Rett said. "I'd forgotten that. She'll love you."

Harry shrugged. "That's less important than me getting my project off the ground. The sooner I can do that, the sooner I can get home."

Rett scoffed. "Listen, we love you and all, but your work is everyone's top priority. You take your time, make your connections, collect your data, whatever."

"Whatever?" He laughed. "What exactly do you think grad student research assistant life is like?"

"Oh, you know, a continuous round of cocktail parties, faculty dinners, all tweed jackets with elbow patches, and very elevated discussion."

"Mum!" Mason's voice was insistent. "Maggie took the remote. It's my turn to pick the show!"

Harry stifled a laugh. "Elevated like that, you mean?"

She turned away for a moment to say, "Mason, you are the older brother, and I expect you can figure out how to handle this." Then she turned back. "No, that was escalated. Big difference." They shared a smile.

"How's the, uh, work thing?" he asked awkwardly. He knew the kids could hear, even if they were too busy fighting to listen.

She shrugged. "Nothing new. I've checked in with Kathryn Gallant, that detective, but there is no news. They're still looking into those deaths. As if there was something criminal about people dying. I'm just caught in the politics of it. The company had to look like they were doing something, so they put me on leave."

"Still stinks."

"Yes, but at least nobody is blaming me for anything. It seems to be all optics. I don't like being caught in somebody else's view of how things are supposed to look. Reality is reality. People die. If they are lucky, they die where they live and not in some unfamiliar hospital bed."

"You're getting red," he said.

"Yeah, okay," she said, settling back down on her stool. "Preaching to the choir. You've heard me on this topic before."

"So still no news on going back to work?"

"Not yet. I don't know what to tell the sitter. She's expecting full time childcare work."

"Can we just pay her like half salary or something until you go back?"

Rett looked doubtful. "Maybe. I wish I knew how long this is going to go on."

"I know you'll figure it out," Harry said. "I have every confidence in you."

"I think I appreciate that," Rett said. "I'll let you know what we work out."

"Don't worry 'bout a thing."

Without missing a beat, she added, "Every little thing..." and together they said, "gonna be alright." She giggled.

"Okay," he said. "I've got to go to my meeting, so can I say bye to the kids?"

"Sure," she agreed. "And bye from me, too." She smiled before calling the children to come throw kisses to Daddy.

Harry slipped the phone into his backpack with a wave of sadness. Home was warm and cluttered, noisy and familiar. This library would probably feel more like home in a few weeks, but right now, it still was like a foreign country.

He resolutely hiked his bag to his shoulder and headed out to his supervisor's office.

Joyce McGinty, Ph.D., he read on the brass plate beside the heavy oak door. The clouded glass showed nothing of the inside of the office, except the bright light within. He knocked, straightened his shoulders, and pushed his glasses up his nose.

"Come!"

The office was like something from a movie; floor to ceiling bookshelves filled to overflowing, a massive oak desk cluttered with papers, two overstuffed armchairs and a straight chair in front of the desk. A woman sat behind the desk, tiny and birdlike, out of proportion to the imposing surroundings. Her imperious bearing belied her tiny frame, however.

"Sit," she said, gesturing to the straight chair.

"Hi," he said. "I'm Harry Brown."

"Yes." She squinted at him. "My new grad assistant. Welcome."

"Thank you," he said. "I'm glad to finally meet you."

"You're not what I thought you'd be. It's hard to tell on paper."

"I'm not?" he said, curious.

"Older. You're older. That's probably a good thing." She stood up. "Now we've got a week before we head back out into the field, Harry, and we've only got four weeks there, so no time to waste. Let's go to the lab, so you can meet the team." She picked up a laptop. "Or at least Marie. She's sure to be there."

She headed out and down the hall without a backward glance, Harry hustling behind. They travelled a bewildering maze of corridors, staircases and fire doors to a small room on an upper floor. Dusty light filtered in through high windows. The old plaster walls were pale, contrasting with the ancient wooden floor, scarred from the footsteps of generations of grad students, all determined to make their marks in science. His heart lifted. This is where he would do what he'd been waiting to do, study and write, see what he was capable of. He briefly recalled his thesis supervisor, just before Mason was born, saying, "Harry, don't stop here. You have a contribution to make." Then there was Mason, and Harry's agreement with Rett that he'd take the at-home parent role with their child. Harry breathed in the air of the lab and sneezed.

"Bless you," said a voice from the corner. From behind a wall of computer monitors rose a vision of tumbling brunette curls attached to liquid dark eyes and a welcoming smile. "Ahh, the new research assistant," she said.

"Oh, Marie, you are here," Joyce said. "Good. This is Harry. Get him oriented."

"Hello, Harry," Marie said, reaching to shake his hand. Her grip was firm, and she held on a little longer than he liked. Pulling his fingers away, he looked around the room and away from her gaze.

"Okay," Joyce said. "I'll leave you to it." She turned to the door.

"Wait," Harry said. "What about...?"

Joyce turned back, frowning. "What?" She cut him off. "Team meeting tomorrow. Marie will tell you what to do. There's no time for fiddle-faddle. One week and we're back out there."

"Okay," Harry said weakly. She marched out the door, and he turned back to Marie, eyebrows raised.

"She's not at her best on campus," Marie said. "She's happiest out in the field. But don't worry. Things might be confusing at first, but you'll get the hang of it."

"Okay."

"There are four of us on Joyce's summer team. Denys and Alpha have both been here for two years. We'll add a couple of undergrads in September, when they arrive for classes. I'm project manager."

"How long have you been working with Joyce?"

Marie scoffed. "My whole adult life, I think. She's amazing, you know. You probably studied her theory of ecosystem movement when you were an undergrad."

Harry shook his head. "I'm a little older than that," he said with a laugh. "She'd started publishing when I was doing my master's though."

"Anyway, I've been here for a long time. I manage Joyce's projects. They take priority, so it's hard to focus on my own." She gave a little laugh. "Except the university has limits. I have this year to finish or else."

"Or else what?"

She shrugged. "You know. Out on my backside without a degree. Ten years and nothing to show for it."

Ten years. Could it really take more than ten years to finish a Ph.D.? Harry felt cold just thinking about it.

"She needs you to keep her projects running, but if you finish yours, you'll leave. That sounds like a bind."

"Well, I'll be leaving, finished or not," she said briskly. "But let's get you started. We need to get your accounts set up, but you don't need lab space. We're in the field for the whole summer, and you could be there all fall."

"Really?" Harry felt disoriented. "She said four weeks."

She looked at him curiously. "She'll be out for four weeks. Her schedule isn't necessarily ours. Things change around here. Don't get tied to your expectations."

Well, so much for his studio apartment. He made a mental note to let his landlord know he'd be a very short-term renter.

She made a phone call, then turned back to Harry. "The tech will be up around noon to get you logged on. You'll have access to our internal database. First rule of the lab: data stays here. You can access anything you need remotely, but you don't download anything."

"Even my own data?"

She looked at him seriously. "Any data collected while you're working in this lab stays here. Joyce has a document she'll have you sign on Monday in front of the team. It's a thing."

"Okay," Harry agreed. He wasn't about to rock this boat, not when it had taken him years to finally get aboard.

Marie made more calls, then sent him to Human Resources. When he returned an hour later someone from technical services had arrived to set up his system link. Time passed, Marie at her own keyboard, Harry sorting himself out, until his morning coffee was a faint memory. At two, food became a requirement.

"Marie? Sorry to bother you, but where's a good place to get lunch?"

She looked up, frowning. Then her face cleared. "Food. Yes, what a good idea. I get busy here and forget. Yes, let's go find some food. I'll show you a great little sandwich place. Come on."

Despite Rett's belief that she'd be called back to work any moment, the moment didn't arrive. On Friday, when she was scheduled to work the evening shift, Rett called Mrs. Adamson.

"Oh, Loretta," Mrs. Adamson said. "Yes."

"I'm looking forward to getting back to work," she said. It was almost true. Mostly she wanted to know what was going on. "When I talked to the police detective, they said they'd be wrapping things up quickly."

"You talked to them?"

"Well, of course. They asked me."

There was silence during which Rett could hear papers being moved around. "Mrs. Adamson?"

"Yes, oh, yes, Rett," the other woman said. "I didn't know you'd talked to the police. I wish you'd told me."

"I did just tell you. I don't even know what this leave is about, and I want to get back to work. What's the delay?" She tried to keep her voice calm and soothing, the way she might talk to an agitated patient, but it was difficult.

"We are still waiting for the police to close the file," Mrs. Adamson said, with great finality. "What that happens, we will call back the people who will be coming back."

"Wait. You mean there's more than me? Who's out? Why?"

"Rett, I won't discuss this with you."

"Well, who will? I've been the full-time evening shift supervisor for years, Mrs. Adamson. Who will tell me what's going on?"

"Rett, that's enough. I can't disclose more information to you. You'll hear from my office if, and when, you can come back to work. In the meantime, you're on paid administrative leave. I would appreciate it if you let me know if the police talk to you again, and I appreciate your discretion in not talking with other employees."

Rett was sure her eyes were popping, her mouth was open, and she seemed to have lost her voice. But her hearing was fine. There was a distinct click as Mrs. Adamson hung up on her.

To heck with discretion. She'd been quiet for nearly a week, awash in shame about an unknown something that was costing her the right to go to work. Whatever that something was, she wasn't the only one affected. Who else?

Pondering over her contacts, she sent a quick text to the night-shift supervisor.

Her phone rang immediately. "Why didn't you call me right away?" Ellen asked. "I should have known something was up when they asked me to add three shifts a week."

"Are you really working that much? Is that okay?"

"Not really, but I expected it to be short-term. But it's been five days and I'm just hearing from you now."

"Did you know I was on admin leave?"

"No." Ellen was suitably shocked. "I just thought you took days off because of Harry going away to work."

"Well, that is true, but that was planned. No, actually I'm barred from the workplace. Who else is missing?"

"Well, Angelica."

"Angelica! Who else?"

"That's all I know about, and only because I've had to work extra. You know you can't keep secrets in a place like this. I'm shocked I didn't know you were on leave."

"Well, now you do." Rett felt impatient.

"Why? Why you and Angelica?" Rett didn't like the curiosity in her voice.

"I have no idea. I was hoping you'd know."

"There were reporters hanging around the other night. Mrs. Adamson showed up in a big rush one evening, but Darcy was already talking. Mrs. A. was some annoyed." Ellen sounded like she relished this information. "People got stirred up by that MNN story, for sure."

Rett felt exasperated. "Old people die. When they go to long-term care, they don't expect to go home. I don't get it."

"They think you've been killing them off?" Ellen chortled.

"That is not funny under any circumstances," Rett ground out. "Cut it out."

"Sorry. But you know, stupider things have happened. Emotions get high and people start saying things."

Maybe, thought Rett. But stupid things like that don't happen to me.

"Yeah. Well, I didn't do anything wrong, and I want to go back to work, so keep that in mind."

"Will do."

Later, Rett poked around on the internet for Darcy's interview. It was amazing how many little news items the network had gotten out of that original story. The news website had trickles of information for the last week, including an abortive attempt to get a statement out of Mrs. Adamson ("I'm sorry but you're on private property here,") and Darcy tearfully saying to the camera how hard it was to be with dying people.

Rett grimaced and snapped her laptop shut. The sooner this quieted down, the sooner she could get back to work. She wondered briefly about Angelica. Should she say something? She'd already broken the rules by talking to Ellen. She sent a quick text. *Thinking of you. Hope you're well.*

Chapter 6

The next week was a long one for Rett and the children. June was Rett's second-favourite month. Not always the warmest, but she and Harry loved taking the kids to Saint Martins to explore the caves that were open at low tide. Last year, they had rented a cottage on Grand Manan. The island in the Bay of Fundy was a long ferry-ride across the water, where the foghorn could ruin a night's sleep but it was so beautiful that it didn't matter. No vacation this year, Rett thought glumly. Or maybe...

She called her sister Dorie.

"Busy? Want to come out to Grand Manan for a couple of days with the kids and me?"

Dorie was breathless, as usual. "Rett? Hold on. Let me get this guy towelled off." Dorie was probably washing a dog. Her youngest sister bathed and groomed the dogs at her sanctuary for old dogs.

"Okay, what? You're going away?"

"Well, maybe. If I can round up another grownup to hang out with."

"I don't think I can, Rett. Sorry. I can't leave Chad with all the work here, and we haven't been able to hire anyone yet."

"Hmm."

"Besides, don't you have to work?"

Rett paused. "I didn't tell Dad, but I'm on leave. Admin leave pending an investigation."

"No way. Investigation of what?" Dorie's disbelief was clear.

"Listen, you can't talk about this. I don't want Dad to worry about anything."

"Yeah, okay," Dorie agreed absently. "Oh, wait, is this about the deaths on the news?"

"Yeah, I guess so." Rett heard her own words, and her heart sank a bit. "Or I think so but nobody has confirmed that for me."

"Chad used to work for them, you know. He said they'll make news when things get slow."

"I guess that's what investigative journalism is," Rett said. "In this case, I don't think they're investigating anything real."

"But you're off work! You've been so tired lately. Maybe this is a break you need," Dorie said.

"I don't need this much time off. It feels terrible actually. It isn't like being on vacation."

"Why not? You get paid. You don't go to work."

Rett scoffed. "It isn't like that. I'm waiting every day to get called back. My babysitter is probably going to quit before we get started and the kids are going a little stir-crazy. Plus it's hot."

"No wonder you want a couple of days on the island. I can't though."

"Okay," Rett said. "That's fine. Listen, really don't tell Dad, okay? I don't want to worry him."

"You can count on me," Dorie said stoutly.

"You sure?" Rett asked. "I remember when you couldn't be trusted to keep Mum's Christmas gift a secret."

"You forget, sister, I'm a real grown up now," Dorie said with a laugh in her voice.

"You're right, I do forget," Rett said. "Bye now."

There would be no vacation. What was Plan B?

Harry developed a bit of routine during the week before field camp. An early morning run, home to shower and dress for work, walk to the university, all day perched in the lab learning how analyses were done, quick meals with Maria and Denys and Alpha, culminating in his video chat with the kids before they went to bed. Then there were hours to fill with reading, to catch up on being out of his field for the past eight years.

Friday evening, Maria reminded them all to be at the lab early the next day. "She wants us ready to go before five on Monday," she reminded them. "Everything has to be ready in advance."

"So, what do we have to do?" Harry asked.

Denys laughed. "Oh, you'll see. Listen, just come ready to work. Tomorrow we'll load up. You'll be tired."

Starting early on Saturday, the four finished packing and loaded the two trucks they'd be taking into the field. Harry enjoyed the experience. It was a new way to connect with his colleagues. His back and shoulders felt pleasantly tired when they finished. The four went out for a beer afterwards.

"We should let Harry know what to expect," Maria said.

"Yes, please," Harry agreed. "I'm willing to listen to anyone's words of wisdom about working out there."

"Well, first we have to drive forever," Alpha deadpanned. "It's at least twelve hours, isn't it?"

"Really? Are you sure?"

Marie pulled up a map on her phone. "They're right," she said. "Look here."

"Wait. Is this the site? I thought..."

She looked at him, eyebrows lifted. "I told you. No expectations."

"But I don't even know..." Harry stopped. He didn't know if his work could be completed in this setting. This was not at all what he'd thought it would be. He looked at Marie and subsided. "Okay. I'm dropping my expectations."

"Good idea. If you have expectations, you might think you can be prepared," Alpha said.

"Ha," Denys scoffed. "I'm not sure you can prepare for it."

"Ooh, Denys, what's that about?" Marie teased. Even Alpha looked up and smiled.

"They're teasing me about being scared in the woods," Denys said to Harry. "They don't remember what scared me." He mocked-glared around the table.

"Now you're scaring me," Harry said with a grin. "Let's hear it."

Denys leaned forward. "I grew up in the woods, up in northern Quebec. My father, he worked in the woods, always. He still prefers being way out instead of being inside. He supported all us kids with cutting and hauling logs, and made a whole business of it. He hoped I'd go into the business, but I disappointed him, obviously."

His eyes darkened briefly, then lit up. "Anyway, so I'm not afraid of the woods. I grew up in the woods. But we were out late on my first field trip, two years ago in August. Like we're going to be in a few weeks. We were out so late it was getting dark."

Harry looked around the table. Even though Marie and Alpha had presumably heard this story, maybe many times, they were rapt.

Denys' voice dropped. "I was out a long way. I knew my way back, it was familiar, but in the waning light the trees even looked different." He paused, took a drink of his beer. "I knew I needed to get back. I was on my way when I realized I was being watched, followed. I didn't see anything or hear anything, but I knew it, right in my bones. There was a chill inside of me. I looked around but couldn't see anything, of course. They are skilful hunters, know how to hide themselves. I turned back toward camp and started to hurry, but I couldn't shake this feeling of being watched, being followed, being tracked." He took another drink.

"So I knew they were after me. I worried about the camp. If I led them back to camp, we would all be at risk. It was one thing for me to be stalked and hunted, but did I have the right to take them right back to where my friends and colleagues were waiting? I decided I would take a different route, a devious one. Maybe I could throw them off.

"I had my compass, of course, and I knew where camp was, so I made a plan." Denys' voice was softer now, and Harry leaned forward. "I veered to the east, because I knew there was a stream there, thinking I could lose them in the stream, where they couldn't use scent. So I hiked to the stream and then hiked in the water, downstream, but still not directly to camp, a kilometre or more. When I stepped out, I waited."

He took another sip of his beer. "My mouth gets dry, just telling this story. Anyway, I waited, and then I heard the smallest sound, a crack of a twig, and I knew, I knew, they were still on my trail." His voice got louder. "Truly scared then, I started to run. Running, I knew I made so much noise that anybody could tell where I was, and I couldn't hear the noise of them behind me, but I was terrified. I was so scared that I ran right up against a cleft, a rock wall, basically, and had to turn northward again, the wall on my right, the woods thick, and darkness deepening, and no longer did I know where I was in relation to the camp. I felt my heart ready to burst and a scream in my throat but I was running and then I fell and knocked myself out."

Harry's chest was tight. He unclenched his hands with effort and wrapped them around his glass.

Denys took another drink and then went on. "The next thing I knew, I felt a grip on my arm and someone, something, flipped me over. My eyes were squeezed shut, but I had to see...what was hunting me? I heard a terrible growling and roaring and opened my eyes to see—Sasquatch!"

With that, the three burst out laughing. Marie elbowed Harry. "Did he get you?"

"You guys," Harry said, and chuckled. "Gotta try to scare the new guy, right?"

"It's reasonable to have respect for the wilderness, for the woods," Alpha said. "People get lost or injured, many people who take precautions and have good skills. It's an unpredictable environment."

"Not unpredictable," Denys argued. "We just don't have all the parameters to make the best predictions."

"Did you at least take a picture?" Harry asked. "My kids would love to see a picture of Sasquatch."

Denys laughed and continued his discussion with Alpha. Marie turned to Harry and asked, "Kids? You have kids? Plural?"

"Oh, yes, I do," Harry said with a smile. "Three of them. Mason is eight and his twin sisters are five."

"And their mother?"

"What about her? She's thirty-eight. Is that what you were asking?" He smiled at her, liking a chance to tease a little.

Marie smiled back. "No, just, how is she about you being out here for a long stretch? Are you guys together?"

Stunned, Harry answered, "Yes, of course we are. She totally supports me being here to finish my degree. It's been a long time coming." He didn't want to defend his years as a stay-at-home parent to her. "What about you? Kids? Family? Partner?"

"No," Marie answered shortly. "None of the above. I've been working here with Joyce since undergrad."

"Does that preclude other interests?" Harry was curious.

"It has for me," she said. "I'd rather not discuss it, actually."

"Okay," he said mildly. "That's fine. Maybe you can tell me what I should be bringing on this four-week, expect-the-unexpected, trip? I have everything on Joyce's list, but what do I really need?"

"Scotch," Alpha said. "Everybody seems to require scotch." With a burst of laughter, the group energetically engaged that topic. When they left the bar, Harry had a list of additions to his pack to acquire before Monday at 5 a.m.

Sunday afternoon, he talked with Rett. "They tell me there's no cell coverage out at the camp, but we go into town on Thursdays, and that's a good day to check in with everybody. Apparently it's also when the data gets sent to the university, we pick up supplies and a bunch of things have to happen."

"Only once-a-week contact? Not even email? That's going to be weird."

"Yeah, I don't like it either. Apparently my wishes are the last thing on anybody's list. I'm the new guy."

"Are you excited?" She sounded a little wistful.

"Yeah, I am," he said. "Not jump up-and-down kind of excited, but it is pretty cool to think about getting out there. I've never done real field work. I'm excited to see really old boreal forest for real, not just in a video."

"I thought you were studying permafrost."

"Permafrost underlying boreal forest. The biggest carbon sink of the planet. To literally study climate change where it's happening. Yeah, I'm excited."

She smiled. "It's nice to see you so excited, truly. You'll take lots of pictures for us non-scientists, too, right?"

"Of course. Don't I always take pictures?" He chuckled gently. "Digital cameras are the greatest invention ever."

"I don't know. I kind of liked visiting you in the darkroom," Rett said dreamily. "You know, way back when."

"Those were some good times," he said huskily. For a moment, he could recall the feeling of her hugging him from behind as he leaned over a developing tray, her warmth inciting his own. Those pre-kid days had their moments.

A sudden ruckus rose on the other end, Charlie barking and Mason shouting. "Hey, you guys," Rett said. "Hold on, Harry."

Mason came on the line. "Hi, Daddy. Mum lets Callie watch cartoons all day. And eat gummy bears."

Harry sighed. "It sounds like you're tattling, son. You like gummy bears, don't you?"

"Yeah, I do."

"Maybe you could just enjoy it. I'll be back in a few months. You can help Mum, okay?"

"But she used plastic bags. I wish you were here," Mason said. "She doesn't do things like you."

"Well, no, she wouldn't, because she's her own person," Harry explained. "Things don't have to be the same to be good, Mason. We've all got to be flexible here. Okay?"

"Okay," Mason said begrudgingly. "Mum wants to talk again."

He heard Rett in the distance. "Okay, everybody outside. Now! You, too, Charlie."

Then her voice was closer as she picked up the phone. "They're out." She was a little breathless. "Did you get the list of my latest faults? I'm contributing mightily to climate change, not like Daddy, who does everything right."

"He'll get used to it," Harry said. "It does surprise me though. What's going on?"

"People get inflexible when they're anxious," Rett said. "We see it in residents. I didn't expect to see it in my kids though."

"Yeah, well, I expect he'll soften up. Don't take it personally."

"I'm trying. I would love to be able to run a low-waste system like you did, but right now I'm just getting through."

Harry wished he could hug her. "You're doing a wonderful job. I appreciate everything you and the kids are doing to let me have this chance."

"I am so proud of you," she said, eyes glistening. "I know you'll do a great job out there. We're all counting on you. I hope you love it."

He chuckled. "I expect I will, but I don't have to. I just have to get there, do what Joyce and Marie tell me to, and figure out a project for myself. Collect the data and come back home." He thought about Marie's statement all data stayed in the lab and wondered how that would affect his plans to complete his work while at home. Well, that problem was for another time.

"I know the details aren't all clear yet," Rett said.

"I am coming back home," Harry corrected. "The only unclear part is when."

"Right," she said slowly.

"Tell me about things," he invited. "We haven't talked without the kids. What's up with work?"

She harrumphed. "Work is still a mess. Ugh."

"It's really bugging you, isn't it?"

"It sure is. I don't do well just sitting around, as you know."

"Three kids, summertime. I bet you're not really sitting around."

"Well, no, of course we're not. But still. It's so frustrating. Work should fish or cut bait, Mum would have said."

"There are even more colourful metaphors," Harry said with a grin. "Like spit or get off the pot, as my father would have put it."

"I don't think Harold would have said 'spit,'" Rett said, grinning back. "I just wish they'd figure out that I didn't have anything to do with those deaths and get me back to work."

"Is that what the issue is?"

"I guess so. The police interviewed me, the news keeps harping on a pattern, and Dorie told me that Chad told her that Briar Ventures stock has fallen. Nobody from work has said why I'm off though. I believe it's just about optics."

"You're paying a big price for some company's optics."

"All of us." She was sober. "You, and me, and the kids, we're getting squeezed."

"Maybe I should be at home," Harry said.

"No, you should not," Rett stated with some aspersion. "We discussed this. I have this under control. You just need to call me and let me vent every now and then."

"You're a rock, you know that? I could throw myself into this work, but only if you're okay. I appreciate how you're handling stuff."

"That's what we do. We're a team. At the moment, there's a little more distance than usual, but nothing else has changed."

Harry was not as sure about that. "Well, we've kind of switched positions, but of course we're a team. I've got to go finish packing."

"I've got to wrestle these kids to bed. It's past bedtime here. They get up early."

"You get up early," he reminded. "They're your kids. But I get it. It's been a week, and I think my brain adjusted to the time change, but I remember it's late at home."

"I miss you, Harry, especially at bedtime," she said softly.

"I miss you too. After tonight, I'll be on a cot in a tent out in the woods somewhere. I'll be missing you, and missing our bed at the same time."

"Ooh, no shower. You'll be ripe."

"Streams and lakes. I'll be clean but parts could be frozen off."

"In the summer?"

"Take a look at the latitude we'll be at. I'm taking lots of wool and fleece. I'll call you on Thursday. And I sent you the satellite phone contact in email, in case of emergency."

"Let's not have any emergencies. Bye, Harry. I love you."

"Love you, too." He hung up with a sinking feeling, but resolutely he turned his mind to the work at hand. Get ready for field work.

Chapter 7

When Mrs. Adamson finally called, Rett was picking her way across the wide mucky low tide beach at Saint Martins. Cassie sat with her legs in the small stream that drained the salt marsh as the waters of the bay continued to withdraw. Digging with her hands, Maggie made a hole at the edge of the stream and giggled as the water poured in and eroded the sides. Mason climbed the red rocks a few meters away.

"This is Rett," she said, straightening her spine. "Hi, Mrs. Adamson."

"Loretta." She didn't sound cheerful.

"I'm glad to hear from you. I hope you're calling me back to work."

Silence. Then Mrs. Adamson sighed heavily. "No, Loretta, I'm not calling you back to work. I'm calling to tell you that your status has changed."

Rett's chest was tight. What could have changed without her return to work?

"What are you talking about?"

"We're putting you on leave without pay, effective at the end of this pay period."

"Without pay? What are you punishing me for?" Equanimity crumbling, her voice got louder. "This is unacceptable. You can't do this. I haven't done anything wrong."

"I certainly can do this, Loretta," Mrs. Adamson retorted. "You forget yourself. You're at the center of an investigation, and Briar Ventures is not going to continue to support you in your leisure."

"In my leisure! I'm here because you won't let me work. This is the most messed up thing I ever heard of. And what investigation? Nobody's talked to me about anything." Well, except Kathryn Gallant, and she wasn't making office policy.

"Loretta, contain yourself. I won't be harassed."

"I'm not harassing you. You haven't explained anything to me. What happened? My daily work, my reputation, and now even my source of income, all gone because of something you won't even explain. This just stinks to high heaven. What's going on at that corporate office of yours, anyway?"

The silence was of a connection severed.

Rett wondered when she'd been hung up on. Hopefully before that entire tirade flew out of her mouth. She winced, thinking of what she'd just said to her boss. But then, it was so unfair. As the adrenaline surge receded, Rett's eyes filled. What had she done?

Mason called to her from the rocks, and the little girls, muddy and wet, were heading his way. Rett swiped at her eyes, stuck her phone in her shorts pocket, and lifted her chin.

"Coming!"

Pondering the state of her finances was no fun. She chickened out and told the sitter by email her services were not needed, but she couldn't bear to look at her bank balance. She snapped her laptop closed, perhaps a little hard. Her face was warm.

"What's wrong, Mum?" Mason asked.

She pushed her hair back. "Nothing, Mason. It's just grownup stuff. No worries." She looked at his concerned little face. "Really. No worries for you. You can go play."

He stayed though, looking at her. "When are you going back to work?"

"What? Now you want me to go to work? I thought you liked having me at home," she said cheerily, but her insides twisted. She knew she was misdirecting, but she didn't want to have to discuss her employment situation with her eight-year-old son. She squatted to his eye level. "Listen, buddy, everything's going to be okay. I don't know when I'm going back to work. I'll be sure to let you know."

"But Mum, why aren't you going? Did they find somebody they like better?"

Rett laughed. "I don't think so. It's not supposed to work that way. No, there's just some confusion at work right now, and Mrs. Adamson wants me to stay at home."

"I do like it when you're at home, but parents have to work." He still looked worried, so she changed the subject.

"What are you going to collect on our hike today?" she asked, and they started a discussion of the rock colours at the park compared to the beach.

Later, she thought about his words. If she were off very long, they would have to hire someone into her position, and it could very well be someone they liked better. Just that idea made Rett unaccountably jealous, as if the Streamside Residence couldn't function without her. It took effort but she pushed away the thought. No point in worrying about something that hadn't happened yet. She had enough to worry about.

She called Helen for advice. Her older sister was gratifyingly angry on her behalf.

"Cut your salary, but stopped short of firing you. Well, that's a way to keep you in suspense, isn't it?"

"It feels suspenseful, but not only that. It's downright frightening. Harry's barely making enough to cover his own living expenses. We need my salary to keep things going just like we've done all along. I can't get EI, since I technically have a job. I don't know how long we can hold out like this."

"No indication how long this situation will be, right?" Helen sounded thoughtful.

"Not from work. I wonder if that detective would have some ideas." Rett mirrored her thoughtful tone.

"What's the most immediate problem?" Helen asked. It felt good to have her sister thinking with her. Helen could think beyond the obvious.

"The mortgage. That payment comes out of our account, no matter what's in there. I don't have salary coming in after next week."

"Sell the house?" Helen asked.

Rett cringed. "Where would we live? It's barely big enough for us as it is. I can't imagine trying to squeeze into some apartment. Plus paying rent requires money."

"No matter what happens at Streamside, this situation is temporary," Helen confirmed. "If they fire you, you get another job. At some point, Harry's going to finish his work out west and come home, and have a job. This isn't a lifetime situation."

Rett thought for a bit. "That's helpful. Yes, this is temporary. I didn't think about quitting Streamside and looking for another job."

"Well, it's an idea."

Rett was frowning. "I don't like it. It feels like admitting wrongdoing. They really need to reinstate me."

"We're just brainstorming here, right? No idea is a dumb idea at this point."

"Okay, but I don't like that one."

"Have you thought about renting out your house and moving in with Dad?"

Rett spluttered. "Certainly not. With Dad? I've got a pile of kids and a big dog, Helen."

"Ideas. We're generating ideas."

"I could sell the kids. They're pretty cute, you know."

Helen chuckled. "Okay, maybe some ideas need to be off the table."

"We could rent out the house, and go camping in the van across Canada. Homeschool the whole way. Go out west and meet Harry," Rett mused.

"That's an idea," Helen said approvingly.

"Can't I do anything to Briar Ventures for disrupting my life like this? Come on, Helen, what's the legal remedy?"

"I think they have the upper hand here. Do you have a union?"

"No. Professional organization. Not the same."

"Well, at least you have some ideas to work with. I've got to drive Jake somewhere, so I have to go."

"Hockey, no doubt," Rett said. Her nephew lived for hockey.

"Actually," Helen confided, "he's meeting a girl for a movie."

"No," Rett said. "In what universe is he that grown up?" In Rett's mind, her nephew was about Mason's age.

Helen laughed. "Yes. He can meet a girl, but he still needs his mother to drive him. Thank goodness for that. I don't know what I'd do without Jake to take care of."

"Other people's kids grow up fast," Rett said. "Based on the condition of my family room, it's taking longer than expected here." Toys and books were scattered all over, and snack wrappers littered the floor in front of the TV.

They said goodbye and Rett absently started to tidy. She could hear the kids' voices as they played in the backyard. Tossing toys into bins, stacking books on shelves, she thought about her options. Then she sat at the kitchen table with her laptop, gathering information.

Chapter 8

R ett was sick of waiting around for something to happen. She bought groceries and remembered there was no money coming in. She took the kids to the park and thought about money to pay for gas. When Mason asked her to buy a treat, she reminded him they had ice cream at home. She didn't like feeling so pinched.

She called her father for a chat.

"Rett! How you doing?" James was jovial.

"Hi, Dad," she said. "Do you have a few minutes? I have something to run by you."

Half an hour later, she posted the house for rent—furnished—on a local social network and went to the liquor store to collect cardboard boxes.

"Why are we packing?" Maggie asked. "I want to play."

"We can play putting all this stuff in boxes," Rett explained. "We're going to go visit Grandpa for a long visit. We need to pack the things you'll want at Grandpa's house."

"See, my stuffies are going to sleep in this big box, Maggie." Callie showed her. "I put in a blanket and now I'm putting them to bed."

Maggie, mollified, decided her box was a toy store.

"Mum, we never did this before," Mason said, frowning. "Does Grandpa need us?"

Rett stopped to look at her son. "Grandpa is fine, Mason. He's fully recovered and he's better than ever." Mason had been especially worried about his grandfather earlier in the summer when he was suddenly hospitalized, but James' diabetes was well-controlled now.

"Why, then? Because Daddy left us?"

Rett sat on the floor. "Daddy didn't leave us, baby. He's working and his job is out west. You know that."

Mason's lip quivered, so she pulled him to her. She was surprised when he let her tug him onto her lap. "I can't go to work right now, and staying with Grandpa is going to save us some money. That's all."

"But what about our house?" Maggie asked.

"I'm going to find some nice people who need a house in Saint Jacques for a while," Rett explained. "They pay to use our house, we stay with Grandpa, and there's money to buy food and ice cream."

"I don't want somebody sleeping in my bed," Callie objected.

Rett blew out her breath, gave Mason a gentle push off her lap, and stood up. "Nobody really wants to do this. I get it. I don't want to do it either. But I don't have a job, and we are short of choices." She heard her words get clipped and short and saw her kids' expressions fall. Right now, she didn't have the bandwidth for this, but she tried to soften a bit. "Lots of times we have to do things that we don't really want to do. We don't always get to decide. Sometimes you just have to do what the grownups decide is best for the family."

Mason, a little disgruntled, probably by her unceremoniously dumping him from her lap, looked like a thundercloud. "Does Daddy know about this?"

"Mason, come on. You can be your helpful self here. Take a couple of boxes into your room and pack the clothes from your dresser, okay?"

"Does Daddy know?" He was insistent.

"Daddy and I are a team," Rett said pointedly. "You know that."

He gave her another dark glance but took a box and headed down the hallway.

"Thank you!" she called after him. After checking how the girls were doing, she then went to pack up the personal items from the kitchen, things she couldn't do without. These included her favourite wooden spoon, her stovetop espresso maker, the kids' sippy cups for the car, and a single framed photograph from the counter. She held the picture in both hands to study it.

Four girls, young women, sort of, and an older woman. Rett shook her head at her own twenty-year-old self. So young, she thought. They were all so young. Helen, in her university graduation garb, Rett in her favourite dress, Evie looking away, and Dorie, still babyish, holding their mother's hand. And Agnes, Mum herself, so happy. Absent, but present because he was behind the camera, was her father, James. This was her family, the one she came from. They had never moved at a moment's notice, never dealt with job loss, separation. Well, her current family was just going to have to manage. Keeping the family going while Harry was gone was her job. They would just do it in another house. Home could be wherever they made it. That's all there was to it. She would do whatever she had to.

She wrapped the picture in a tea towel and tucked it into the box.

It took some doing—more than Rett had anticipated—to decide
what stayed in the house as a furnished rental, what went into storage,
and what they would take with them. The house was promised as soon
as she advertised it.

Her neighbour took the kids one afternoon. "The new people need
to get in right away," Rett told her. "Apparently, there's a real shortage
of rentals, and they offered me a hundred a month more than I was
asking, so I'm happy to move things along. Thank you so much for
entertaining this crowd."

"Oh, well," said Julie, looking around. "Your three, my five...it's just
kids. Besides, it's summertime, and they're all outside anyway."

"It's a big help though. Thank you."

There was little fanfare to moving home to James' house in Stella
Mare.

Rett reminded her father it was a temporary situation. "Once I get
a little money coming in, Magda's going to find us another house. We
won't be in your hair forever."

James nodded. "It's fine. You know I like having the kids around.
You too." He smiled at her.

"Thank you. I appreciate that. It's going to be a little crowded
though, with Evie already there." Her sister Evie had moved home after a breakup and now worked at selling her paintings and researching
hooked rugs.

"Crowded is just family being together," he said stoutly, but Rett
was less certain. Dad hadn't had little kids full-time in his house for a
long time. She hauled the last box of kid stuff up the stairs and into
the room her three would be sharing.

"I want to sleep on the air mattress!" Callie squealed.

"No, me!" shouted her sister. "I get to!"

"Well, you guys are both wrong," she said cheerfully. "Mason gets to choose because he's the oldest."

Mason preened a little, and Callie stuck out her tongue at him.

"Callie," Rett warned. "Mason, think carefully. You can have one of the beds or the air mattress."

Mason reverted to his usual serious self. "Can Charlie sleep on the air mattress with me?"

"I don't think he'll like it," Rett said, matching his serious tone. "Also his toenails might pop it, and then where would you be?"

"On the floor?" he asked. The little girls giggled.

"I want a regular bed so Charlie can sleep with me," Mason decided. The dog had slept with him since puppyhood, and the loyalty went both ways. "I wonder if Mallow will come sleep here, too?" he wondered, referring to one of his grandfather's enormous Bernese-New-foundland mix dogs.

"Mallow and Custard stay downstairs," Rett reminded him. "It'll be you kids and Charlie."

"What about you, Mum?" Maggie asked. "Where will you sleep?"

"Don't you worry. I've got it covered," Rett said energetically. "Here, can you guys get your stuff put away? Clothes in the dresser, toys on this bookshelf?" She gave a silent prayer of thanks to her sister for cleaning out her old bedroom earlier in the summer. Evie was going to faint when she saw the house all cluttered up again.

As the sun drew close to the horizon, Rett cooked pasta and fresh vegetables while James grilled chicken, and the kids and dogs played in the backyard. They were all settling down to dinner when the crunch of tires on the driveway made Rett get up to look out the window. "Oh, Evie and Corinne," she said with delight. "Here, Mason, let's set some more places. Your aunt and my aunt are here."

There was a flurry of activity as they came in, and Corinne set a bakery box on the counter, with a guilty look at James. "Never you mind, Corinne," he said. "I can look without eating."

"Good." She smiled and took her place at the table. "I wanted to celebrate Rett and the kids coming home."

"This family celebrates everything with food," Evie said, pulling out her own chair. "No worries, Dad. I have fruit salad."

He rolled his eyes and they laughed.

"How's everybody doing?" Corinne asked the kids and got a crescendo of replies. While she was chatting with the twins about the bugs they found in the backyard, Evie leaned over to Rett. "How's it going?"

"I didn't realize how much stuff three kids require until I unpacked it. All your hard work decluttering, Evie, it's disappeared under a layer of kid stuff."

Evie demurred. "It can't be that bad."

"Just wait and see," Rett said. She turned in time to see Maggie gazing at Corinne.

Maggie said, "Do you know my daddy?"

Corinne laughed. "Of course I do, sweetie. He was just here a few weeks ago."

She looked very serious. "He's far away. He's out west."

Corinne bent her head close to Maggie's. "Is that so?"

"Yes. But what if he comes home? He won't be able to find us."

"Sure he will," Corinne said. "He knows where Grandpa lives."

"But he doesn't know we're here," she wailed.

The sudden escalation brought the big dogs out of the sunporch to investigate, and a general commotion ensued. Dogs nosed around to comfort, Callie yelled at her sister, and Maggie's wails became a full-on meltdown. Meanwhile James and Mason placidly ate their pasta. Finally, Rett carried Maggie away from the table to help her calm down.

They sat. Rett cradled the child against her chest, arms firmly around her, rocking in the chair in the living room. Maggie's sobs subsided, and her thumb found her mouth. Woman and child rocked slowly, dogs drifted back to their beds in the sunporch, and the conversation from the dining room floated past.

Rett felt the weight of her youngest against her body. Maybe she'd gone about this wrong. The kids had worries too.

"We'll call Daddy tonight," she said to Maggie. "We'll show him your new room."

Maggie turned her tear-stained face up to look at her mother. "But it's a surprise. You said."

"Well, we're here now, right? So we don't have to keep the surprise anymore." Rett didn't like the idea of secrets between her and Harry, so she'd told the kids it was a surprise. He didn't have anything to do with her solution to being without a salary.

"But he's out west." Maggie started to wail again. Oh, right, Rett thought with annoyance. "Out in the field, you mean, Maggie. You're right. He can't get a phone call."

She tried to press down her frustration. "I know what we can do," she said suddenly. "We'll make a video of you kids in your new room and send it to Daddy. He won't get it until he goes to town on Thursday, but for sure he will know where to find you, if he should happen to come home. How does that sound?"

Maggie sniffled and nodded. "Okay."

"Now, do you want to eat your supper?"

"Yes, please."

As they returned to the table, James gave Rett a brief look of irritation. "The kids said moving here is a surprise for Harry. You didn't tell him?"

Rett avoided looking at her father while she settled Maggie back into her chair. Slipping into her own chair, she said, "He's out in the woods someplace, out of touch, and I didn't think he needed the worry." She glanced up to see the adults around the table gazing at her.

Evie looked shocked, James looked annoyed, and Corinne looked kind. She decided to look at Corinne.

"It just seemed like it was better to do it and then discuss." Corinne nodded at Rett's explanation and turned back to her meal.

"We're going to make a video of the kids' room tonight," Rett announced to the whole table. "He won't get it for a few days, but we'll send it."

"Hmm," James said. Rett knew he'd have more to say after the kids were asleep. Maybe she could go to bed early and skip the lecture.

Rett felt some pleasure and relief knowing dinner cleanup was being managed by other adults as she monitored baths, showers, pajamas and the making of the video. That old adage about the village it takes to raise kids might be right. At home, dinner dishes would have been waiting to be washed until after the kids' bedtime. The sound of Evie and Corinne chatting over the washing up was comforting in a way she didn't expect. Maybe she didn't have to avoid everyone tonight.

Before she'd finished the third story, Maggie was asleep with Callie close behind. The twins had opted to share the air mattress, leaving one of the twin beds free. She looked at it longingly, but instead, she tucked in Mason and perched on the side of his bed.

"Where's Charlie?" he fretted.

"Don't worry," she assured him. "Charlie will be up soon. He's hanging out with his cousins, you know?"

Mason giggled. "You mean Mallow and Custard."

"That's right. They'll all go out for a last visit to the backyard, and then I'll personally make sure Charlie knows where to find you."

"Okay," Mason murmured. "Goodnight."

He turned over toward the wall, holding his old rabbit, a ragged stuffed toy that still, sometimes, made it to his bed. The first night at Grandpa's was the perfect time for rabbit, Rett thought. Mason knows what helps him cope. She wished maybe she had a rabbit, or a Charlie. Coping was getting harder.

She pulled the kids' door closed and headed down the stairs into the kitchen. "Need any help?" she asked her sister and her aunt.

"Good timing," Evie said, as she wiped her hands. "We're just finished. Want a glass of wine?"

Rett shook her head. "No, thanks. I'm about ready to turn in myself." She went into the living room and sat on the couch. James looked up from his paper, peering over the top of his glasses.

"They're still printing the newspaper here?" she asked. "I figured the little towns would lose their papers first."

"Still going, though not going strong," James said, folding it up. "Everybody asleep?"

"Pretty much. We've all had a big day." She sank deeper into the cushions. This old couch had seen a lot of years and had provided comfort to a lot of girls in distress. She sighed and then yawned. "It's good to be home," she said.

"Rett," her father began, but she held up her hand.

"Are you going to scold me for something? Because I just can't, not tonight."

"I don't scold, daughter. I advise. Admonish. Support," he said wryly. "You girls are too grown-up for scoldings."

"Right."

"All I want to say is that you and the children are welcome. You stay as long as you need to." She waited. "And I'm very surprised that you kept all of this from Harry. Does he know about your work situation?"

With effort, she pulled herself out of the cushy couch to sit on the edge. "Dad, Harry's finally getting to do what he's wanted for years, finish his Ph.D. He put everything on hold to take care of Mason and we figured when Mason was five, he'd be back at it, and we'd be a happy working family of three. But the twins happened."

"Happened."

"Well, yes. I wouldn't have it any other way, but they were not part of our playbook, and so that set Harry back more. He agreed to be the stay-at-home parent, so I could really work at my career—" She choked on the word. She coughed a bit. "Now it's his turn. I don't want to interfere with that."

"I hear you, but secrets between partners, well, that's not good for the partnership." His look was kind.

"There's nothing Harry can do, Dad," she said rationally. "There's no need to bother him with details I'm going to handle myself anyway."

James was silent for a moment. Then he said, "This thing with your job, that's been pretty hard on you."

"Well, yes. Nobody ever accused me of wrongdoing before."

He frowned. "Who accused you?"

"That's the problem. There's no accusation, no information, just that I can't be at work. And, as I told you, they yanked my salary too. I'm not laid off, not fired. I have a job, but I can't go, and they aren't paying me. It stinks."

She leaned back into the comfortable couch. "The good side is that the rent from the house pays the mortgage and some extra, so we do have income. Harry's stipend barely covers his expenses and the plane flight home for Christmas. I'm so grateful that you've taken us in."

"You think you'll be here until Christmas?"

She sighed. "I just don't know. I hate feeling like somebody else has control of my life, so I talked to Helen about options. She thinks I should just quit and find another job, but I hate to let them win. Besides, I helped develop that program." Her heart hurt at the thought of leaving Streamside forever.

"Well, there's no rush," he said, smiling at her. "You can stay here."

"Thanks." She returned his smile.

Corinne came in, followed by Evie. "Catch me up," Corinne said. "I didn't know you were coming, and I certainly didn't know you were moving in. Tell Auntie Corinne."

Rett stretched her arms over her head. No sleep right now, especially if the couch was her bed. "Okay. It's not a pretty story."

Chapter 9

W as it possible to travel any further north? After driving over sixteen hours, then leaving the paved road in the tiny town for tracks through the woods, they were in real wilderness. There was a lot more north to be found, but he'd never been at this latitude before. It was full daylight by four a.m., and never really, truly got dark, though the sun set at eleven. This meant hours and hours of available light to work; to hike through habitat, set out cameras, collect tree counts and soil samples in places Harry never thought he'd see. Most evenings, they cooked and ate and worked in their tent camp. He now understood why they brought so much with them.

Other times, they were invited to go with Joyce to visit families who lived in the far outskirts of Gillam, people she'd met over her years doing fieldwork. Despite his initial shyness, Harry found these family visits to be the best part of being in the field. There was nothing like a pack of kids and dogs swirling around the house, mothers waving wooden spoons, the men waxing poetic about their experiences, the kids playing hide and seek and play fighting inside and out. While at first he felt uncomfortably like the scientist observer, he soon found himself playing silly games with the kids under the parents' watchful eyes. Being welcomed by a pack of kids was encouraging, and Harry loved being included in Joyce's invitations. Marie almost always opted to stay at camp, along with Denys. Alpha, Harry and Joyce were becoming regular visitors to the closest cluster of homes.

"It's good that you two come out," Joyce said to them on the trip back to camp one night. "Our connection with the folks who live here is what allows us to keep coming back."

"It's Crown land though," Harry objected. "Belongs to the government."

"Hmph." Joyce was dismissive. "Legally, yes, but practically and ethically, no. This land is its own thing. It grew the plants and animals we study, and it also grew the people who live here. That's what we get wrong about land ownership. The land generated the people. Those of us from colonial backgrounds, like me and probably like you, we're so far away from the land that grew us we can't even feel that connection."

Harry thought about that as he drove the truck over the jolting ruts. He wondered where his own ancestral lands might be. England? Would he feel a connection, recognize it, if he were there?

"Anyway," Joyce said, continuing, "making relationships is what's important. We have to be clear about our intentions, and we have to have the blessing of the locals. There must be mutual benefit here. Otherwise, there's just no point."

"Isn't there a point to getting the data regardless?" Alpha asked. "We want to know how climate change is affecting the permafrost. We don't have to have the locals' blessing for that, do we?"

"I think we do," Joyce said firmly. "They're not just the locals. They're the traditional stewards of the land. Some of them know things in their bones that I'll never experience, no matter how much data we collect. There are people here and in town who know more about the land and its occupants than we'll ever figure out."

Harry knew about indigenous knowledge-keepers who held vast stores of information and experience, both from their own lives and from being told by ancestors. He'd attended talks at the local university by New Brunswick wisdom keepers. He wondered how different things would be in Manitoba. "Will we be working with elders?" he asked.

"We always work with them. Weren't you paying attention? Jason invited me to come and sit with him next week."

Harry felt abashed. "I was playing with the kids, I think. Sorry I missed that."

Alpha was looking at him. "You miss your kid, huh?" they asked.

"Kids," he corrected and nodded. "Yeah. Three of them."

He'd enjoyed the children, even though they spoke a mishmash of languages, a smattering of French, English and Ininímowin, the local tongue. They didn't need language to communicate; kids were kids were kids. He missed his children, but these guys had helped a little.

Back at camp, Marie barely looked up from her laptop when they trooped into the main tent. After Joyce said goodnight and left, Marie muttered to Harry, "Well, I hope you had a good time."

"I did," Harry said mildly, but her annoyance disturbed him. "What's wrong?"

"Nothing," she said, but she still didn't look at him.

"What? What did I do?"

She shook her head. "Nothing. I need you to gather core samples. We're getting behind already. You and Alpha can come with me. We have three locations tomorrow."

"Sure," Harry said. "You're the boss."

She shook her head, irritated. "I'm not the boss. Just the project manager. Tomorrow."

"Right, tomorrow. Good night." Whatever was eating her wasn't his problem.

He slept immediately upon laying on his cot, but when he woke in the night to relieve himself, a light was still on in the big tent. Too tired to be curious, he returned to sleep. Two more days until the trip to town and he could call Rett. He hoped things were back to normal at home.

Settling into a routine at her father's house meant sleeping in the same room as the kids. Clearly the couch was not an option. Too many people kept peculiar hours, plus there was always the risk of being assaulted by canine kisses. Fortunately, the twins seemed to like sharing the air mattress, so that made a twin bed available for Rett. She tiptoed in well after the kids were asleep, and usually she was up with the sun, which was pretty early this time of year. When she slipped out of bed, Charlie jumped off too, waking Mason.

She, Mason and Charlie had developed a morning ritual that involved Rett sleepily making coffee, Mason curling up on the couch with a blanket, and the dogs, all three of them, taking their turns outside. Before she had a sip of coffee, she filled bowls with kibble, put away last night's dishes, and took a quick inventory of the refrigerator.

Mallow and Custard burst back into the house with Charlie behind them. He went to the living room to climb on the couch with Mason, but the big dogs sat in front of Rett, drooling. There was no avoiding the jangling of dog tags, Mason's giggles, or the clank of dog bowls as the canines licked them clean across the floor and into each other. James invariably got up within fifteen minutes of Rett.

"I'm sorry, Dad," she said when he descended the last few stairs. She'd heard him overhead, of course, old houses being creaky. He was dressed right down to his shoes, as usual, and she was aware of her ratty t-shirt and pajama pants. She went to give him a hug. "Sorry we woke you. Again."

He shrugged. "No big deal. Coffee ready yet?" He looked toward the coffee maker.

"It's coming," she said. "Hungry?" She held open the refrigerator door.

"Too early to eat," he said.

"You'd think so," she agreed. "Not for the dogs though."

"Well, dogs," he said. "There's no bad time to eat if you're a dog."

Mallow bumped his head lovingly against James' thigh, then headed into the living room. Mason's giggles escalated.

"That boy loves that dog," James commented, as he always did. Custard, not to be left out, galumphed out of the kitchen, a noise followed by a mighty thud, crash, glass breaking and then, silence.

Rett and James stared at each other. "Mason?" Rett called. "You okay?" She stuck her head around the corner.

Mason was hurriedly trying to put the end table upright and rescue the lamp. James' papers were scattered across the floor. "He didn't mean it, Mum," Mason said quickly. "He was just playing."

"Right." She helped turn the furniture around. "Did the lamp break?"

"I don't know." Mason was close to tears. "I'm sorry."

"I don't think you did this," she said. "We'll get it fixed up."

James was leaning in the doorway surveying the scene. "It's okay, Mason. Just dogs getting a bit excitable."

Rett gave a short laugh. "I never thought of Mallow and Custard as excitable."

"I think they've got a new lease on life with the children here," James said. "Reliving their puppyhood."

Within ten minutes, the kitchen was full of kids and adults, coffee was being poured (thank goodness, thought Rett) and cereal passed around. The clock said five-thirty. It made Rett tired just to look at it.

Evie came down, too, in rumpled pajamas. "Good morning, everybody," she said lightly. "Where's that coffee?"

Rett handed her a mug. "I'm so sorry. You probably didn't plan to get up this early."

"I might be getting used to it," Evie said, taking the cup in both hands. "I'm going"—she gestured vaguely—"there."

She disappeared into the living room. James followed.

Maggie giggled on the floor with Custard, who was licking her face and head-butting her. Between bouts of licks, she scratched his big silky ears. Dog and child looked blissful, but Rett tripped over them when she tried to get food on the table. "Come on, Mags, let Custard go. He likes to nap. You need to wash your hands now." She probably needed a bath too, Rett thought, but that wasn't happening. She poured milk, cut up fruit, and handed out toast, all while sipping at her mug.

She leaned over Callie to put something on the table. "Cal, your pjs are wet." She leaned in for a sniff. Callie gave her a guilty glance.

She whispered to the child, "It's okay, Cal. Go upstairs and get those wet things off. I'll be right up to help."

Mason watched. "Did Callie pee the bed again?"

Maggie, still playing, barely noticed Rett feeling her pajamas and giving her the sniff test. "Yeah, maybe," Rett said to her son. "Don't tease her."

"What?" Maggie suddenly tuned in. "Did Callie pee again?"

Rett didn't answer. "Are you dry, Mags?"

"Yep," she said. Rett had no idea how that was possible, given their bed sharing, but she was grateful. Only one kid to put in the shower this morning. She prevailed upon Maggie to sit at the table with her breakfast and headed upstairs.

Later, she hung the sheets to dry in the backyard. Fifth day in a row, she thought. Adjustment. It's all adjustment.

Everyone was trying. Evie asked her if it was okay to use the washing machine, as if Rett was now in charge. She was doing laundry daily though, so no wonder. Rett just grabbed Evie's laundry and James's too. She might as well do it all.

The refrigerator was full, but it seemed like there was never anything to eat. Harry had always managed the kids' food, and Rett found the continuous demands for snacks wearing. James had particular dietary needs and so did her kids. It was one more thing to keep in mind, but when the little people got hungry, food was necessary. Immediately.

Pinning wet sheets to the line, her mind went to Harry somewhere out in the wilderness of Manitoba or Nunavut or something. Maybe she should have paid more attention. Probably his Thursdays in town included a trip to the laundromat. Maybe living in a tent by yourself wouldn't be so bad.

She dropped the empty laundry basket on the back porch when she returned to the house. Evie was in the den, off the kitchen, that she'd turned into her office, and Rett stuck in her head.

"How's it going?"

Evie turned tired eyes her way. "Fine," she said, but her face belied her words. Rett walked in and sat.

"Pardon me for not believing you," Rett said with a little smile.

Evie rubbed her eyes. "I'm just tired. I'm not used to getting up at five."

"Sorry about that," Rett said.

"I have to change my habit of working late," her sister said. "It's just so quiet then. You can hear yourself think."

"How's the project?" Rett asked, nodding toward Evie's laptop.

"Good, good. I've got attributions for almost all the hooked rugs and I'm collecting family stories about them now. Next is to learn how to display them, and I'm going to Fredericton next week to meet someone who will help me."

Rett nodded. "Good."

"How are you doing? This sure isn't what you're used to."

"It's not," Rett said briskly, pushing herself up. "But chaos is chaos. I'm a nurse. I've got this."

"Anything new about work?" Evie asked before she could get out the door. She looked over her shoulder and shook her head.

"Sorry I mentioned it," Evie said.

"I'll let you know about any developments."

She picked up an armload of toys on her way to the living room where Mason was arguing with Callie about cartoon shows while James tried to divert his attention. Mason, usually quiet and reserved, had his father's dogged determination about some things, and watching his sister's cartoon show for the third time was one of them. "It's my turn to pick. She's been watching for a long time." His chin was out.

Rett tossed the toys into one of the baskets she'd arranged on the floor by the door to the sunporch, then intervened. "Come on, everybody, let's go for a hike. Callie, you've had enough Puppy Police for now, and Mason, use your calm voice, please. Turn it off, Callie. Now."

Callie was motionless, holding the remote, so Mason grabbed it and clicked. She erupted with an enraged howl, he shouted back at her, and James got up and went to the kitchen. Rett looked after him. In a furious whisper, she said, "You two stop it right now. You've upset your grandfather! Stop it."

"But he..." Callie turned her tear-stained face up to her mother, but Rett was having none of it.

"You were told. Now both of you, get upstairs and find your jackets. We're going out."

She went into the kitchen. James was looking out the window, leaning on his palms before the sink. She had a flash of memory from earlier in the summer, her father lying motionless in a hospital bed, tubes snaking out of his arms. With it came a stab of dread. Maybe all this was too much for him.

"Sorry, Dad," she said.

He turned, looking a little surprised. "You know, seeing all that laundry out there and the energy in here, reminds me of how it was when Aggie and your grandmother, and all you girls were living here with me. It was a busy time." He smiled at her. "Don't apologize, Rett. Kids are kids."

Mildly comforted, she said, "I never intended to dump my houseful on you, Dad. This is temporary, that's all."

"I'm not complaining. If I find something to complain about, I'll let you know."

"Thanks. We're going to Minister's Island if the tide is right. Want to come?"

He shook his head. "No, thanks. I've got my old-guys-drinking-cof-fee meeting."

Minister's Island was only accessible by car at low tide, and she was lucky. Without checking a chart, she'd managed to get them there with hours to hike and run around. As she released the kids to start their hike, she called Magda Allen, the realtor with whom Dorie had connected her.

"It's getting more urgent," she said to Magda. "I'm willing to lower my expectations a lot."

"What do you mean?"

"Right now, four of us and a dog are sharing a bedroom. We have one bathroom for six people. Anything better than that would be excellent."

Magda sounded like she was taking notes. "Okay. Anything else?"

"Like what?"

Magda cleared her throat delicately. "Like any change in what you're looking to pay?"

Rett squinted. "No increase, if that's what you mean."

"Well, yes. The reason I haven't brought you any possibilities is because they're hard to find at that price point."

"I told you my situation. It's temporary."

"Right, but I can't put you into a rental where you're not going to be able to pay. That's not fair to you or the owner."

"I know this," Rett said irritably. "No, I don't have any more money than I told you before. But I need a place and I need it soon."

They said goodbyes, but Rett was not encouraged. She set off after the kids, Charlie's leash in hand, but her mind was not on hiking.

The solution to the housing crisis arrived on its own, as solutions often do.

That very evening, Mason was playing in the wooded area behind the house. Rett called the kids to come in for supper, but he didn't arrive. She set off to find him, following a trail he'd apparently made. She wasn't worried, but it was irritating to have to go find him at mealtime.

"Mase! Where are you?"

Following a crashing through the underbrush, Charlie arrived, ecstatic to see her. Mason was right behind. "Hey, Mum, want to come see my hideout?"

She looked at her watch. "Mason, it's dinnertime."

"Come see. It'll only take a minute. Please?"

His excitement reminded her of Harry. She made a quick decision to ignore the schedule. "Sure. Let's see it." He led her through the woods to a broken-down wooden fence, where a downed maple sagged, making a kid-and-dog-sized cave under the trunk. Mason slipped inside, Charlie following. The little boy grinned. "Come on in. It's cool."

She scoffed but squatted down and squeezed into the tree cave beside him. Charlie whined a little and moved over, but there was room for all three of them. She sat, arms circling her knees, gazing into the thin forest from Mason's little hideout. It was suddenly quiet.

She smiled at the boy. "You're right, this is very cool." The scent of soil, decaying leaves and old wood, and the fresh smell of green leaves surrounded her. The silence settled around her shoulders like a blanket, calming her and holding her closely. As her mind quieted, she looked out of the cave, gazing absently, and then with increasing focus.

"Have you been over there?" she asked Mason, gesturing beyond the wooden fence.

"No. Grandpa said stay on this side of the fence."

"Want to go look?" she asked him.

"Okay." She jumped up and he followed. "What is it, Mum?"

She clambered over the fence. Mason and Charlie slipped beneath the rails. "I think it's a house. Maybe we have a neighbour." They approached through the thinning trees and across an unkempt lawn.

"I hope they're nice," Mason said. "It looks like a haunted house."

Rett looked again. Haunted? "Well, it's old. And it's got that big turret."

They followed Charlie past an overgrown garden and around the side of the old wooden structure to find a weed-filled driveway, a broken-down front porch and a sign, covered with a vine. Rett tore the vine away.

"For rent," Mason read. "For rent. What's for rent?"

"It means that you can pay money to live here." She looked again at the outside of the house. "Let's go look in the windows."

"Mum, you can't," Mason objected. "Privacy."

"We don't disturb people's privacy, that's right," she agreed. "But look at this place. Nobody is here. Maybe not for a long time." She headed for the broken boards of the porch. Peering through a dirty window, she saw a nondescript living room and the room beyond was full of long afternoon light. "This has possibilities," she muttered to herself.

"Come on, let's look for the kitchen." She tossed the words over her shoulder as she jumped off the porch and headed around the other side to the back of the house. Mason trotted behind and Charlie led the way.

The back of the house held windows, the southwest corner the most windows of all. Oddly placed and out of alignment, they contributed to the haunted house look, but those windows were fully illuminated by the sun. She tried to jump up to see inside, but couldn't. Instead, she found an old wooden box to stand on. She picked Mason up so he could look too.

"Well, what do you see?" she asked him.

"It's a mess."

"It sure is," she agreed. "But there's a lot of space in there. And it's practically in grandpa's backyard."

"Can we go home? I'm hungry." Mason's attention had shifted. Rett wasn't really ready to leave, but she snapped a couple of pictures with her phone and they headed back. On the way, she texted her picture of the sign to Magda with a note.

Viewing please. ASAP.

Magda replied before they got through the woods to James' backyard. *Eight a.m. But are you sure? I don't even know if it's safe.*

I'll leave the kids at home. See you then.

Finally feeling a sense of something happening, Rett followed Mason up her father's back porch, welcomed by the fragrances of spaghetti sauce and garlic bread. Things might be looking up.

Chapter 10

Joyce called on Harry to go to the village again. "You got along well enough," she said. "They need some help with the community center. I'm volunteering you."

"Sure," Harry agreed. "What's involved?"

"Work," she said shortly. "You don't seem to be allergic to it. I can afford to lose you for a couple of days."

"Wait, lose me? What are you talking about?"

"They need another body and I need their goodwill. Marie, Denys, and Alpha are all deep in the project. You're the body I can afford to send."

"Thanks, I think," Harry said. "I'm not valuable enough on the project, that's what you're saying." He wondered if Marie, as the project manager, would agree.

Joyce gave him a sharp glance. "On the contrary. Your value right now is in keeping our relationships working smoothly. Do you have a problem with that?"

"Well, no, I guess not," he said. It felt like blowing in the wind, whatever wind Joyce wanted, but she was in charge. She must have some idea of when he'd get to start his own work. As he loaded the ATV with his needs for the day, Marie came by.

"Where are you going? We're collecting core samples on Site 24."

"Joyce sent me to the village."

She huffed. "I need you here. We have a certain amount of time to cover a specific territory and I need all hands."

"What do you want me to say?" He turned up his palms. "Joyce told me to go. She's your boss as well as mine."

"Joyce wants too much," Marie said. "But you go. Whatever." She stomped off, scowling, but he noticed she headed away from Joyce.

He threw his pack and himself onto the ATV. Restraining an impulse to peel out of camp, he kept his speed down, but he wanted to tear down the rugged road. They'd have to sort that out themselves. He only knew Joyce sent him out, and what Joyce wanted, Joyce got. Besides, if he were scrupulously honest, he wasn't all that excited about core sampling, even for his own project. He was beginning to think he lacked some internal fire, some drive that made the others pore over data and engage in excited conversation about minutiae. Spending a couple of days doing construction would be welcome.

His arrival was noted. A few of the men gathered around, checking him out. "Hi," he said, offering his hand. "I'm Harry. I came to help."

"You with Joyce, up in the forest?" someone asked.

He nodded.

"Okay. Good that she sent you," a man said. "More hands. You want to see Paul, over there." The man gestured across the way.

Paul and another man were moving a sheet of galvanized steel at the side of the new building. Harry tugged on his work gloves and jumped in to help carry the load. When they had it settled, Paul turned to him. "You must be Joyce's new recruit."

"That's right," Harry said, taking off his gloves to shake hands. "This is quite a project. Looks like it could stand up to alien invasion."

"That's just about right," Paul replied with a smile. "I think I met you last weekend. Right?"

"Probably," Harry said. "I met a lot of people and I'd just arrived, so I'm afraid I don't remember great. But tell me, why does your new building need so much reinforcement?"

Paul looked at him, deadpan. "Oh, you people from the south."

"My first time this far north," Harry admitted. "I'm trying."

"Where are you from?"

Harry laughed. "I'm a Maritimer. Born in Nova Scotia."

"Do your people fish?"

My people, Harry thought. "Well, my great-grandfather fished. He was in Newfoundland and moved to Nova Scotia for a better life. I'm not so sure he found that, but he ended up staying."

"Fishing?"

"Well, fishing when it was good, working in the woods when it wasn't. Like a lot of people."

"And you?"

"I think it's been bred out of me," Harry admitted. "I don't fish. I camp and take pictures in the woods. My grandfather had a general store, and he was able to send his sons to school. My father was a teacher."

"What about you?"

He wondered how to explain himself. "I've been raising kids," he said. "I studied science before that."

"Now you're doing science again." Paul nodded his understanding.

"Now I'm trying to find out if I'm really going to be a scientist," Harry said, surprising himself.

"You're already working with Joyce. That seems like a big commitment."

Harry straightened. "Yes. I left my family for the duration, too. I'm here working on my Ph.D. research project."

"I've been to Nova Scotia," Paul said, in an abrupt change of topic. "My cousin had an art show in Halifax."

"I live in New Brunswick now," Harry said. "I don't get to art shows much, except my sister-in-law is an artist. What kind of art?"

"Sculpture," Paul said. "I don't know about that. I make buildings."

"Right. And why are we reinforcing this one?"

"Bears."

Harry wondered if Paul was teasing him, being from away and all. But he wasn't sure. "Polar bears? Due to climate change?"

"Nah, we're too far inland for polar bears, though I wouldn't be surprised by anything these days. But the grizzly population is increasing, and we have black bears and brown bears. They're looking for food wherever they can find it," Paul explained. "The polar bears are interesting though. Used to be, they would be out on the ice, fishing and hunting there. We saw them when we were hunting. Polar ice has receded and they're in trouble. You've seen those news stories. Churchill's been overrun. The bears like the town dumps."

"This isn't town here though," Harry said. "You don't have a dump."

"No, no dump. But we have food and I'm not interested in sharing with bears. Any bears."

"Hence the heavy reinforcements for your building. I thought you were joking."

Paul gave him a long look. "Those guys are no joke. You should hear my grandfather's story. He lost his arm to one a long time ago."

"Really? Would he tell me about it?" Harry was fascinated.

Paul shrugged. "Could be. After we get this building up, we'll have a big meal, and the old people will tell stories. He might tell that one."

He headed toward the front of the building and Harry followed. "Okay, Harry from Nova Scotia, we're going to put you to work. Come on."

The work was physical and demanding, but progress was visible and satisfying. Harry was tired at the end of the day, but it wasn't time to return to camp. The group gathered at Paul's grandmother's house to eat, drink, and ultimately sit and tell stories. Harry leaned back against a log, letting the talk wash over him, hearing sounds of kids playing, the women laughing nearby, men joking with each other. His shoulders held powerful fatigue. He knew if he didn't leave soon, he'd be sleeping out here on the ground.

Heading downhill toward the house, he found Paul with an older woman. Paul introduced him to his grandmother Jeannette, and Harry offered his hand, but also his goodbyes. "I'm about to drop," he admitted.

"It was a good day," Paul said. "Don't forget to come back."

"See you in the morning," he promised.

Back at camp, he drove past the main tent to park the ATV. Joyce sat outside, cup in hand. He walked toward her to check in.

"How did it go?" she asked.

"Paul said it was a good day," he reported. "I'm about done in."

"They're testing," Joyce said. "Seeing if you're up to it."

Harry chuckled. "I don't feel like I have to prove anything. But I do want to help."

"They'll make you work," she said. "Testing the new guy."

Just like here, he thought. Except here I do have to prove myself. Have to prove my worth to Joyce, to Marie, and maybe even to me. "Yeah, maybe. Paul told me to come back tomorrow. Maybe that means I passed."

"They can have you tomorrow." A small smile tugged at her lips.

"Marie was surprised that you sent me," he said. She shrugged.

"Well, goodnight." He walked away, thinking only of rest as he crawled into his sleeping bag.

Waking before the sun was up meant outrageously early. The middle of the night, actually. But there he was. He took his notebook to the main tent, where he made coffee on the camp stove. Taking his mug outside, he settled down to write impressions of the people he'd met, the stories he'd heard, and make sketches of Joyce's thin face, Paul's big smile, and the skinny dog he'd befriended at the worksite. Scribbling down images, ideas, words that seemed to fit, he made some sense of yesterday. Today he'd take his camera. So much felt noteworthy, to see and experience.

Driving to the village yesterday had meant crossing an open area just as the daylight began to overcome night. He'd stopped and watched the light grow before the sun crested the horizon, feeling his presence as a tiny dot on a massive landscape of wilderness and sky that extended far beyond his capacity to sense it. Perched on the ATV, he was simultaneously a microscopic particle and an expansive presence, part of the vast consciousness of the earth. He'd felt that way once before, as a child on a fishing boat with his grandfather, chugging into the Atlantic. At the time, he thought it was because he was only a boy, small in the adult world, but when he turned to his grandfather for reassurance he was there, that they both were real, the old man wore a faraway look Harry, even then, had recognized as his own. Another time, he'd seen the Milky Way spilling over a night sky in Newfoundland, and that, too, had brought the feeling.

He struggled to write about those moments. The vastness of the wilderness, the big sky overhead, the abundance of nature that took no notice of him. Important as he might be to himself, it reminded him of his smallness, his human fragility. At the same time, it called him to awareness of his own place within the vastness. Fragile though he was, he had a place. As a living person or as a dead body, it was all the same to nature. But the very fact of his existence meant something. His particular collection of molecules, held together by unseen forces at this place and time, meant something.

It was an encounter, but he couldn't name what he was encountering. Anyway, here he was, living it. He was in it right now and trying to capture the experience on paper. He scribbled a few more notes, tried to sketch yesterday's sunrise. Finally he put away his pencil. Scoffing at himself, he swallowed his coffee and prepared for a day of work in the little village.

Chapter 11

Rett took Evie with her the next morning. James stayed at home with the kids.

"No point in getting Mason all excited," Rett explained to her father. "Who knows if this is going to work out?"

James scoffed. "I think someone else is in danger of getting all excited," he said. "Don't be impulsive, Rett."

"Ouch," she said, straightening her back. "When have I ever?"

"Oh, like when you rented your house out without talking to your husband," James said, though his tone was mild.

She subsided. "You have a point. Come on, Evie," she called. "Let's get going."

They were a bit early to meet Magda, but she wanted to approach the house from the street, and that required walking around a very large, irregularly shaped block. It might be immediately behind James' house but streetwise, it was half a kilometre away. Evie kept pace.

When they turned the corner, Dorie's van was visible on the street. Rett turned to Evie.

"Yes, I called her," Evie responded to the glance. "I knew she'd want to see it too."

Dorie's fiancé Chad stood beside the van, and Magda's little coupe with the real estate sign on the side was in the driveway. Magda, Dorie, and a tall man with sun-streaked hair chatted in the driveway. Dorie waved to Rett and Evie, and Chad joined the group as they came together.

"Hi, Magda," Rett said. "This is my sister Evie, and it looks like you met Dorie and Chad."

"I did, thank you," Magda said. "I already knew Dorie, but it's lovely to meet more of the family." She indicated the tall man. "This is Jürgen Stern. Jürgen lives next door." She gestured to the right of the old house.

Rett smiled politely. "I assume there's a house there," she said, nodding toward the thick growth of bushes and trees.

She reached for a handshake. He held her hand with both of his, looking closely at her eyes. Her face warmed and she pulled away her hand.

He spoke smoothly. "Yes, there certainly is. I've been watching this place for the Pickfords and I'm glad someone is finally interested." Rett shoved her hand in her pocket.

"Watching it do what?" Dorie asked. "It looks pretty rough."

Evie kicked Dorie's foot. "Rude," she whispered.

Dorie shrugged. "It's true."

"It is true," Jürgen agreed. "I should have been clear. I'm not responsible for the place. I've just called the police a couple of times when kids were breaking in, partying, you know."

"Oh," Rett said, looking at the house again. "So that's been going on."

Magda walked briskly toward the front porch. "Maybe we can try the back," she said, looking doubtfully at the broken floorboards.

"No, it's okay," Rett said, jumping up onto the porch. "I was up here yesterday. Just don't step on the obvious spots." She tapped her foot as Magda fitted the key into the lock and wrestled open the old door.

"Allow me," Jürgen said, stepping ahead of all of them.

"Is the electricity on?" Magda asked.

"Maybe," Jürgen said, sounding doubtful, but as they all stumbled in, he flipped a switch. The dim overhead bulb flared, then sizzled out. "Incandescents," Jürgen noted.

After a lot of thumping on the front porch, Chad came in, a little dusty. "That porch is pretty solid," he announced. "It's just got some broken floorboards. Easy to fix."

The shady front yard made for a dark front room. An old wood stove stood in the corner. An overstuffed sofa, ratty rug, and a couple of end tables filled out the space.

"Probably full of mice," Dorie said with distaste, skirting the sofa.

"I don't care about mice," Rett said. "Does it have working plumbing? Are there bedrooms? I don't need much."

"Oh, Rett, I don't know about this place," Evie said, looking around. "It's pretty bad." She opened a door, and something fell out.

"Did the ceiling just fall down?" Dorie asked. "What is that?"

Evie studied the closet floor. "No idea."

"Just close the door," Dorie advised.

"Let's keep looking," Rett said, marching down the hallway. "Where's the kitchen? Oh, yes."

She walked into the room she'd seen the afternoon before, with the tall windows on the south and west corners of the house. It was a dining room, probably, based on the table and a couple of broken chairs. It opened into a kitchen with another wood-burning stove, a deep sink, and an ancient cook stove. Magda turned on the faucet and Rett held her breath, but the water flowed clear and fast.

"City water," Magda said triumphantly. "Sewer, too."

"That's one good thing," Evie said. "Hey, there's a bathroom down here."

"Probably the only bathroom," Magda said. "These old houses had plumbing on one floor only."

"I want to see the haunted tower," Dorie burst out. "Hey, Chad! Where did you go?"

Footsteps sounded overhead and Chad called down, "The stairs seem safe. Come on up."

Upstairs had four bedrooms, wallpaper peeling off several walls, and no closets anywhere, but the rooms were full-size. A door that opened on a twisting staircase led to the turret room. Rett clambered up, Dorie following behind her. Magda stayed at the bottom, offering commentary.

"This is a classic widow's walk," she said, "where sea captain's wives would watch for their ships to return. Can you see down to the harbour there, Rett?"

"Hardly," Rett said with a laugh. "I can barely see the roof of Dad's house. There's a lot of trees here." She turned all the way around to take in the full view. One of the windows was broken, and she could see some damage from rain. Overall though, it was charming, despite the dirt and ravages of time.

Dorie knelt at the south facing window. "You could make a trail back to Dad's house," she said, gazing at the wooded area, "and it would be almost like being in each other's backyard. The kids would love that."

"Dad might, too," Rett said. "I wouldn't mind being close. Right now we're too close."

"I can imagine," Dorie said.

When the women went back downstairs, Chad and Jürgen were in the kitchen, looking at fixtures and talking.

"It's pretty bad," Rett said to Magda. "Probably not a lot of competition for renters."

The realtor laughed. "Did you see that sign? I don't know if anyone has ever looked at it before today."

Jürgen said, "It would be great to have neighbours. The place has been a magnet for troublesome kids, as I said. It just needs to be occupied."

Rett said, "I'll remember those words. I have three kids and a dog, plus a lot of relatives. It might get a little wild around here."

"Wild is better than too quiet," he said. "I'm going now, but please do let me know if you decide to move in."

"Thanks. It would be good to know the neighbours."

Magda was busy on her phone in the far reaches of the dining room. "Well?" she asked, returning to the sisters, clustered on the front porch.

"Four bedrooms, a bathroom that works, a kitchen, and a big yard. With a garden just waiting for me to plant food."

"Mice, ceilings falling down, filthy, broken up furniture, and an overgrown yard probably full of critters," Dorie said.

"Oh, Rett, it's just so much work," Evie said.

Rett shrugged. "I have time right now. For the first time, maybe, I have time."

"Ugh. I'm done cleaning out old houses," Evie said with a shudder.

"I don't know," Rett teased her. "There could be treasures in this house, too. Maybe you'll want to help."

Evie shook her head. "It looks like any treasures were looted a long time ago. Rett, this is a big project."

"It's close to Dad and it might be in my budget," Rett said tightly. "Besides, it has a certain charm."

"If you like haunted houses," Dorie added darkly.

"You can't talk like that around the kids," Rett warned. "They'll take it seriously. Mason already asked me how you can tell if house is haunted. He thought the turret was a key indicator."

Dorie chuckled. "Okay, I'll keep it to myself."

Chad, always a few steps behind, stepped onto the porch. "It's not bad. I poked in the basement, and the sills seem to be solid. There is an oil furnace, too, along with those stoves. The pipes aren't as old as the rest of the house."

"Thanks, Chad. Hey, when did you get so good at house stuff?"

"Well, I've been living at Nan's for a while now and watching a lot of YouTube."

Rett said, "To my benefit. I appreciate it."

Magda tapped her pen on her clipboard. "Do you want to come down to the office?" she asked Rett. "See if this is going to work?"

"Sure," Rett agreed. "Evie, are you going home? Can you let Dad know?"

"I was going over to the house to see if Mason wanted to come help us this morning," Dorie said.

"Sure, just talk to Dad," Rett said, distracted. "I'd like to get this sorted."

Chapter 12

"Can you even sign a rental agreement without your husband?" James asked.

"I don't know if I can, but I did," Rett retorted. "It's done. We're moving in as soon as we can get it more or less habitable."

"Moving to Stella Mare," James mused. "Not just for a visit."

She sat on the couch facing him. "Dad, this is a new start for me. I've been so busy my whole adult life, trying to get ahead at work, extra hours at the care home, keeping things going there during staffing crises, during outbreaks of viral illness, helping support the families, and trying to help the business grow. When Briar Ventures took over, I thought it would be the same, but it wasn't. But I just kept on."

"You did. You were looking pretty thin and stressed earlier this summer," he recalled.

"I didn't even realize it. We were pretty sure Harry was going to get this opportunity to do his research, and we just figured I'd keep on at Streamside. But this situation at work might have an upside. I never thought I'd like being at home with the kids, but I think at this house, well, we can take it to the next level. Like have some chickens and a garden, maybe, and the kids can do projects. Earthworm composting, maybe. Weaving. Stuff like that. They call it urban homesteading. Back to basics."

James was quiet. "Your kids aren't exactly back-to-nature types. They like to watch cartoons."

"This is such a great opportunity to get them off the screens. To get them to really live life! You know. Like it was meant to be."

"Harry...."

"Harry would love this," Rett said firmly. "He's all about living sustainably. Growing your own, minimizing waste. Like in the old days."

James raised his eyebrows. "Your mother and I wanted you kids to have an education so you wouldn't have to live hand to mouth like we did, but it sounds like that's what you want to do."

"Well, frankly, with my money situation, hand to mouth is about right."

"I can loan you money, you know."

She shook her head. "Thanks, but it's not necessary. I'm just going to practice frugality for now."

"For now. That's not forever, Rett. Just until you get your job back."

She looked off into the distance. "I think I'm going to quit."

"What?"

"If I quit, I can apply for employment insurance. As long as they keep me on but don't pay me, I can't get any financial help and I can't look for another job."

"So you'd look for work?"

"Well, yeah," she said.

"How are you going to do this urban homesteading and work, too?"

She heaved a giant sigh. "I don't know how I'm going to do anything really, but I always manage to do something." She looked at him. "I know it sounds a little crazy right now, but I think I can probably work part-time while the kids are in school, plus we can grow some food and keep our expenses down and have some fun, too."

"What about Harry?"

"What about him?"

"When does he get to have an opinion about this?"

"When he comes home."

"Are you mad about him leaving?" James sounded curious, not judgmental, but Rett's anger flared anyway.

"Of course not. It's his turn to, you know, spread his wings." She consciously made her voice low and calm.

"He's not flying away. He's coming back, but he's going to be some surprised."

"Dad, he would approve, really. But he's not here making these decisions, or even helping. I don't even get to talk to him while he's out in the field, so I can't wait for his agreement." She knew her tone was getting sharper. "It's my call, and this is how I'm calling it."

"I can see that. I hope you're not doing this because you think I don't want you at the house," he said. "Having the kids around is good for an old man."

She softened. "That's why this house is perfect. It's practically in your backyard, but we have our own bathroom. You know?"

"It might be getting a dite small here," he agreed. "I don't want you to disappear over there, though."

"Mason's already got plans to build his trail between the houses, so no worries. I'll need your help with the garden, too. You and Mum used to grow vegetables, right?"

"I know when I'm being placated," James said. "I do have an old garden journal of your mother's here, though. It might have some useful ideas for you." He headed to the bookshelf and Rett relaxed against the sofa. Things were finally moving along.

When Thursday came, Joyce asked Harry for his list.

"What list?"

"Let me know what you want from town. You're going to work in the village today."

He sighed. "Can you send my wife a text? She's going to expect to hear from me."

Joyce looked irritated. "She'll hear from you. Just not this week."

He wrote a brief message and Rett's number on a piece of paper and watched Joyce tuck it into her jeans pocket. "You better get going," she reminded him. "Paul's going to be looking for you."

"Right."

He enjoyed his time in the little cluster of houses and not only because the kids had adopted him. He liked the men, who gave him a nickname and teased him mercilessly. He was creating a real friendship with Paul, too. He felt closer to Paul than to Marie or Denys or Alpha, that was sure.

The two men sat on a log having lunch and sharing tea.

"Why did you come here?" Paul asked. "When your family is so far away?"

"I thought I was going to be studying the way local ecology is affected by changes in the permafrost. That's why I wanted to work with Joyce. She's an expert. I'm supposed to be formulating my Ph.D. project in relation to her work."

"Supposed to be? But instead you're helping us," Paul said. "Why?"

"This is where Joyce sent me," he said simply. "She thinks it's important."

Paul looked at him.

"I think it's important, too," he assured. "In fact, I like it. I like meeting people and seeing how folks live so close to the land here. I'm learning a lot."

Paul nodded. "It's a particular kind of life here. It's the way my ancestors lived, and I hope the way my descendants will live."

"My parents wanted what they called 'a better life' for their kids," Harry said. "One where you didn't risk your life fishing, where there was food every day, and where you were safe and warm all winter."

"Did that work out?"

"Sure," Harry said. "Now we have the stress of commuting, food that's made in a factory, and we're so safe and warm we're all out of shape and dying of chronic illness."

"A better life."

"A safer life. Not the hardships that they endured."

"We want safer for our children, too. Safe from hatred. From the trauma of colonialism. From discrimination and prejudice."

"That would be a better life."

"We want that, and we don't want to lose our ancestral heritage."

They both chewed meditatively. "I don't have much of my ancestral heritage," Harry said. "I wish I knew more. My family came to Nova Scotia from England in the mid-1800s."

"England is your ancestral land?"

"I guess so," Harry said, a little surprised. "I've never been there."

"That must be hard, to not know the land that bore you and your family line."

"You know, every time I come here, you give me something else to think about."

"Good. Right now, we need to think about getting back to work, or this building will never be done."

"Right."

Chapter 13

Getting the house clean enough for human habitation was a big job. Magda negotiated with the owners for a professional cleaning service, plus someone to repair the broken planks on the front porch, but after that, Rett was on her own. For what she was paying in rent, it seemed fair.

Moving in was easy because they didn't have much, but the kids were excited anyway. She took pictures to send to Harry. She figured he couldn't be mad if he saw how happy the kids were. Not that he would be mad, she reminded herself. Not like I would be, if the situation were reversed, she acknowledged. Harry is just a better human than I am.

"It's too bad we got rid of all that extra furniture when we cleaned out Dad's house last spring," Evie said as she helped Rett pack up. "You could use it now."

"Oh, right! That reminds me that I had Dorie store two twin beds out at Alice's. I have beds for the girls, at least. I just have to get them." Rett picked up her phone.

A minute later, she reported to Evie. "Dorie says Chad will bring the beds into town, but she also said I should see what else is in the barn."

Evie squinted. "Really? I wonder what she means by that."

"I don't know. Do you want to come with me to look?"

The kids accompanied Rett and Evie to the dog sanctuary. Chad's grandmother, Alice, came out of the house with a big smile.

"Hello, hello!" she called out. "Mason, look at how big you are!" The kids said cursory hellos but headed to the dog enclosure, while Rett gave the old woman a hug. "How are you, Alice?"

"Pretty good, pretty good," Alice said. "The house must be busy now over to James's."

"Well, we've just found a place practically next door," Rett explained. "Dorie's got a couple of beds stashed in the barn. We're here to get them."

"I don't know what's in the back of the barn anymore. Let's go take a look." They walked toward the cacophony of barking that came from the barn and the fenced play yard. Mason and the twins were squatting by the fence, making friends with a shepherd mix.

Dorie came out the door. "Rett, have you seen the sign?" She gestured over her head to a wooden sign.

"No, I hadn't seen it, not in place," Rett said, gazing upward. "That's so nice." 'Best Friends Dog Sanctuary' was followed by 'In Memory of Agnes Madison and Marjorie Bartlett'. Mrs. Bartlett's estate supported the sanctuary.

"Mum would be so proud," Rett said.

"It looks nice, doesn't it?" Dorie said with proprietorial pride. "Now you need furniture. Let's go out back."

She led the way through a low door to the big back room of the barn, away from the dogs. "Here's your twin beds," she pointed out, sweeping her arm across an expanse filled with furniture.

Evie walked around as if in a daze. "Dorie, you kept all this stuff. I thought you were selling it to raise money for the dogs."

Dorie, a little shamefaced, shrugged. "I thought I was, but I didn't quite get around to it. Not yet anyway, and see, it's a good thing! Now Rett has some furniture to use."

"This stuff was all in Dad's attic?" Rett asked. "How come I didn't know?"

"Because you were too busy, remember?" Evie said. "You tried to help us sort it out, but work kept calling you in."

"Right." She wandered among the pieces of furniture. "Well, this is fortunate, I guess. I can use this table and chairs for sure. And there's two dressers."

"There's even a little lady's desk, if you want that," Dorie pointed out. "I figured that to be a good item, if we ever have a fundraising auction, but if you can use it, you should. It's just sitting here in the barn."

"You know, Rett, I probably have some stuff in the house you can have. Do you need dishes and pans and things like that?" Alice offered.

"I probably do," Rett said, "because I left my house in Saint Jacques fully equipped. I figured we'd be at Dad's, but that was just too chaotic for all of us."

"Well, I think we can supply you," Alice said. "Not elegant but utilitarian."

"That's all I need," Rett said. "I've never been much for elegance anyway."

Chad stuck his head through the open door from the dog part of the barn. "Did you find anything?"

"Oh, a treasure trove," Rett said.

"And Nan has more," Dorie added. "Can you drive?"

He chuckled. "It's good to be the guy with the truck. Everyone wants to be your friend."

By the middle of the second week in the field, when Harry hadn't been able to call home at all, had no idea about his own project, and was days behind in the jobs Marie assigned, he was feeling pressured. At least the building project was done, so he was available full time for field work.

Waking up at four every day, he went to the main tent, fired up the stove to make coffee, and pondered. Scribbling ideas almost always led to noting observations, sketches, writing descriptions to match the pictures he'd been taking. This was not about permafrost ecology, but about the land, the people, and the feelings Harry had about being there. He couldn't get his head to focus on finding a research question. Instead, he found himself writing a story for his children.

His days and nights had been filled with Joyce's consuming make-nice-with-the-locals plan, and Marie's get-Joyce's-data-collected-and-managed plan. He found it disturbing that his own research interests seemed to have evaporated.

He had made an optimistic plan to nail down his question, collect data, and be ready to analyze and write. He had completed none of it, and the calendar held shockingly few days before they were scheduled to leave. Marie was so cold to him he could feel the freeze. Denys and Alpha were busy and tired, and Joyce was inaccessible except to give him orders about staying connected to the village. It had been a lousy trip, except for his connection with Paul and his extended family. Harry looked at his incomplete list of things to accomplish. How was this supposed to work, anyway?

Marie showed up at five as usual, poured her coffee and then sat with her own notebook and thoughts. Stirred up, Harry approached her.

"Got a minute?"

She looked up annoyed, but said, "Go ahead."

"This trip isn't going how I thought," he said. "I haven't gotten near enough done."

"You, too?" She wasn't as nasty as he'd expected.

"I thought you were right on track," he said.

"I thought you were going to be part of the team," she retorted. "We've been trying to get the data collected with one man down, and she's breathing down my neck daily." She whispered this, looking toward the front flap of the tent.

"Joyce?"

"Who else? This trip was supposed to be my last one. My final push to get a project finished this fall. I don't think I'm going to make it."

Harry was surprised. "I thought I was the only one not getting stuff done."

"I should have known she'd have some agenda for you. She's kept me from finishing for years now."

Puzzled, Harry asked, "How is that possible?"

"It just happens. She really doesn't intend to create obstacles. There's just work for me to do; work for all of us."

"Isn't that the deal? We work for her, we get to work on her projects and ours?"

"Sometimes that works out and sometimes it doesn't," Marie hissed. "How's it working for you?"

"I figured I'm new, just learning," he said. "I do what I'm told."

"She likes that," Marie said. "But you'll never get any of your own work done. Trust me on that."

That couldn't be true, he thought. Lots of students finished their degrees while working in Joyce's lab. He knew three of them himself, or at least he had read their research.

"I have to," he said, more to himself than her. "I've got a family."

"Lucky you," Marie said soberly. "Priorities."

Harry felt unsure. "Circumstances. I left grad school to care for our baby while my wife finished her master's and started her career. Then the twins arrived, a little unexpectedly."

"At least you've got your kids."

He remembered the discussion he and Rett had before trying for a baby. Harry had been determined his children would be at home with a parent. Rett was determined she would finish her degree and start her career. It had sounded fine and, when she got pregnant almost right away, they thought they were the luckiest people in the world. Staying at home with Mason, even in the first six months when Rett was also on maternity leave, was the best thing Harry could have imagined. He learned to recognize Mason's little sounds, when he was fussing, or when he was really getting wound up to wail. Tucking a baby under his arm while he ate, pushed the vacuum cleaner, or picked up milk at the store became second nature. He could wear that baby as well as any mom, he'd thought with a tinge of satisfaction. Cooking, rather than a chore, became a mode of creative expression, and even a way to take personal action on climate change. Who knew that being the at-home adult could be fun? By the time Mason was two and in preschool, Harry had started to feel a little constrained though, and he took a graduate seminar to get updated on the research in his area. He could feel himself gearing up to get back to his work as soon as Mason was occupied during the day.

By the time Mason was in school, Harry was up to his elbows in diapers again, this time twins. Then Rett's mum had gotten sick and they headed to Stella Mare every weekend, kids and all. Nobody had any time to think, including Harry. It wasn't what they had planned, and it certainly wasn't what he'd expected.

Marie was right. The kids were his priority, even if he hadn't anticipated three of them. He couldn't feel any regret about that. Sitting here though, he did have some regret about the years he could have been doing research. Funny how you could both regret something and not regret it at the same time.

He realized he'd been silent for a long time. "You make me think," he said to Marie. "Maybe I need to be doing that a little more."

"Joyce has that effect. She tells you to do something and you do it. Later you wonder how your own work disappeared."

"What she's doing is important though."

"Absolutely. That doesn't mean my work isn't. Or that your work isn't."

If only he knew what that work was. But her point –being on Joyce's agenda might not help him move forward – was worth considering. He returned to his side of the table and gazed at his calendar again. For the millionth time, he wondered what Rett thought when she didn't hear from him. He couldn't help that though, so he just settled back into the information in front of him.

Marie's assigned tasks, Denys' project, what Alpha was doing, Joyce's big vision about permafrost – all these ideas swam in front of his eyes. Rather than parsing them into a research project he could do, Harry found himself sketching and scribbling. The impressions of his experience became the Labrador tea plants on the bog, the wildly twisted black spruce near the village, the story one of the men had told about a relative whose knowledge of caribou migration patterns was legend.

When Denys arrived to do breakfast preparation, Harry was startled to see how much time had passed. He tucked away his notebook and turned his attention to the work of the day.

Chapter 14

"Helen, I think it's time for me to quit this job," Rett said. Rett was in her living room at the rental on a video call with her sister.

"Why now?"

Rett sat up very straight. "I know I said before that I'd be letting them off the hook, or maybe acting like I did something wrong, but the financial pressure here is getting to be too much. I need to get a job."

"Are you sure, Rett? Dad said you were doing some farming or something?"

"Urban homesteading. Yeah. That's the plan. I've started the garden for fall, and I'm cleaning out the shed for chickens. We're going to make some money selling eggs, I think."

"Eggs? Really?"

Rett was getting tired of this response. "Well, it's a plan, anyway. I'm getting chickens and we're going to sell eggs. But a job would help."

"Who will watch the children while you work? This doesn't sound like you."

"Oh, I think it'll be okay. I can probably do a few shifts at the downtown clinic. Maybe Dad can watch the kids."

"Dad's got a lot of stuff already, doesn't he? Cardiac rehab and appointments and things."

"Maybe Evie, then. They'll be in school soon, anyway." Rett was impatient. "Listen, I don't need you to vet my life choices. I just want to know if there are legal ramifications of quitting, so I can get a job where they actually pay me."

Helen let out her breath slowly. "Okay. I'll just answer what you asked me. If you state clearly in your letter of resignation that you have no culpability, and that their decision to refuse your salary is why you are leaving, you should be fine."

"Okay," Rett replied with energy. "Thank you."

"Rett!" Helen said before she could hang up. "Take your time. Be aware."

"I'm aware," Rett said, laughing. "You know I'm always aware."

The kids were busy with paper and crayons at their little table in the kitchen, so Rett tapped out a letter of resignation on her laptop. Reading it critically, she thought about sending it to Helen for a second opinion, but then decided against it and sent it off to Mrs. Adamson and to Briar Ventures' department of human resources. "There!"

She opened a browser to look at jobs, and then she drafted a letter of interest, including her credentials and experience, and sent it to the downtown clinic. Firmly closing the laptop, she thought about Dr. Hackett. He'd remember her. She'd done a high-school project shadowing his office nurse for a week, and he'd written letters of recommendation for nursing school and her graduate program. She wondered why she'd waited so long to take this step.

Standing and stretching, she looked out the big windows of the dining room. An untidy pile of firewood sat in the driveway, waiting to be stacked.

"Hey, kids," she said. "Who wants to help me stack wood?"

Charlie jumped up immediately. "Not you, you big lug," she said, scratching his ears. "You don't have arms."

Maggie giggled. "Charlie can't stack wood because he has no arms."

"Right, but you can," Rett said. "Come on. Everybody with arms needs to help!"

The three kids left the table easily. Rett noted that for later: outdoor activity was preferred to colouring, at least early in the morning. Charlie came too, despite his lack of arms, and the small troop went outside to reconnoitre.

Forty-five minutes later, Rett looked at her half-finished woodpile and the girls, who'd each lasted about ten minutes, were off playing in the tall grass. Mason was actually sweeping out the shed to get ready for the chickens. Sweating and ready for a break, Rett headed inside for a drink.

She rapidly scrolled her emails, looking only for Streamside, Briar Ventures, or the Downtown Clinic. She felt mocked by her overflowing inbox, full of junk of no interest. Annoyed, she left her phone on the kitchen table and returned to stacking firewood.

About the time her body was calling for another break, Mason shouted from the back of the house. "Mum! Your phone."

"Thanks," she panted, jogging past him to grab it from the kitchen. "Rett Madison," she said, trying not to sound like she'd been running.

Mason watched her curiously. "Is it Daddy?" he asked.

She shook her head and put her finger to her lips. "Yes? Oh, hi, Angelica."

"Rett, I'm sorry to bother you," Angelica said. "I just, well, I need to talk to you."

Rett walked slowly to a chair. "How are you? I haven't heard from you in forever."

"There's an investigation," Angelica said.

"Yes, I know," Rett said. "I'm being investigated."

"You are too? I thought it was just me."

"Well, I talked to Ellen a while ago, and she said you and I were both off work."

"They told me not to talk to anybody from work," Angelica said thickly, "so I didn't. I didn't know about you. This is so messed up."

"It sure is."

Angelica sniffed. "They think I did something to those residents. The ones on the news."

Rett was shaking her head. "It's just so stupid. I had to talk to the police, too. When did they put you off work?"

"July eighth," Angelica said. "Worst day of my life, at least so far."

Rett thought. "We worked together on the seventh, right? That night Mrs. Adamson put me on administrative leave but I had to finish my shift."

"You didn't say anything. I had no idea."

"Yeah, well, they tell you not to talk to anyone," Rett said bitterly. "I guess we just followed directions."

"She called me the next morning while I was trying to sleep. She said don't come in to work, don't leave town, don't talk to anybody. Then the police called."

Rett was thinking fast. "Who else? Is anyone else off?"

"I don't know. I truly haven't talked to anyone. I just had to talk to you. We've worked together so long, and you know I would never hurt a resident." Angelica sobbed.

"Of course you wouldn't," Rett reassured. "Why now? What happened to make you call now?"

"They took away my license. My nursing assistant license."

"Who did?"

"The college." The college was the licensing body for certified nursing assistants in the province.

Rett felt a chill run up her spine. "Why? How could they do that?"

Angelica was frankly crying now. "I don't know. Maybe it isn't taken away, but it is suspended. I can't work as a nursing assistant right now, that's what I know."

Rett's mind was racing. "Can you file a protest?"

"I don't know," she said. "I don't have any idea what to do next. You know how my mother is. She's worried I'm going to prison, and I'm afraid this is going to kill her."

"Oh, honey," Rett said, sitting down. "Take a breath. You didn't hurt anybody and you're not going to prison."

"How do you know? Back in Mama's country, the police can just take you. She's praying every day."

"How are you managing?"

She sniffled. "It's okay. I use the food bank. Mama's church has been helping. She cooks, too, she can make food out of nothing, I swear, and my landlady has said we can stay here. Ricky's been good, too. He got a part time job after school. It's okay, people have been kind. Losing my license, this is scary. I just thought it was Briar Ventures being paranoid, but maybe something really bad is happening."

"Is it just us?" Rett wondered out loud. "Was anyone else let go?"

"I saw Darcy downtown once and she asked me about you. That's why I wondered if you were off, too. She was fishing for information."

"Maybe it was just us two," Rett mused. "Well, we can't read minds. If they don't tell us what they're thinking, we don't know. Do you want to come out here for a visit?"

"Where is 'out here'?"

Rett gave a short laugh. "I forgot; you don't know. The kids and I are in Stella Mare where my Dad lives."

"Really? You lost your house?"

"Well, not lost. I rented it out."

"Oh, that sounds smart," Angelica said.

"I'm not sure how smart," Rett admitted, "but it seemed like the best option at the time. Can you come down?"

"No, I don't think so," Angelica said. "Too far, too much gas, and my old car isn't really inspected. You know."

Rett did know. Angelica not only supported herself, her son and her mother, she sent money every month to support her mother's sisters in El Salvador. Even when she was working, things were tight in her household.

Well, in mine too, Rett thought with some surprise. I guess we're both just doing what we have to.

"I was getting ready to look for a new job," Rett said. "Now I'm a little worried about that."

"Yeah, well, I found out when I applied at the hospital," Angelica said. "It was hard enough to hold up my head, knowing that somebody thinks I've done wrong, and then to have the head of human resources tell me I don't have a license anymore was awful. Just awful."

"I'm going to write a letter to your college," Rett said. "Losing your license is just ridiculous."

"Thanks. I don't know if it will help, but it can't hurt," Angelica said. "I'll look at how to protest their decision, too. There must be a process."

"I'm sure," Rett agreed. "Let's keep in touch. This thing that happened is terrible enough, but at least you're not totally alone with it. I'm in it too."

"I do feel better," Angelica agreed. "A little guilty because Mrs. Adamson said not to talk, though."

Rett scoffed. "I don't think she gets to dictate that. Not at this point. I'll call you next week, but if anything happens before that, we'll get in touch, right?"

"Right. Thank you, Rett. You take care of yourself and those kids."

Rett smiled. "You bet. You too. Give your mama a hug for me."

As she clicked off, Mason and the girls tumbled into the kitchen, arguing about something, banging into the refrigerator and cupboards, looking for snacks. She turned her back and went to the living room, staring at her phone. She found the website for Angelica's professional organization. Clicking the Contact Us link, she tapped out her message.

How dare they, she thought. What a terrible thing to do to a good person.

She sat on the couch as she typed on her phone. Mason followed her into the living room. "Mum?"

She absently patted the couch next to her. "Just a minute, okay? I've got to finish this."

He sat but wiggled impatiently while she tapped and scrolled. Narrowing her eyes, she read over her note, then signed it Loretta Madison, RN. How dare they suggest this excellent nursing assistant could ever do something so terrible? Her letter would make their mistake clear.

"Mum? Mum, are you okay?" Mason's voice was far away. She felt him shaking her arm.

"Yes, yes, Mason," she said, coming to awareness. "I'm okay. What do you need?" She dropped her phone and watched it slip between the sofa cushions. Good. She was sick of the crazy outside world anyway. It was better to pay attention to home.

"The twins were fighting over snacks, so I gave everybody three cookies." He looked a little scared as he spoke.

She mustered a smile. "Well, Mason, three cookies. That was very generous of you," she said, standing up. "Did you take three cookies, too?"

He nodded slowly, watching her face.

"I suppose we could call that enlightened self-interest. Thanks for keeping the girls from fighting, Mase. Maybe next time only one cookie, okay?"

He looked up at her with Harry's thoughtful expression. "Okay. But they only promised to be good for three."

She chuckled and ruffled his hair. "Come on. Let's go for a drive. I need to get out of here."

She drove across the narrow road that linked Stella Mare to Minister's Island, noting the tide. They probably had a few hours before the road would become impassible, long enough to tire the kids and the dog, she thought. Gunning her engine up the hill, she parked the van in the field, found Charlie's leash, and grabbed a backpack full of sweaters and water bottles.

"Come on, kids," she said. "Let's go exploring." She set off with the dog, with only a quick backward glance to see the three children in her wake.

"Mum! Wait for us!" Maggie called. Rett plowed on. They'd keep up.

She turned at the top of the hill to see them all clambering up behind her. Already she felt better. At least her body was doing something. "Isn't this fun?" she asked brightly.

"Yes!" Callie shouted.

"Hey, Mum, there's a trail here," Mason pointed out.

"Let's go," she said. The kids took off, and she released Charlie to bound off toward Mason. She followed a little more slowly. The summer sun warmed her back like a blanket. She sighed, dropping her shoulders.

Mason ran back to her with a palmful of berries. "Can we eat these?"

"They look like blueberries, but show me the plant where you got them." Together they peered near the ground where red leaves shone in the late afternoon light. "Aren't you lucky, Mason. Look at all of those berries. Yes, you can eat them. We can pick a bunch and make blueberry muffins."

He called the twins. "Hey, you guys, want some blueberries?"

"Mum, these are little baby blueberries," Callie said. "Not like at the store."

"Right," Rett said absently. "These are wild ones. Your grandmother used to pick buckets of these and make pies."

"Pumpkin pie?" Maggie asked.

"No, silly," Mason corrected. "Blueberry pie."

Rett thought about her mother's pies. "Hey, kids, I'm going down to the car to get a container. Let's see how many of these we can gather. Maybe I'll make a pie. Mason, keep an eye on your sisters."

She jogged down the hill toward the van. The world was a crazy place when good people like Angelica could be accused of bad things, but at least there were wild blueberries and the possibility of pie.

Chapter 15

H arry didn't know how it had happened, but he lay at the
bottom of a steep grade with his leg bent at an unnatural angle
under him. When he opened his eyes, daylight filtered through the
heavy canopy. He had a raging headache and a pain in his lower right
leg that was beyond description. Nausea overcame him. Leaning over
to let the vomit clear his mouth felt like a hundred sledgehammers
landing on his brain. Spitting, and cautiously moving his head, he
leaned back against a rock as everything faded to black.

Some time later, he came alert again. This time, he shifted his weight
slightly and moved his hips to take the weight off his right leg. The
pain was still there, yes, but so was thirst, deep, penetrating and urgent.
He realized his pack was still on his back; he'd been leaning against it.
With extreme economy of motion, he slid one strap off his shoulder
and fumbled for a water bottle.

For a brief moment, as the cool water slid over his tongue, he felt
bliss, then the pain of his head and leg returned. As much as he wanted
to drink down all the water, some part of him was aware enough to

keep a limit. A mouthful, he cautioned himself, and managed to stop after two.

Thirst abated, he noticed the sun through the trees. Slanting now, shadows lengthening. Where was he? Who knew where to look for him? Thoughts were fragmented but still starting to link together. He remembered that morning—was it only that morning?—telling Marie which quadrant he'd be headed to, but then, did he deviate? Was there something that took him off course? He couldn't remember and settled, instead, for looking in his backpack. Yes, he was equipped and no, this was no fun at all. He found painkillers in his first aid kit and swallowed four, using a scant amount of water to wash them down.

Could his right leg move? Harry reminded himself pain was only a signal. It might mean he genuinely couldn't move, or it might just mean moving was a bad idea. He tested it out.

It was a bad idea. Really bad, but movement was possible. The pain was so exquisite that nausea threatened again, so he stopped, breathed, and waited until his mind cleared a little. Economy. Economy of movement. What did he need the most right now?

He focused on his breathing until it slowed slightly, and then asked himself the question again. Unbidden, Rett's face appeared. "Harry, come home."

He was nearly overcome with longing but forced his mind to work. Remember, pain is a signal. Panic is not an option, he reminded himself. It's a signal, that's all.

That's what he needed—a signal. He'd fallen off the trail, obviously, even though he wasn't certain how he'd landed wherever he was. People would be looking for him, wouldn't they? He thought about Marie's obdurate silence of the last days and wondered if she'd be happy he was lost. Would Joyce even notice? He slumped onto the rock, but the pain in that tiny movement alerted him once again. This is not time to fall apart, he counselled himself. Make a noise. Build a fire. Create a signal.

He dug deeper into his pack and found a box in the very bottom, something Alpha had insisted on, but he'd never looked at it. He dug it out. The Emergency label mocked him, but he used his pocketknife to get it open anyway.

Daylight was receding, so he knew it was getting late as he pried the top off the metal box. The inside was clean and dry, two things Harry was not. He pulled out a whistle, a small pile of emergency flares, and a metal tin of matches. Blowing the whistle hurt his leg and his head, but it also felt he was taking useful action. The sound reverberated. Better than trying to shout. Looking around at the ravine he was in, he wondered if the sound was getting out of this ditch. Regardless, he continued to send out blasts, first at random, then in a pattern he remembered from childhood, the SOS his uncle had taught him.

Taking a break, he ate a protein bar and washed it down with a small drink. The pain in his leg was not less, but something about trying to help himself made it, well, not really easier, but not as hard. He tried once again to shift so his leg was straight and, this time, with a mighty effort and a scream of pain, he was successful.

Okay, so now he knew. Moving was a bad idea, but it was not impossible. Not impossible, he said to himself. Not impossible. This is not impossible.

He turned to look uphill at the side of the ravine he'd slipped down. Not impossible. He needed to keep his pack with him though, since it held food, water, and those emergency flares. Not impossible, he muttered to himself and manoeuvred the pack back onto his shoulders and turned to the steep rocky face. *Not impossible.*

The long reach of late-day light shone on the rocky incline, highlighting his way. He moved in tiny increments, reaching with one arm, supporting his dragging leg, wincing and trying not to gasp with each shift of his weight. He looked up only the inches he needed to see the next handhold, and then the next. He was surrounded by the scent of freshly disturbed soil and crushed green plants; his hand grasped rocks, soil, and roots. Inch by excruciating inch, he moved back up the slope.

This is not impossible. He looked up to find an earthy overhang, perhaps where he'd slipped originally. He was quite literally under this overhang, which made an effective ceiling. To his right he saw a clear way to the top, but he'd have to get over there, and his right leg was dragging. This was too much. He leaned his head against the dirt and rock under the overhang. Though it felt solid here for the moment, he knew he was neither safe nor likely to be seen, but he just couldn't move any more. He fumbled for the whistle around his neck. Summoning energy, he gave a weak tweet. Then another, and then stronger, blast after blast. Blast, blast, blast and...

"Harry? Harry?" He heard a man's voice. Paul's head looked over the edge to his right. "Okay, Harry, just hold on, man," Paul said. "We're going to get you."

Rett was in major problem-solving mode in the soon-to-be chicken house. She was measuring and sawing when she heard a man's voice calling to her. Her heart leaped. Had Harry come home?

Before she could even note that thought, her neighbour Jürgen stuck his head inside the little shed.

"Good morning," he said.

"Oh, hi," she said, brushing away her excitement as she dusted off her hands. "What can I do for you?"

He shook his head. "Not a thing. I was wondering if I can do something for you? Looks like you've got some plans for this old place." He looked around the shed.

"Yes, chickens," she said. "I'm trying to figure out how to turn this shed into a nice chicken coop."

He raised one eyebrow. "Chickens," he repeated.

"Yes, you know, egg layers," she said. He was smiling at her. "What? Do you think I'm crazy?"

"Oh, no, not at all," he said, still smiling. "What do chickens need?"

"Well, I got this book at the library," she said, gesturing to the open manual. "I read some stuff online, too. They need nest boxes, and places to roost, and mostly need to be safe from foxes at night."

"Hawks and eagles during the day," he added, soberly.

"Really? I didn't know that," she said. "Well, we'll just have to figure it out. We're having chickens."

"Well, let's see what you're trying to do in here, and maybe I can help. I've got a garage full of old lumber, power tools, and a lot of free time."

"That's so nice," Rett said, finally smiling back. "I'm good at some things, but carpentry isn't one of them."

"Well," he said, "I don't know how good I am, but I can follow a blueprint and saw a straight line."

"Two things I'm not so sure of," she said. "I appreciate your help."

He wrote down her measurements and they went together into the kitchen to plan the next step. Mason and Charlie, fresh from visiting Grandpa through the woods, burst in as they sipped coffee at the table.

"Hi," he said, startled.

"Mason, do you remember Jürgen? He helped us move in," Rett said. "He's going to help with the chicken house."

"Hi, Mason," Jürgen said. "Nice dog you've got there."

Charlie, sitting at Mason's side, thumped his tail on the floor.

"His name is Charlie," Mason said in his quiet voice. "We visited Grandpa and Mallow."

"Mallow is one of my father's dogs," Rett explained to Jürgen. "Mason built a trail that goes from our backyard right to my dad's house. Being so close was the most attractive thing about this house."

She looked around the kitchen. The spotless windows now spilled morning light onto the ancient linoleum. "Well, and the rent."

"Yeah," Mason said, "it was cheap." Rett laughed in surprise at her eight-year-old's comment.

Jürgen laughed. "It needed to be cheap considering the condition. I'm really glad to have you as neighbours, though. It's made a big difference to the street, just knowing you and the kids are here."

"And Charlie," Mason said.

"Charlie, too," Jürgen agreed. "It was pretty lonely here last winter."

"The house has been empty longer than one winter," Rett said.

"Yes, of course, but I've only been here one winter. I used to spend my winters in Portugal, but not any more."

"Why not?" Mason asked.

"Shh," Rett said. "We don't ask personal questions, Mason. Remember?"

"Things change," Jürgen said. "I'm just glad to have such good neighbours." He leaned his head closer to Rett's as she pored over the chicken manual.

"My dad's coming home soon," Mason announced, much louder than usual.

"Is he?" Jürgen said, looking up. "That's great. I can't wait to meet him."

Rett, puzzled, said, "Not for quite a while, Mason. He's got a lot of work to do, remember?"

Mason's reply, if he had one, was lost in the kerfuffle of the girls arriving at home, accompanied by their Aunt Dorie and Frou-Frou, the white poodle.

"Hey, everyone," Dorie called from the front door. "We're here!"

"Unnecessary announcement," Rett said, going to greet her. "The kids were hard to miss. Come on in."

Dorie looked up and past Rett's shoulder, surprise on her face. Rett looked behind her. Jürgen, tall and lean, lounged against the door frame. His streaked hair was swept back and his jeans hung on his hips.

Rett looked back at Dorie, whose mouth was making an o. "Jürgen is going to help me with the chicken house," she explained. "You guys met, right, when we first looked at this place?"

"Oh, right, Jürgen, hello." Dorie said, finding her manners. "That's nice of you to help Rett out."

"It is my pleasure," he said formally. "I have time, and I am happy to have such lovely neighbours."

"Right," Dorie said, still looking a little stunned.

"You want lunch?" Rett asked her. "It's time to feed the kids anyway. Come in."

"I'll be leaving," Jürgen said.

"You can have lunch, too," Rett said, "as long as you like KD." At his blank look, she explained, "You know, mac and cheese in the blue box."

"No, thank you," he said, and headed out the front door. "I'll come back later with some lumber for your project."

Rett waved him off and turned to the kitchen, where kids, dogs, and running water were making conversation impossible. She wasn't too sure she liked how Dorie was looking at her.

After a big rush of boiling water, hand washing, table setting, and tea-making, the kids were settled with their bowls and Dorie and Rett took sandwiches to the backyard. Perched on a chunk of a log that served as a patio chair, Dorie asked, "Chicken house?"

Rett and Dorie burst into a spate of giggles.

"He's the most attractive chicken-house helper I ever saw," Dorie spluttered. "What's his angle?"

Rett shrugged as she wiped snorted tea off her face. "I don't know and I don't really care. I need the help. I thought I could just follow directions, but it turns out you need skills. He might help us get chickens before winter, you know?"

"This guy knows you have a husband, right?" Dorie sounded suspicious.

Rett giggled again. "Well, if he had any question about that, Mason set him straight. Besides, he's probably just what he says he is, happy to help out the new neighbours."

Dorie's eyebrows were up, but she didn't say any more about Jürgen. "What do you hear from Harry?"

Rett's giggles subsided immediately. "Nothing. He was supposed to be getting in touch on Thursdays, but I have heard exactly nothing since they went out into the field. They have a satellite phone for emergencies, so I know nothing terrible has happened, but he was expecting to get into town weekly and check in then."

"So you have no idea what's going on with him?"

"Right. The kids and I sent email updates but I have to assume he hasn't gotten them yet. He'd call or at least text, if he could."

"That's not how you thought it would be, is it?" Dorie's eyes were sympathetic.

"It's okay," Rett said. "He's working. I'm sure he's working super hard so he can get his data collected and get back here. He's planning to do the balance of the analysis and writing from the university here, but he needs these months in the field and working with Joyce McGinty."

"Have I ever heard of her?" Dorie asked, face scrunched up.

"Probably not. I never had, and I've lived with Harry's obsessions for all these years. She's extremely well-known in her field, but it's not trending, you know. Except in science circles."

Dorie pondered while she finished her sandwich. "Does Harry know?"

"Know what?"

"Well, all this," she said, gesturing widely. "This house, chickens, you know."

Rett paused while she finished her sandwich. Then she said, "No."

"No?" Dorie pressed. "No? Harry has no idea?"

"I've sent those emails but he hasn't gotten them, so yeah. It goes both ways. I have no idea about Harry and he has no idea about all..." She mimicked Dorie's gesture. "...this."

"Wow." Now Dorie was silent, gazing over the scrubby backyard toward the treeline. "Hey, is that Mason's trail?"

Turning a sharp gaze on her sister, Rett said, "Yes. Thanks for changing the subject."

"You're welcome. There's not much to say about that. If you're out of touch, of course it goes both ways." She leaned toward the trees. "I like how he's put a flag up there. Did he make that?"

Rett peered toward the trees. "I guess so," she said. "He keeps himself busy."

A crashing sound came from the woods, and Custard and Mallow bounded into the backyard, James following behind.

"Dad!" Dorie shouted, with a big wave. The kids burst from the house. Grandpa hadn't come over often and never with the dogs.

Rett sighed, gathered her dishes and Dorie's, and went into the house. Watching the reunion of kids, dogs, grandpa, and aunt through the wavy glass, she felt overwhelming sleepiness. This life, it was a little too much. Too many people, too many problems, too much to do. But she'd always been at her best with too much to do. When it feels worst, then you do your best, she reminded herself. That philosophy had gotten her through a lot of hard times.

Doing her best, right now, meant going back outside to see her father, continuing to try connecting with Harry, keeping in touch with Angelica and, somehow, clearing her own name. She'd done nothing wrong, but this new life was a continual reminder that somebody thought she had.

Chapter 16

Harry spent four days at Paul's grandmother's house in the village, being fed and fussed over. He slept through the first two days, blessed relief that sleep was, though Jeannette kept waking him and checking his pupils. When Harry finally came to himself, he found that his leg had been bandaged, his scratches treated and his headache, while not gone, was more manageable.

"So you're awake," said Jeannette.

Harry pushed himself up to sitting on the cot. He was in the kitchen. "Yeah, I guess so," he said, swiping a hand over his hair and looking around.

"You looking for your glasses?" she asked, and handed them to him. "Amazing they didn't break."

"I guess it is," he agreed, looking at them then putting them on. Ah, now he could see his surroundings. "Thanks for taking me in."

She nodded, then handed him a mug. "Tea," she said.

He sipped and grimaced. "Tea?"

"Medicine tea," she said with a grin. "Drink it. It will help you heal."

"It's pretty nasty," he said.

She nodded again. "Drink it anyway."

"Does Joyce—"

"She knows. She sent Alpha around to see."

"Guess they weren't worried," he said. He swung his feet around to the floor. He started to get up, but the room swirled, so he sat back down.

"You wait a minute," Jeanette said. "Paul's coming. We'll help you get up."

A couple more days passed before Harry was allowed to leave Jeannette's care.

"Exhaustion, dehydration, a lot of banging and bruising, a very bad sprain and a concussion," Paul announced, as Harry leaned on a stick to walk with him. "That's according to my grandmother, who I'd trust over any doctor."

"Nothing life-threatening."

Paul laughed shortly. "Except all of it would be, if you were out in the forest. Being lost was more dangerous than your injuries."

"Yeah," Harry said soberly. "Thanks for looking for me."

Paul shrugged. "Joyce came over and asked us to help search. More eyes and ears, you know."

"Thanks for taking care of me," he said. "Jeannette has magic hands, I think."

Paul laughed. "She's been doctoring all of us forever. She tells us if we need to look for a different kind of doctor."

"It sounds like you've got medical experience."

"Mostly first aid. She knows more, truly. More than anybody I know."

A roar of engines announced Denys on the side-by-side. Harry hoisted his pack. "Thanks, man. I can't say it enough." Paul clapped him on the shoulder, but gently. Harry climbed into the vehicle, trying not to wince.

Denys looked at Harry. "Well, man, good to see you," he said over the roar of the engine. "Glad you're coming back to camp."

Harry nodded, but he had all he could do to hold onto his composure as the vehicle bounced over rocks and ruts on the rough trail back to camp. The twenty-minute ride felt longer, his head pounding from the noise and his leg aching from hip to toes. When they finally came to a stop, he was thinking only about the painkillers in his pack, but Joyce and Marie came out of the main tent to greet him.

"Good to see you, Harry," Joyce said brusquely. "We're getting behind. We need every pair of hands." She nodded at him, then turned toward her own tent.

Marie reached out a hand to him as Denys roared away to park the ATV. He took it, grateful for the support. "How are you?" she asked. "Sorry I didn't come to see you. We've been busy here."

"I'm okay," he said. How to explain he was different now, that he would quite possibly never be okay again in his life?

"Paul's sure nothing is broken?" she asked.

"Paul and his grandmother," Harry said. "I'm sure too. My head might be a little broken, but no broken bones, if that's what you mean."

"Right," she said. "Well, good. We really need you at work. I'm glad you're better."

He followed her into the main tent. Denys came in behind them. "Did you call my wife?" Harry asked Marie. "Did anyone let her know?"

"Know what?" Marie asked. "We go into town on Thursday, so no. Nobody called your wife."

He sat down.

"What?" she demanded. "You were okay. It wasn't an emergency, you know."

"It felt like an emergency to me," he said softly. "But okay. I get it."

"Harry, you don't seem to understand that we're fighting nature here. On a deadline due to fall and the next semester."

Her voice came from far away. "I get it," he said again. "I do understand."

She kept talking, but he couldn't make any sense of it. He stood up, picked up his pack and walking stick, and made his way out of the main tent, past Denys. He walked past the kitchen area, where Alpha stirred a pot of chili, and on toward his tent. Pushing open the flap, he sank down on his cot and rummaged in his pack for pills and water, then pulled off his boots and lay down, sinking into blessed slumber.

On Thursday, Rett carried her phone everywhere. When she was working in the kitchen, she plugged it in so there would be no possibility of running out of juice. She turned the ring volume up as high as possible and pulled it out so often she thought she was wearing a hole in her jeans pocket. This was the fourth Thursday since he'd gone to field camp.

Finally at three p.m., the familiar sound of a video call came while she was digging in the garden with the kids. She looked at Mason and headed for the house, pulling the phone out of her pocket. He followed, calling to his sisters. "Daddy! Daddy's calling."

The four tumbled through the kitchen, Charlie jumping with shared excitement, to land on the couch in the living room.

"Shh," Rett said, and then she spoke into the phone. "Harry? Harry, are you there?"

The kids leaned on her, everyone all piled together on the couch. She held the phone at arm's length so they could all see, and yes, there he was. The video cut in and out but they could see and hear him.

"Daddy! It's Daddy," said Callie.

Maggie shouted, "Hi, Daddy."

Mason leaned closer to his mother and smiled at the phone.

Harry looked tired. "Hi, you guys. It is so good to see you."

"Why didn't you call us?" Mason asked. "Where have you been?"

Rett wanted to ask those same questions. Instead, she said, "Hi, Harry."

"Daddy, we got a new house," Callie shouted.

"I saw that email from Mum," Harry said. "Is it nice?"

"We have a big yard," Maggie shouted.

"And a trail to Grandpa's house," Mason added, apparently getting over his annoyance. "I built it myself."

"Oh, a whole trail," Harry said. "That's great."

"Harry, are you okay?" Rett asked. He really didn't look great. She expected he'd be maybe thin and very tanned, but he was pasty and looked dark under the eyes.

The kids were listening. "I'm okay, of course," he said. "It's just been a little crazier here than I thought."

"Exceeded your expectations?" Rett asked.

He nodded. "I'll have to tell you, uh, later." She wondered what had happened that he couldn't talk about in front of the kids. He was right, that would have to be later. The kids needed this time.

"We're getting chickens," Mason announced.

"We made a garden and Mum's going to get some baby goats," Callie said.

"Daddy, can you come home?" Maggie asked. "I want to show you my room."

"Not right now, Mags. I'm sorry I haven't been able to call until now."

"That's been hard, Harry," Rett said firmly. "I'm sure you're doing your best, but we really need to hear from you."

"Daddy, can you read me a story?" Callie asked.

"Not right now," Rett said.

"No, I can't, baby, not now," Harry said. "I wish I could, but I have to get ready to go back to camp."

"What's at camp?"

"Oh, it's amazing," Harry said. "I live in a tent. And I work in another tent. And I go out into the woods to look for animals and plants and dirt and take measurements and then come back to a tent."

"But Daddy! Where do you pee?"

"Callie," Rett started.

"That's a valid question, Callie. We have a latrine. Mum can tell you what that is."

"Do you take a shower there?" she persisted.

"No showers. We wash up in the lake. It's the coldest bath you could ever take," he said, smiling at her. "Do you want to take an icy cold bath?"

"No!" The twins were clear. "That's yucky." He laughed along with them.

Rett felt her shoulders drop. That sounded like Harry. He might not look like himself, but he was definitely their daddy. After a few more minutes, Harry said to the kids, "Hey, guys, can I have a conversation with Mum?"

"No!" Maggie whined, but Rett gave her a little glance and she pouted but agreed. The three waved to Harry and Maggie kissed Rett's phone, then they headed back outdoors.

"So," Rett said into the sudden quiet.

"So," Harry said in return.

She waited.

"You moved into a house in Stella Mare," Harry said. Her belly tightened.

"You've been out of touch for a month, Harry. I had to make some decisions."

"I know my going away would make some changes, but I didn't expect my home to be gone," he said with some bitterness.

She was immediately enraged. "Do you think I did this to you? This is a solution to a problem, Harry. A big problem."

He sighed and his shoulders slumped. "It just seems kind of extreme, that's all." He didn't look at her.

"Extreme measures were called for. You were gone, out of touch entirely, and I had no money coming in, except what was left of your stipend after your expenses, and now, now, I can't even get a job." Her voice caught.

He shook his head. "What do you mean? You have a job, don't you?"

"You don't know everything that's been going on."

"No, obviously. But tell me."

She shook her head. "It's too much and it's too hard. I'll write you about it."

"Rett, I won't get that until next week, if then. Can't you tell me?"

Her eyes threatened to overflow. "No, really. I have to take care of things here. I'm just doing my best, Harry. You can't be second-guessing me."

"Okay. You're right. You're handling things there."

"Why haven't I heard from you?" She hated the way she sounded, whiny and needy, but she couldn't help it. "What's been so important that you can't be bothered to call your family?"

He sighed. "I can't even tell you what it's like here. First, we have to drive over two hours to get within cell and internet coverage. Joyce is frantic about getting the work done in the limited time we have, and then, there was an incident..."

She interrupted. "You don't go to town because of work?"

"We don't all get to go each week. Somebody goes to get supplies, but Joyce says we can't waste the time it would take for everyone to go. And there have been some other things, too."

"You won't get there next week either?"

"Probably not, because it's the end of field camp. But listen, I've been thinking about leaving the project. Coming home."

"Oh, no," Rett said firmly. "We're okay, Harry, really. Stay there. This is your chance, your work."

"I don't have to..."

"Yes, you do," she said. "We've all made changes to support you in getting this project going, and we're not going to be the reason you don't get to do it."

"But it's not you," he started.

"The kids are fine, honestly. We have a lot of good projects going on here, and school starts soon. Chickens and goats, and I'm baking bread, and we're going to sell blueberry pies."

"Goats? What about your job, Rett?"

"Oh, that," she said, airily. "Well, I think with the chickens and the garden we'll be okay. I might get a little job in the village. We'll be fine."

"Be okay? Just okay?"

She sighed. "It's no big deal. Don't worry about it. You look tired out."

He sighed in turn. "Yeah, well, I got banged up last week, but I'm doing fine. Nothing to be concerned about."

"What do you mean, you got banged up?"

"I just had a fall on the trail. No lasting damage."

A scream erupted from the backyard, making Rett look. "Oh, somebody skinned a knee."

"You better go," he said. "I miss you."

"I miss you too," she replied. "Maggie's bleeding though. Gotta go."

"Rett, wait."

She stopped, watching his face, feeling her chest tighten. "Harry, I can't. The kids need me now."

Eyes swimming, she ended the call and lifted her chin. How could it feel worse to talk to him than to live with the silence? Dropping the phone on the couch, she headed to the kitchen, where Mason was shepherding in his little sister. "Okay, let's take a look at that knee."

Chapter 17

Something truly had changed for Harry.

When it was time to head back out to collect data, he felt a little sick. Not scared, not exactly, but he couldn't imagine how he'd found it easy and even fun before. The first day back, he asked if he could hang with Denys.

"Sure, I guess so," Denys agreed. "But there's not enough for two of us to do in one quadrant."

"It's silly, but I just don't feel okay about going out alone today," Harry said, shamefaced. "Just for today, okay?"

"It's gonna put you further behind, you know," Denys said helpfully. "Marie's gonna have your hide. She's annoyed already."

"Yeah, well, I'll just have to take it, I guess," he said. "She can be mad. I could be dead, and she wouldn't have my data either. She'll just have to suck it up."

Denys shook his head, but he took Harry with him very early the next morning. Pouring coffee into his thermos, Harry shook off a lingering feeling of dread. He'd be fine; they would have a good day and he'd get back in the saddle, so to speak. Just for today, he told himself.

They headed out shortly before sunrise on the side-by-side to get to the general locale, then worked on foot together through the forest.

They returned late, but with a full complement of specimens and pictures, measurements and other data. Marie had her storm-cloud face on, but Harry was undisturbed.

"Good day," he commented to Denys.

"Yeah, not bad," the other man agreed. "Productive, at least."

Harry nodded. "I did more today than I've managed any day on my own," he noted.

"Working entirely alone isn't for everyone," Denys said. "I don't mind it, but today felt easier and more fun, and you're right, we were productive. Maybe we should try it again. Tomorrow we could work your quadrant."

"Would you do that? Really?"

"Yeah, I think we got a little ahead today, so maybe I can help you catch up."

"Hey, what's going on?" Alpha wandered into their conversation.

"Denys and I went out together today," Harry explained. "It turned out to be more efficient than we expected."

"Didn't want to go out alone, huh?" Alpha asked him. "I can understand that. How was it more efficient? Two people on a quadrant sounds less efficient."

The men looked at each other. "You'd think. But in terms of actual data collected, number of specimens and observations, we did well."

"Well, you can't argue with data," Alpha observed. "Maybe you're onto something."

"Maybe," Harry said, "but you're right, I was squeamish about going out alone."

"Anybody would be," they said comfortingly. "You don't have to confess it, Harry. It's normal."

"Thanks," he said. He turned to help Denys unload the new specimens, avoiding Marie's black look. She wasn't happy, that was clear, but Harry didn't particularly care. Everything would have to go into their main tent to be catalogued and packed for the return trip to the university.

Joyce roared into the campsite, parked the ATV, and strode to the main tent. "Harry."

"Hi, Joyce." Between Marie's dark looks and Joyce's demanding voice, Harry was feeling some tension, so he consciously lowered his voice.

"Come take a walk with me," she said.

Harry looked at Denys, who waved him off. "Go. I've got this."

She was walking faster than he could, so he was behind her, like a dog at heel, he thought with some bitterness. She stopped abruptly and turned back to him. "Sorry," she said. "I forgot your wings are still pinned."

"Yes. I'm still a little slow," he said. "I did get a full day in today, though."

"That's fine," she said, brushing it off. "Listen, what did you do over there?" She gestured to the west.

"Where? At the village?"

"You made an impression."

"I don't know how. I just laid around in Jeannette's kitchen until she said I could leave."

"Well, that's not the story I hear. They have a pet name for you."

"Well, only because they were making fun of me," Harry recalled with a smile. "Paul called me wet-behind-the-ears, and Jeannette said I was like a moose calf."

"And?"

"Well, it wasn't complimentary," Harry said with a short laugh. "If Paul hadn't found me, I don't think I'd be here talking to you."

"Oh, you weren't in any real danger," Joyce demurred. "No risk of hypothermia, and we'd have located you sooner or later."

"Dead or alive," Harry said.

"We weren't worried," she said.

"I was," he said frankly. "I didn't expect to get out of the woods that day."

"I've never lost a student yet," Joyce said stoutly. "In the lab maybe, but not in the woods. But that's not what I wanted to talk to you about. How's your project shaping up?"

Harry was glad to look across the landscape. "I'm having some trouble," he admitted.

"What kind of trouble?" She was direct, but it didn't sound unkind.

"I can't quite see where I can make a contribution," he admitted. "I respect and appreciate what everyone here in camp is working on, and I'm glad to participate, but no part of this work seems to be calling me. It's a great honour to work with you," he added, stumbling over his words.

"I wondered," she said simply. "You're busy every minute, but with what?"

He sighed miserably. "I record observations from the work in the village. Been listening to Jeannette talk about healing. Taking pictures of just about everything. Sketching plants, landscapes, faces. I've probably learned more in the last four weeks than in all my years in school. I just haven't figured out what to do with it."

"This place can have that effect," she said. "It rearranges your brain, makes you different."

"Yes," he agreed with enthusiasm. "That's just it. I've lost my footing, and I don't just mean when I fell off that cliff." The only other time he remembered feeling so disoriented was after Mason was born. He didn't know if Joyce could relate. He recalled the long nights of wondering if he'd ever feel like himself again. This was similar, only with sleep.

"What do you have to take back to the university?" Joyce asked. "Do you have a hypothesis? Data? Something to work on?"

He shook his head. "Plenty of work, but not my own work. I really don't know what to do."

She stopped and faced him. "I have an idea about that."

"I'm listening."

"It sounds like you need to be here a while longer."

He shrugged. It wasn't what he planned, but she was probably correct. He remembered Marie talking about being here in the fall, dropping his expectations.

"We didn't get everything done either, partly because you were banged up," she went on.

And because you kept sending me on other errands, he thought, annoyed, but he kept quiet.

"I think you should stay," she said abruptly. "You can finish collecting our samples, keep connected with Paul and Jeannette, and sort yourself out. You're an asset in our relationship with the local people, by the way."

Stay? Maybe this was what Marie had meant about things changing. "By myself?"

"No, Marie is staying on for a couple more weeks. She can use your help. I've got to get back for the start of fall semester, but you're not teaching. You can stay here. Otherwise, what are you going to do?"

She had a point. He hadn't formulated a project, and when he did, he'd have to collect data, so going back to the university wasn't going to be productive. He could spin his wheels here as well as there. If he stayed here, he might get some traction. But with Marie? "I guess that's okay," he said.

"Of course it's okay," she asserted. "Good. Now let's tell Marie she's going to have some help. The rest of us are leaving in ten days."

"Is there a trip to town in those ten days?"

"Probably not. We've got to make the best use of the days we have left, and that takes everyone away from work for a whole day. Anything that needs to be done on a Thursday can wait until the following Sunday."

Great. He couldn't even tell Rett the news that he'd be staying in the field camp. With Marie. Until who knows when.

Chapter 18

Late July days were hot. Blue, blue skies and unrelenting sunshine made the tomatoes set fruit, bleached out the lettuce, and generated zucchini beyond Rett's fondest garden dreams. She and the chickens poked around in the garden for bugs, but when she realized the chickens were more thorough, she left them to it.

By early August though, mornings felt cooler.

"Bye, Mum," Mason called from the driveway. Dorie was there with Chad's truck.

"Wait a minute," she called back, picking her way across the garden fencing. "What's the plan?" she asked her sister.

"I'm going to work," Mason said importantly.

Dorie laughed. "That's right. I have an appointment in town at two, so I can bring him home then. Is that okay?"

"Sure," Rett said. "If we're not home, go to Grandpa's, okay?"

"Where are you going?" Mason asked.

"Oh, probably nowhere, but just in case, Grandpa's. Got it?"

"Got it."

"Have fun with the dogs." She waved them off, but before she could get back to the garden, Jürgen walked up the driveway carrying a cardboard box.

"Good morning, Rett," he said, smiling. "I hope you can help me."

"Sure," she said. "That box looks heavy." She noted his muscular forearms.

"Not bad," he said. "I thought you might be able to do something with these."

"Peaches! Look at all the peaches."

"More than I can ever use. Can you help a guy out? Take these off my hands?"

"Well, yes, of course. Thank you. Do you want to come in for a cup of coffee?"

"I would like that," he said, and followed her around the house to the kitchen door. The twins were playing in the little sandbox Rett had set up.

"Look, girls," Rett said. "Jürgen's here and he brought peaches!" Immersed in play, they barely noted his arrival.

Inside, he put the heavy box on the table while Rett made a fresh pot of coffee. "What should I do with these?" she asked, picking up a heavy peach. "Are they for eating or cooking or what?"

"I have no idea," Jürgen said frankly. "I just know I have no use for an entire case of peaches, no matter how delicious."

"Peach jam," Rett said. "Peach pie. Peach cobbler. Peach ice cream."

He chuckled. "I knew you'd come up with something. You're a bit of a peach, yourself."

She looked at him sharply. "I don't know what that means."

He looked entirely relaxed, sitting at her kitchen table. "Your colouring. Soft blush on your cheeks. Sweet."

"If you knew me better, you'd never say that." She scoffed. "Sweet is not a word anyone uses to describe me."

He shrugged and picked up the mug she put on the table. "Maybe they don't see it."

"Jam, I think," she said, turning back to the fruit, ignoring the warmth in her cheeks. "I've never done it, but I saw my mother make jam lots of times. Maritime women have done it for ages. It can't be that hard."

"I'm sure you'll be successful," he said. "Look at what you've accomplished with this house."

"There is still so much to do." She sighed, looking around. "At least right now, nothing is falling down, falling apart, or failing to work."

"That's good news. Remember, you can call me when something does happen."

"I know. I appreciate that. I miss my neighbours from Saint Jacques."

"I didn't really have neighbours until you moved in," he said. "But I've told you that before."

Maggie came inside. "Can we play with the hose? It's hot."

Rett had visions of the sandbox-turned-mudbox. "I'll fill up your pool instead. How's that?"

"No! I want to play with the hose," Maggie shouted.

Callie, following her sister, joined the chaos. "No, Maggie, Mum said the pool. I want the pool!"

"Girls. No need to scream. We'll figure it out."

Maggie was crying. "But I want the hose. Callie always gets her way."

"That's enough, you two." She spoke louder to be heard over the twins' squabbling.

Jürgen stood. "Well, this is where I exit. Have a good day, Rett."

"Bye. Thanks for the peaches." Out of the corner of her eye, she saw him leave the kitchen. The front door opened and closed.

Remarkably, the girls settled immediately. "I like your talking voice so much better than your screaming voice," Rett said to Maggie. "Let's figure out how you can get cool."

By the time Dorie returned with Mason, the girls were wrapped in towels watching TV, bathing suits hanging on the line. Peaches simmered in a big pot borrowed from James, and Dorie and Mason carried in cases of canning jars. Mason was wearing a big smirk.

"Thank goodness, you didn't let Evie get rid of everything," Rett said to her sister. "And what are you grinning about?" she demanded of her young son. "Did you and Dorie get in trouble?"

"No trouble, not exactly," Dorie said, setting her box of jars on the table. "Here, Mason, I'll take those."

"What do you mean, not exactly?" Rett's suspicion was justified. This was Dorie, after all.

"This, Mum," said Mason, reaching into a shoulder bag and pulling out a little white kitten. He cradled the tiny cat in his arms, then looked up at Rett. "Isn't she cute?"

Rett cut her eyes at Dorie. "Yes, of course she is," she said to Mason. "Hey, girls, come see what Mason brought home."

"Dorie..." she started as the kids erupted in squeals and giggles.

"Don't say a word," Dorie said, holding up her hand. "Mason has to ask your permission. We agreed."

Rett scoffed. "This is a set-up," she retorted. "There's no way to say no at this point." She reached over to scratch the tiny cat under the chin. Tiny, yes, but the purr sounded like a lion.

"Mum, what's that noise?" Maggie said, near tears.

"Listen," Mason said. "She's purring."

"See, Rett! Your kids need life experiences. They don't even know that a cat purrs."

"It's okay, Maggie. That's what they do when they're happy, see?" Rett glared at Dorie, but turned kind eyes to her little girl.

"Well, now you have a cat," Dorie said with satisfaction.

"I guess so," Rett agreed. "Thanks for the canning jars. What else did you snag from Evie's big clean-out? It's all hidden in Alice's barn."

"I'm not really sure myself," Dorie said.

"Well, it's worked out well for us more than once. Even though a kitten was not on my wish list."

Dorie smiled. "Kittens are on everybody's wish list. But you're right about the barn. I did save a lot of the house stuff. Maybe I inherited the packrat gene. Dad's house looks bigger and better than it ever has since Evie made all that space, but I didn't like seeing everything just disappear."

"I'm not judging," Rett said. "I'm grateful. Not so much for the kitten, but for the jars. There's no extra money."

"Well, you do have to buy new lids," Dorie said practically. "But they're cheap."

"I have a box here already," Rett said. "I can finish this batch of jam today."

"Peaches can be canned, too. Without making jam."

"Do you know how?"

"Ha! Who are you talking to? I shouldn't even have mentioned it."

"Well, you have been living with Alice for a while," Rett said. "Maybe some of her kitchen skills have rubbed off."

"I doubt it. I lived with Mum for almost twenty years and didn't learn to cook anything."

"You said you're trying," Rett objected.

"I am, but I'm still in baby steps. Nothing major like canning."

Rett looked at her kitchen, the big water canner simmering on the stove, bowls of peaches, a hot, sticky pot of jam on the counter. The kids were on the floor, playing with the kitten. "I might be in trouble."

Dorie laughed. "Rett, everything you do turns out okay. You'll be fine. See you later. Bye, kids!"

"Bye, Dorie."

Chapter 19

L ife in field camp was hard but not harder than taking care of babies, Harry thought. Instead of dealing with the competing demands of three small children, he was dealing with the competing demands of one big boss, one project manager, and his own pressing feeling of being behind in his work. In his life.

At the same time, he loved his visits to Jeannette and made a point of seeing her often. She didn't seem to mind him trailing her as she did her usual late summer collecting and preserving of medicines. She seemed to like teaching him and tolerated his incessant questions with grace.

He squeezed a couple of hours out of a morning and showed up at her doorstep early.

"What are we doing today?"

"What do you know about mushrooms?"

He shrugged. "Good with steak?"

"Oh, man." She scoffed. "You are a mess, aren't you?"

"I'm pretty ignorant," he agreed good-naturedly. "What should I know about mushrooms? You pick them and eat them."

She scoffed. "Don't tease me, wet-behind-the-ears. You eat whatever you find, you die. Every little kid knows that."

He laughed. "First thing I taught mine while hiking. You can look, but don't put it in your mouth."

"People learn by doing, but sometimes the doing can be fatal. The ancestors who survived did it by paying attention."

"Then passing their knowledge along."

"There are always some who have to try things out," she said, giving him a dark look.

"I'm teachable," he assured her.

"We're selective about what we gather. We use what we can and thank the provider for giving it to us. Then we make sure we give something back."

"You know, I learned a lot of things in college that were wrong."

She raised her eyebrows.

"Well, not wrong exactly, but incomplete. Like we thought things worked a certain way, but it turns out to be a lot more complicated. Things are more interrelated."

"You ever look at weaving?"

"What do you mean? Like a tapestry?"

"Like this. Here." She picked up an old blanket and held it out to him. "See here? When my daughter was young, she picked at this thread. It was loose, and she was sick and bored and lying around, and she picked and picked here. But look at where I had to make repairs. Not just where she picked, but in other places too."

He gazed at the pattern. "Yes. I see where you fixed it. And here, the shape got distorted. Here, too, it probably looks different than when it was first made."

"Well, of course," she said. "It's old. I look different than I used to, also. You're right, though. Her tugging on this thread changed the pattern way over here."

"I think we're a lot more aware of the interrelatedness of things than we were," he said. "What I was taught twenty years ago isn't what students are taught now. We didn't know back then."

She hefted her gathering basket onto her hip. "In twenty more years, today's students will say the same thing. We can't see the whole. But we have to assume that there is a whole that is bigger than what we can see. You ready to go?"

After a few days of rain, the early morning forest smelled like humus, rich, redolent and almost delicious. A cluster of boreal chickadees fled their arrival but soon returned to the birches to twitter and cheep.

Jeanette's eyes were on the ground. "Look at this mushroom. What do you see?"

Harry squatted to see. "It's a pancake mushroom, edible, and pretty typical here."

She scolded him. "No, Harry, that's what you think. What do you see?"

"Oh," he said, reconsidering. "It's bigger than my palm, brown like, uh, brown like that dark chestnut wood your cupboard is made of, and it's probably heavy, heavier than you'd think, just looking at it. And the underside is whitish and the spores are starting to scatter. The stem is thick, as big around as my thumb. Is that what you mean?"

"Why is it here?"

"Uh, because it likes these kinds of trees? The pancake is the fruiting body of an underground network of fibers."

"Can you see that?"

"Well, I'd have to dig around and look. Right now, no."

"So you see what is available to see. When others have seen the network and told you the story of how the mushroom grows, then you also know."

"Right," he said slowly. "What is your point?"

"We see what we know to look for, that's all. I see medicine everywhere out here. You're learning to see it. But you didn't see any medicine before you got hurt and stayed with me."

"Right. That's true. When I was in college, I mostly saw animals because I was studying wolves. When I'm with you, I mostly see plants."

"When we pick one part to dig up or take away or kill, we affect other parts. We can't see it because we are just human."

"We humans have done a lot of damage while trying hard to do no harm."

She shrugged. "Trying hard means nothing. When you ignore what your ancestors saw and knew, you are a wilful child hitting his mother."

"You're like Yoda, you know that? Without the weird ears."

"I'm a lot taller than Yoda," she said with aspersion.

"Okay," he agreed. "But the wise story thing, you've got that down."

"Paul said more like Obi Wan," she said modestly.

"Why only male figures? Why not a major wise woman?"

"And who would that be in popular culture?"

"Hmm. Well, I'm going to take some time with that question. In the meantime, you're just you, and I appreciate what you've done for me. What do you need from town this week?"

"Going again? So soon?"

"I need to talk to my family," he admitted. "The rest of the team is heading back to the university, but I need to let Rett know about the change in plans. So let me know what you want me to bring back."

"I'll think on it. It's good to talk to your wife, Harry."

"Yeah. She's never had the kids on her own before," he said. "I think she's had a bit of a hard time."

Rett's chickens had started to lay eggs. The twins took on the egg-finding responsibility, but Maggie refused to enter the coop without Callie, ever since one of the hens had chased her around the yard.

The girls had run into the kitchen, Callie slamming the door and shouting, "You leave my sister alone, you frickin' chicken!" and the name stuck. Rett thought the hen deserved a better name, but Frickin Chicken she was. Frickin Chicken and her sisters were good producers, and Rett and the kids had a couple of regular egg customers.

Chickens were not without drama. Rett was doing some kitchen task when a massive bird descended on the garden and pulled one of the hens away in his enormous talons. The sound of his wings and the kids' screams sent her to the backyard, but only in time to see her hen disappearing into the sky. She spent that night sleeping in the twins' room, after a long conversation about the circle of life.

The kitten, named KD after the children's favourite food, was a wily hunter. Since chicken feed attracted mice, Rett was happy to have the cat. The goat plan hadn't quite been realized, but that was okay. They didn't have to do everything all at once.

The early August holiday came, and immediately afterwards came the shift in the weather that foretold fall. Mason, complaining about being cold, scrounged for a sweatshirt.

"I guess we have to find the jackets and sweaters," Rett said, backing out of the little closet she used for storage. "It was hot when we came here, but it won't be hot forever."

"Why not, Mum?" Maggie asked. "I like swimming in my pool."

"Fall, dummy," Mason said.

"Mason! No name-calling. You can explain it to her, but politely."

Callie gave an exasperated sigh. "Maggie knows about fall. We're five. We're not babies."

"I like the warm weather, too," Rett said, stroking Maggie's hair. "But things change."

Her phone rang and she left to find it. It was stuck between the couch cushions, as usual, but she grabbed it in time to answer it.

"Loretta Madison," she said clearly.

"Rett? This is Honey MacPherson. Remember me?"

She did. "Honey from school. Yes, hello." Honey had been in her class; a nice girl despite her too-sweet name.

"I'm the office manager at the Downtown Clinic now. We got your letter and resume. I'm glad to hear you're available for work."

"Well, I am in town," she said cautiously. "What did you have in mind?"

"We're running shorthanded right now, like everybody is," Honey said. "I have a recruiter looking for a nurse manager, but that position won't open until January. Right now, we need part-time coverage for the clinic, a nurse to help with patient visits three mornings a week. Is that something you'd be interested in? I know it's part-time and we don't pay the very best."

Rett was thinking furiously. This was just what she'd hoped for, but still, what to do with the kids? Poor pay was better than no pay. There were problems to solve but she could do that. "Sure, I'm interested. Yes, please. What's next?"

"We're setting up interviews and checking details, but I just wanted to see if you'd be interested in part-time. I'll call you when we have an interview schedule, okay?"

"That's great," Rett said. "Thank you."

Rett hung up, both bemused and a little excited. Taking a position in Stella Mare was kind of like digging in. Like growing roots or finding the roots she'd left behind. It's only part-time, she reminded herself. Not permanent. How could it work? She stopped herself from trying to solve the childcare problem. She could wait until they offered her something. Firmly pushing aside that worry, she returned to the kitchen.

"Was that Daddy?" Mason asked.

She gave him a look. "Of course not. If Daddy calls, we all get to talk, right?"

"Right," he said. "What are we doing today, Mum?"

"Aunt Evie invited us for a barbecue. I told her we'd bring our favourite chocolate cake. With..."

"Peanut butter frosting!" the three kids shouted almost in unison.

"Right. You can help. Wash up, and we'll get started."

The kids tumbled out of the kitchen and Rett washed her own hands at the sink, gazing blindly out the window. It would be so nice to be working again. Feeling competent. Her gaze suddenly sharpened as she spotted a circling hawk dropping lower. She ran out the kitchen door, shouting and flapping a dishtowel, hustling the chickens back into their shed. "Get out of here," she shouted, shaking her fist at the sky. The hawk—maybe it was another eagle—drifted away.

"You're not grabbing another chicken," she muttered to herself. "Not in front of my kids." She stomped back to the house.

Mason was talking on her phone. She frowned at him, but he held on, talking. "Today is fine. Mum said anytime is okay. Yes, here she is." Looking guilty, he handed the phone to her.

"Who is it?" she hissed.

"It's the goat lady, Mum," Mason said. "Goats today!"

Callie jumped up and down, chanting, "Goats today, goats today!" Maggie and Charlie joined in, of course.

Rett, holding her phone but with her other hand over her free ear, carried the phone into the living room. Saving chickens, getting goats, baking, kids...why did she think she had time to work? "Hello? This is Rett."

The kids had quieted by the time she returned to the kitchen, where Mason was presiding while Callie gathered supplies: the big metal bowl, a bag of flour, the jar of sugar, and eggs. Maggie's face was deep in a cupboard under the counter. "How do you turn it to chocolate?" she asked.

Callie carefully carried the eggs to the table. "You put chocolate in it, silly," she said. "We just have to find where Mum keeps the chocolate."

"The goats are coming today," Rett announced. "Right before the barbecue."

"Maybe we shouldn't go," Mason said seriously. "They'll be home-sick and need us."

"You think so?" Rett asked, amused. "I expect they'll be okay. There are two of them, anyway."

The little girls looked up intently.

"What will we name them?" Maggie asked.

"Can I have one sleep in my bed?" Callie wanted to know.

"We talked about this," Rett reminded. "Goats are outdoor animals like the chickens. KD and Charlie come inside, but the other animals have their own homes. They like it that way."

Callie looked sad. "Charlie sleeps with Mason and KD sleeps with Maggie."

Rett gave her a hug. "I know. But chickens and goats are not good to sleep with."

"It's okay, Callie," Mason said. "You'll get somebody."

"Let's get this cake in the oven, kids, and we can go check out the goat shed to make sure it's all ready."

The entire kitchen had a light coating of flour when the cake, all three layers, went into the oven. Rett turned on the oven timer and the timer on her phone, congratulating herself on her foresight. While they all trooped to the back part of the chicken coop, now christened the goat shed, she popped the phone into her pocket.

Mason swept out the shed. While her girls put water in the two buckets, she hauled straw to spread on the floor. The chickens clucked and squawked, and she scanned the sky before she let them back into the garden. Plenty of fish in the Bay of Fundy, she thought. Why do those eagles have to try to get my chickens?

"They'll be happy here, right, Mum?" Mason said, surveying their work.

"It looks pretty nice to me," Rett agreed. "But I'm not a goat."

The twins giggled uncontrollably. "I'm a goat! I'm a goat!" Callie shouted, and they both clambered around on all fours. Charlie barked and bounced with them.

"Go on, goats, out of here," Rett shooed them into the yard. "There's time to play for a while before we have to go to Grandpa's."

The screaming alarm of the smoke detector sent her into the kitchen, where the heat was overwhelming. Smoke poured out of the stove, carrying the distinct smell of charring.

"No!" She turned off the stove and hauled open the oven door. Swirls of smoke poured out, sending her into a fit of coughing. Rubbing her eyes with one hand, she grabbed a cake pan with the oven mitt and put it on the cooling rack. Peering through smoke, she saw charred edges and a liquid center. She wrestled the other pans out of the oven and turned the oven off.

"Mum!" Mason shouted. She ran to the living room to shut down the smoke detector. Just like working on shift, she thought, alarms going off everywhere.

Mason came into the living room where she was standing on a chair, pulling the battery out of the device.

"Mum! Are you okay?"

She brushed the hair out of her face and got off the chair. "Yes, I'm okay. The cake isn't, though," she said.

He turned abruptly and returned to the kitchen. She followed. Together they gazed at the cake. "It was going to be so good," Mason said sadly.

"I don't know what happened," she said. "An oven malfunction."

A roar came from the driveway and an excited squeal and barking from the backyard announced visitors. Mason perked up. "Goats!" he shouted and ran outside.

Rett sighed, retied her ponytail, and followed. Even chocolate cake lost its allure when there were goats.

Chapter 20

R ett took stock of her situation. Some things were working out well, or at least okay. Goats, for example. Even though it had taken a little time for Nanny Goat and Baby Goat to settle in, everyone agreed the goats were fun, maybe even worth the work.

Nanny vocalized whenever she saw Rett. The children insisted she was talking to Mum, but Rett denied understanding anything. Once the children had established themselves as a source of food, Nanny was willing to let Baby Goat play with them, at least some of the time. Maggie got over her shyness, and Callie was learning to read Nanny Goat's body language. Mason took on important tasks, like shuttling Nanny between her shed and her outdoor space. Between the goats and chickens, the kids were endlessly entertained, and had plenty of chores.

Rett didn't have to spend all day trying to pry them off screens, and when they did want a movie or cartoon, it was usually because they were tired from being outside. That was working well.

Selling eggs to her regular customers, mostly family friends, and feeding the family mostly from the garden, felt good to Rett. The garden itself was a wonder; producing despite getting a late start, to the point where Maggie said she would die if she had to eat zucchini again in any form. Evie promised to teach Rett how to make a zucchini cake that would disguise the vegetable, so even that was pretty good.

Those things were good.

Work, however, wasn't good.

When she didn't hear from Honey about an interview for the clinic position, she called.

"Rett." Honey sounded uncomfortable. "We couldn't offer you an interview because of your license."

"What about my license?" Rett's stomach was a tight ball. She remembered Angelica's voice cracking when she told Rett her CNA license had been suspended.

Honey stumbled over her words. "Your professional organization couldn't verify your license."

Stunned, Rett mumbled a goodbye and dropped the phone. "Those miserable good-for-nothings." With trepidation, she unearthed her laptop. Steeling herself, she scrolled backward through the enormous list of items she'd been ignoring in her inbox. Hidden among the messages about continuing education offerings, footwear for nurses, and other useless information was a note from her professional association. A wave of foreboding washed over her as she clicked on it.

She skimmed until she got to the meaty part. "...to inform you that your license/registration is currently in suspension until this matter is resolved..."

Suspension! What "matter?"

She returned to the top of the note. "In the matter of a professional conduct complaint by Briar Ventures/Streamside Residence, and a criminal investigation, the Association bylaws state...suspended until resolved..." The email was dated more than a month ago.

She paced the living room while those words rattled in her brain. Suspended until resolved. License suspended. They had made it so she couldn't work anywhere.

Rett felt suspended in the moment, trying to take in this new information. It was one thing to play at homesteading when she knew she could get a job. Now everything was different.

She scrolled her contacts, pausing over Helen, but then bypassed her sister to land on Angelica. She really wanted Harry, but that was impossible, so Angelica would have to do. Besides, she might know something useful.

She heard Evie's voice from the backyard while the phone was ringing. No way was she letting Evie know about this new complication.

She quickly clicked off, folded the laptop closed, and headed through the kitchen, pocketing her phone.

"Hi," she said to Evie, who was squatting down beside the sandbox with the twins.

"I came by to see if you have any coffee," her sister said. "Can I come in?"

"Sure," Rett said. "We might even have food."

"Eggs!" Maggie said. "We have eggs and zucchini."

Evie laughed as she followed Rett into the house. "No food, thanks. I just wanted to check in, see how it's going, and ask you something."

"Sure," Rett said. "I'll make coffee." She busied herself at the stove, trying to keep a grip on her emotions. Maybe Evie would distract her.

"My local show is coming right up," Evie said. "I'm getting some publicity for it."

Rett nodded. The local gallery was sponsoring Evie's show of the best of the locally made antique hooked rugs she'd been studying for months.

"This is a weird request, but I'm going to ask anyway. The reporter from the Maritime News wants to do a background story on me, and part of that is about my sisters. She wants to interview all of you, Helen included, because she thinks this is a human-interest thing, four sisters from our little village, all so different, and the old rugs and all of that."

"No," Rett said immediately.

"No? Just like that?" Evie looked hurt.

Rett vividly recalled the MNN coverage of the deaths at the care home. "Sorry, Evie, but they got me into this place," she said darkly.

"What? What place?"

"Never mind. You probably don't want your show associated with your criminal sister."

"You're hardly a criminal," Evie demurred. "I thought your urban homestead would be interesting. Like Dorie's dog sanctuary. Something different."

"Those news people turned normal events into a sensational story and got me fired."

"Is that what happened?"

"That's my interpretation, anyway. It's not a good idea. You don't want the news looking too closely at your family right now."

Evie laughed. "I'm not running for office, you know. Just hanging a show at the gallery."

"Exactly. They don't need to interview your whole family."

"Okay," Evie said. "I won't mention the chickens and the garden and the baking and all that."

"Right," Rett said firmly. "Don't."

"Even though it might be good for your business, if selling eggs and stuff is your business."

"Don't, please," she said. "I'd love to support you, but I can't do it that way."

"Okay. I just thought I'd ask. I'll drop it." Rett was grateful the request had come from a sister capable of dropping it. Dorie would not have given up so easily.

"Thank you. That feels safer."

"What is happening with your work stuff, anyway? You don't tell us much."

Rett sighed. "That's because nothing good has happened, and I don't like to dwell on the bad stuff. Doesn't get you anywhere."

"Maybe we can help. We're your family, you know."

Rett threw herself onto the couch. "I didn't want to talk about it, but I'll tell you the latest. I was about to get a job in town, but my nursing license is suspended. Has been suspended for a month."

"Suspended! You didn't know?"

Rett sighed. "I should have. Denial isn't just a river in Egypt, I guess."

Evie snickered. "At least you have your sense of humour."

"Not really. It's annoying because that email has been in my inbox for weeks. I just didn't look. I might have missed the window to file an objection."

"What are you objecting to?"

Rett shrugged. "This whole mess. Somebody made a complaint, there's a criminal investigation associated with the complaint, and so I can't work as a nurse until that's resolved."

"Wait. Who's investigating you?"

"I had an interview with the police last month. I keep emailing the detective to see if this can be resolved, but I don't hear back."

"What do you mean by resolved? Resolved how?"

"I don't know. If the police close the file, and the association thinks I've been punished enough, maybe then." Rett barely recognized her bitter tone. "Grrr. It makes me so mad!" She shook her fists.

Evie's dark eyes were soft and kind. She touched Rett's fist. "That's terrible," she said. "It's unfair."

Rett felt the sharp sting of tears but willed them away. She stood up, shaking off Evie's touch.

"That's why I try not to think about it too much. I can't do anything about any of it. It just stinks."

"Have you talked to Helen?"

"Of course. When this whole thing started. She doesn't know about the license because I just found out myself. I figured getting another job would be easy if I just quit Streamside, even though they were wrong to put me off. But now I've found out I can't. I can't even support my family."

Her voice cracking, she turned away from Evie, hand over mouth. She would not break down in front of her sister. She swallowed and straightened up.

Looking back over her shoulder, she said, "No reporters. Living with this shame is bad enough without parading it all over the province."

"You have nothing to be ashamed of, but I understand. I'll steer her back to the show and away from the family part."

Rett turned all the way toward her. "Thanks."

"Okay, so I've got to get back to it." Evie stood up. "Come over to the house. Have a talk with Dad. He's pretty good at seeing ways out of sticky places."

Rett thought not. Her memory of Dad in the hospital was always close. She wasn't going to burden him with her issues, but a visit might be okay. "The kids get over there all the time," she said, "but I only seem to go when I'm specifically invited. Yes, I'll drop by later to see Dad. Good idea."

Chapter 21

Harry didn't know what to expect about being left in field camp, but it was pretty good. Marie was busy. She assigned his tasks, but after he finished those, the time was his. He worked diligently, but kept his own agenda, planning to talk to Rett and the kids weekly. Thoughts about his future, his project, were always present, but it was like an amorphous cloud that would not take shape. He could only struggle with it so long.

Staying in field camp had not been on the original plan, and when he told Rett, she didn't grasp it easily. "You're not going back to Winnipeg?"

"Well, I will sometime, but no, not right now. I don't have any teaching or coursework responsibilities, and my work is here, really."

"Harry, you got hurt there."

"I know. I'm fully recovered, though. It's going to work out better, you'll see."

She scoffed. "Right. Tell me how it's better."

"Well, I'll be on my own time, so I will certainly get to town weekly to call you."

"Yes, you're right. That's better."

"I let go of that studio apartment in the city, too, and that means money in the account. That's probably better, too, right?"

He heard her sharp intake of breath. "Oh, yes, actually, that would be great."

"Are things tight?" he asked, worried.

"No, no, everything's okay," she said quickly. "But a few more dollars won't be a problem."

He laughed. "Good. See, there's two really good things about this change."

"Except the kids and I thought we'd get to talk to you every day once you got back to the university."

"Right. Except that."

She sighed, and he could almost imagine her straightening her spine. "Well, if that's how it is, that's how it is. We'll be fine."

"I count on that," he said warmly. "I know you'll be fine."

"Will you be fine?" she asked. "That's a big place to be alone."

"I won't be entirely alone," he said. "Marie is here for a couple of weeks."

"Marie. I thought she didn't like you."

"She doesn't," he said with a smile, "but that doesn't matter. She's committed to getting the project completed, and I'll help."

"What about after she leaves?"

"I've connected with some local people who live nearby. Jeannette. She took care of me when I got hurt, remember?"

"Somebody's grandmother."

"Yes. Her grandson has become a friend. Jeannette's an elder who knows more than anyone I ever met about using plants for healing."

"Don't discount real medicine, Harry," she said. "Backed by science."

"I'm not discounting anything," he said. "That's what's so interesting."

"Yeah," she said absently. "The kids are wiggling to talk to you, and they've got to get to bed. I'm going to hand you over."

"Okay," he agreed. "I'll talk to you next week, okay?"

But she was gone, and then Mason and his sisters were fighting over the phone.

Rett was stonewalled in her efforts to make her professional association reverse her suspension. The registrar continued to point out the bylaws that made it impossible for someone under investigation to work as a nurse. She couldn't get in touch with Kathryn Gallant to confirm she wasn't under investigation. Weary after trying to make her case, she dropped it. Besides, it was already September and the start of school.

Rett took the children on the first day. Before they left, she took pictures on the front porch. "You guys look great! Daddy will love to see these."

She felt a twinge of missing Harry. He was the family documentarian for the first day of school. The twins were finally getting to go to school like their big brother, and their father wasn't there to see.

They had picked out matching outfits, and looked outrageously cute in leggings and rainbow shirts. Rett bent down to hug them. "You used to be my babies," she said.

"Oh, Mum," Callie protested. "We're five now."

"I know. But that doesn't change it. You used to be my babies."

"Mason, too," Maggie said quickly.

"Of course, Mason too," Rett agreed. "Nice backpack, Mase. Looks good." He turned sideways to show it off and she snapped another picture. Charlie whined, and all three kids bent down to pose with the dog. Then the whole crowd set off down the sidewalk, the kids dragging their feet a little.

"I like having school so close," she said, relentlessly upbeat. "Look, you guys, it's easy to walk here. Better than Saint Jacques."

Maggie clutched her hand while Callie danced ahead. Mason dogged her heels, muttering, backpack weighing down his narrow shoulders.

She turned to ask him, "What are you saying?"

"I liked the bus," he said a little louder. "I liked riding the bus. I liked seeing my friends. I don't want to go to a new school."

Maggie, plastered to Rett's side, sniffled. "I don't wanna."

"No time for negativity, you guys. You're going," Rett said, hating her sharp tone. "This is where we live now, and this is where you go to school."

"Mum," Maggie whimpered.

Rett looked at her and shook her head. "You girls have been waiting a long time for kindergarten. Today's finally the day. No tears, Maggie."

"But Mum," the little girl sniffled. "I don't wanna."

Rett rolled her eyes and sighed. Where was Harry when she needed him? Squatting down, she pulled Mason and Maggie in close. "Listen, guys, I know this is all new. New things can feel hard sometimes. But look at all the new things we've done lately. We never had goats before, right?"

Mason looked at her skeptically.

Maggie said, "Chickens. Garden."

Rett nodded encouragingly. "New things. Hard things. But they turned out fun. Just like school."

She stood up and started walking again. Kids just had to adapt. They all just had to adapt.

When she got home after peeling Maggie from her side and seeing Mason and Callie into their classrooms, she sat with her coffee on the old couch. The house made little noises around her, and crows and seagulls were racketing outside the open windows. Sunlight puddled on the ancient wooden floor. Why was September such a beautiful month when the kids had to be in school? She wouldn't mind if they stayed home until winter, really.

Looking at the house was like reading her To Do list: clean out the chimney, replace that cracked window, get the roof inspected, and a continuous reminder there was not really enough money. She fished around for her laptop. Maybe she could find a job that didn't require a nursing license. Maybe the darn investigation would end, and she could get back to her real life. She sent another note to Detective Gallant. Then she turned to the help wanted listings.

A frustrating hour later, no further ahead, she got up to punch down the bread dough she'd made in the early morning. From the kitchen, the yard drew her, and she spent some time picking beans and hanging out with the hens who kept the garden bug-free. Frickin Chicken came over to check in. Nanny Goat hollered at her, and Rett went to scratch between her poky horns and give her a treat. Charlie lay on his side in a patch of sunlight, and the kitten prowled through the border, hunting.

A noise from the woods made her look up, and Charlie leaped to his feet.

"Rett!" James was waving and Mallow and Custard picked up their lumbering pace to greet Charlie.

She poured coffee, and they pulled chairs into a patch of late morning sun while the dogs settled into basking.

"First day of school," James observed.

"Yeah. Here's pictures." She leaned over with her phone.

"Everybody looks good."

"Appearances can be deceptive. Maggie cried, Mason complained, and Callie couldn't wait," Rett said. "I hope it's going well."

"Oh, they'll be fine," James predicted. "How are you liking the quiet?"

She looked around. "It's not all that quiet," she acknowledged, "but it's okay. I'd rather it was summer vacation all year, if I'm perfectly honest. I like having them around."

"I do too," he said. "I never thought we'd be like this, with a little path in the woods from your house to mine, but I like it. I like when Mason and Charlie just show up. Pretty soon the little girls will be big enough to do that, too."

"They probably could already," Rett said, "but their mother has city worries."

"S'okay," James said. "It's good for kids to have something to look forward to. Something to grow up for."

"You mean like getting to do whatever you want when you grow up?"

He laughed. "Kids do believe that. I just meant being big enough or old enough to do things that are important to you."

She squinted at him. Where was he going with this?

"Like you, you were always taking care of your dolls, the dogs, anyone who needed it. You couldn't wait to grow up so you could be a real nurse."

"I don't remember that," Rett lied. "I remember soccer and track, and fighting with Helen about our room, and Evie always drawing. I was mostly a jock."

James shook his head. "Your mother and I were sure you were heading for nursing. I can't believe you don't remember. We were so proud of you when you graduated, but mostly because you did what was important to you."

"Really? Helen was in law school and that was a big deal."

"It sure was," he said, a far-away look in his eyes. "Helen in law, you finishing nursing, Evie at Mount Allison. That was a big year."

His gaze sharpened again. "You wanted to be a nurse since you were little, and you did it, and kept on doing it, growing your career. How you doing right now, though? You never had this much time off of work in your life."

"This place is work, Dad," she said quickly. "Don't think it's a vacation here. I'm trying to meet our needs with this piece of property, you know."

"Are you?" He looked around. "I guess I didn't realize it was a program. A thing."

"Oh, it's a thing," she said, laughing a little. "I'm an urban home-steader." She used her fingers for the air quotes. "I'm not too successful at it, but that's what I'm aiming for."

"Why is this so important? Why now?"

She considered. "Harry's doing his thing, and I think that's great. It's his turn. I'm getting my turn at being the person at home. This is how I want to do it."

"You were going to be a stay-home mum when Harry went back to work?" He looked confused.

She took pity on him and explained. "No, not really. This mess at work made it happen. When they cut my salary, I had to do something different. It wasn't until we found this house that I thought about trying to meet some of our needs on this land."

"I figured you'd be looking for a new job," he said. "Going back to Saint Jacques, put the kids back in their regular school."

She looked out at the treeline, feeling shame wash over her. He didn't know about her license, and she wasn't about to tell him. "The tenants signed a year-long contract," she said instead.

"What were you thinking? Was urban homesteading a plan?"

"Not exactly a plan. Just a solution to a problem. No salary, no money from Harry, I had to do something, or risk losing the house," she said flatly. "Don't judge me, Dad. I'm doing the best I can here."

"Did you think about borrowing from your old father?"

"No, I did not," she retorted. "I'm a big girl. You don't have to take care of me."

"You and the kids could have stayed at the house, too," he continued. "You didn't need to move out to this place."

"Dad, we really couldn't. It was too much."

"For you, maybe. It wasn't too much for me," he said stoutly. "You decided to move here. You decided to raise chickens and goats and who knows what. You decided not to get a job."

She stared at him. "Are you mad about something?"

"I know for a fact you were offered a job at the Downtown Clinic. This is a small town, Loretta, and everybody knows. I don't know why you didn't take that job."

"That's right. I decided." Her throat tightened. Narrowing her eyes, she continued. "I don't need you to bail me out, and I don't need you to tell me I did wrong."

He leaned back in his chair.

After a moment, he said, "Maybe I deserved that. I'm not telling you that you did wrong. I don't know if it was wrong or right. You did what you did. But seeing you so far off the course you set all those years ago makes me wonder."

Ashamed of her outburst, she said, "Sometimes I wonder, too. All I'm doing here is what needs doing. Whatever shows up that needs to be done. Every day is something new, and I just do what I have to."

"You're a good girl, Rett, and you always have been," he said as he stood up. "Stubborn, betimes, but a good girl. Just don't forget you have us, me and your sisters. Corinne, too. We always count on you, but you can count on us, too, once in a while." He walked away, calling the dogs. Her tears blurred the sight of him melting into the treeline at Mason's flag.

Chapter 22

Rett was tying herbs into bunches to dry. Maybe she could sell them at the market. When her phone rang, she snatched it up. Anything was better than this boredom. She missed her kids.

"Mrs. Brown?"

"This is Rett Madison, yes," she said, rolling her eyes.

"Mason's mother?"

"Yes."

"There's been an incident. Mason is fine, but Mr. Standish would like to talk with you. Can you come in right away?"

Mason was sitting in the outer office, legs too short for the tall chair. "Hi, Mum," he said with a weak smile.

"Hi," she responded, squatting down to look him in the eye. "Everything okay?"

He shook his head and bit his lip. "I'm going to talk to Mr. Standish," she told him. "It'll be okay." He nodded, and she patted his head as she stood up to look for the receptionist.

Mr. Standish invited her in, shaking her hand and offering a chair. She looked at him closely. "Ryan?"

"I wondered if you'd recognize me," he said. "I didn't realize Mason was your boy, Rett."

"Yes, the last name confuses things," she said. "You're a principal? That's unexpected."

He grinned at her. "I'm good at it, too. Anything a kid does, I've already done and gotten in trouble for it."

"What has my kid done?"

Ryan sobered immediately. "He hit the teacher, Rett. Then he dumped a box of chalk on the floor and ran out of the classroom."

Shocked, she had trouble finding words. "Mason? Are you sure it was Mason?"

"Well, he agreed that he did it," Ryan said. "A lot of people saw it."

Rett shook her head. "That's not really like him at all."

"You might want to talk with the school counsellor about that, but right now it's a disciplinary issue." Mr. Standish's eyes were like steel, his jaw tight. "He can't be hitting anyone, or damaging property, or running away."

She wanted to reach over the desk and grab the principal by the shirt and give him a shake. Instead, she leaned back in her chair and exhaled slowly. Consciously pitching her voice low, she asked, "Was anyone hurt?"

He shook his head. "Nobody. Not even the teacher. We just can't have this behaviour happening, though. Other kids see it, they have to see consequences."

"I understand. Can I take him home now?"

"Yes. He has to stay home tomorrow, too, Rett."

"What?"

"Automatic suspension for this offence. Today plus one more day."

She sighed. "Come on. That's just going to make coming back so much harder, Ryan. He's probably dying of shame right now."

"If it stops the behaviour, it's worth it," he said firmly.

"I couldn't disagree more," she said hotly. "Shaming is no way to help a kid."

"He hit a teacher. He should be ashamed."

"I'm sure he is. I just don't think the school has to capitalize on it. Can't he write an apology or something?"

Ryan indicated a paper on his desk. "He already did that. Suspension is a school rule. We must enforce the rules."

"Whatever." She got up to leave.

"Rett," he stopped her. "Where's Mason's father?" His tone was gentle. She sat back down.

"Harry," she said. "He's away for a few months, working on his Ph.D."

"Are you separated?"

"What? No, of course not. I mean, yes, by distance, but that's all. He's coming home."

"I wondered. The class was working on a project about families and that seemed to upset him."

Rett nodded. "He misses his dad. I don't think the kids can understand why he's not at home anymore."

"You might think about that. Our school counsellor might be able to help. Those kinds of behaviours are problems."

Rett went rigid. This was no way to treat children. Public shaming, treat them like criminals, and then blame them for being upset. No wonder kids needed counsellors. But rage wasn't going to help this situation. Firmly gripping the arms of the chair, she replied mildly, "Thank you. I'll let you know if I think that's necessary."

"Well, let's go let Mason know what's happening," Ryan said.

Rett followed him from the office, trying not to roll her eyes. Instead she looked at her son, seeing a very small boy sitting in a large chair.

Mr. Standish spoke to Mason and shook his hand. Mason led her to the grade 3 cubbies where they gathered his things.

They were nearly finished when the kindergarten class walked down the hall in a neat row, heading to the playground. Maggie fell out of line, clutching at her mother's legs. "I want to go home too!" she sobbed. Callie gave her a scornful glance over her shoulder, and marched along with her class, but Maggie, leech-like, had lost her equanimity.

"Okay, okay," Rett said, rubbing her forehead. "Let's get your stuff and you can come home with Mason. Come on. Stop crying now."

Once at home, she sent Maggie out to hunt eggs while she sat Mason at the kitchen table. She gazed at him, seeing so much that reminded her of Harry. Her heart twisting, she noted the same straight brown hair, falling onto his forehead, the same soft brown eyes. Mason's sweet smile was all his own, though.

That smile was nowhere to be seen right now. Instead, he was looking down and patting Charlie's head on his knee. His occasional sniffles were getting to Rett. She handed him a tissue and thought about wrapping her patience around her like a cloak.

"Tell me what happened," she said, keeping her voice even.

When he looked up at her, she could see his emotions at war on his face. Was that fear? "Mason, really, it's okay. Just tell me what happened."

"Mr. Standish told you."

This note of defiance was new. "Mason, I want to hear it from you," she said firmly.

He was silent. She felt her mantle of patience slipping. "Mason, right now. Tell me."

His lower lip trembled, but he pressed them closer together. His eyebrows came down, but he said nothing.

"Mason James. You'll tell me right now, or you'll be spending today and tomorrow in your room."

"Okay, fine." He got off the chair and, calling Charlie, headed for the stairs. Rett, shocked into immobility, saw them leave the room and heard them climbing the stairs in the living room.

"Well," she breathed, "that's something." Heavy with thought, she returned to bundling her herbs.

Later in the afternoon, she called the children to walk to school to pick up Callie. Charlie came bounding down the stairs, but Mason didn't appear. While Maggie was checking the snacks drawer, Rett went up to find him. He was asleep, half under the covers of his bed, a framed picture of Harry and himself from a summer camping trip beside him. Rett replaced the photo on his dresser and sat down on the bed.

"Mason, wake up. It's time to get Callie," she said gently.

"No," he muttered and burrowed into the covers.

"Come on, Mason," she urged. "I don't want to be late."

"No," he insisted. "I can stay here alone. Charlie will stay with me."

"No," she said. "You're eight. Not old enough to be alone."

"Mum!"

"Maybe Jürgen will come over for a few minutes," she said, thinking aloud.

Mason threw off the covers and jumped to the floor. "No!" he shouted. "I'm coming."

"Well, okay then," she said, surprised. "That's great. Let's go."

They were walking toward school, Rett, two kids, and the dog, when Jürgen came out of his house and saw them. "Hey, family," he called. "Can I come too?"

"We're just going to school," Maggie said. "To get Callie."

"It's a walk," Jürgen said, arriving at the sidewalk to meet them. "A little walk is good, right?" He reached to ruffle Mason's hair, but the boy eluded him and ran on ahead.

Rett scowled. "Don't be rude, Mason," she muttered, but she didn't call him back.

Callie ran up when she saw Mason in the vanguard, and Rett waved to Callie's teacher to acknowledge the pickup. They were headed back home again in a moment, a ragtag group with Mason jogging out in front, Charlie cavorting at his side, Callie talking rapidly to Rett's left, Maggie still clinging to her right hand, and Jürgen bringing up the rear. They trooped past Jürgen's house and Rett barely noticed when he dropped out of their group to go up his driveway. Callie was the one to call out, "Bye, Jürgen."

He waved and Rett said, "Goodbye," and that was that. Mason and Charlie returned to the group.

"Mase, you need to be polite to our neighbour," Rett reminded, but he just skipped ahead with the leash in his hand. Callie was slowing down, too.

"Mum, can you carry my backpack?" she whined. Maggie left her side to catch up with Mason. Rett hoisted the backpack and Callie ran ahead too. Three kids and the dog had disappeared when Rett rounded the corner by the overgrown cedar windbreak. Dorie's truck was parked in the driveway. Laughter and barking came from behind the house.

Instead of heading around the side of the house, Rett went in through the front door. The living room was quiet, dampening the sounds of fun from the backyard. She hung Callie's pack from the hook and went through to the kitchen, taking it in with a glance.

Her bunched herbs hung across the eating nook, dangling with a rich, green fragrance. Loaves of her fresh bread were lightly draped with red checked tea towels. A blue bowl full of brown eggs sat on the counter next to the electric kettle. The walls were hung with the kids' drawings, and she nearly tripped over the bin they were using to collect cardboard for construction projects. She pushed it into a corner, set the kettle to boil, and went out the back door into the yard. How could things look so good and yet feel so terrible?

Dorie and Mason were huddled in conversation, while Frou-Frou, Dorie's frequent canine companion, bounced politely with Charlie. The girls were chattering and giggling in the chicken house.

"Tea, Dorie?" she called.

Her sister looked up. "Hi, Rett. Yes, please," she said, then returned her focus to Mason.

"Mum, me too!" came from the chicken house.

Back in the kitchen, Rett sliced bread, spread jam, made tea, and put everything on a tray. By the time she got it out to the yard, everyone had assembled. She sent the children inside for hand washing and handed Dorie a mug of tea.

"Thanks," her sister said. "It's busy here."

"You got here at the right time," Rett said. "It was boring before."

Dorie raised her eyebrows. "Okay, not boring," Rett admitted. "Just quiet. Did Mason tell you he got suspended?"

"Something about your neighbour," Dorie said, looking puzzled. "But suspended, yes."

Rett glanced toward the house. Nobody coming yet. "Jürgen? I don't know what happened, but he actually hit his teacher and ran out of the classroom."

"Really? Mason hit a teacher?"

"I know. Seems impossible. But he apologized already, so he obviously did it."

"Why is he suspended if he apologized?"

"My question exactly," Rett said, miffed all over again. "I think they just want to shame him. Make an example, or something. I don't like that at all."

"Well, you could keep him home, you know," Dorie said. "Homeschool or something."

Rett gave her the sarcasm face. "It is obvious, dear sister, that you do not have children."

The kids burst out the kitchen door and clustered at the table. Rett was busy for a moment putting food on plates and pouring drinks.

Dorie wasn't dissuaded. "Look how much fun you guys have here. You could totally teach them, Rett, you know you could."

"Right."

"Mum teach us?" Mason asked, looking at Dorie. "She's not a teacher. She's a nurse."

"That's right," Rett agreed. "I'm not a teacher."

"You guys. Look at everything you've learned this summer. Taking care of chickens, gardening, making bread, goats." Dorie was effusive.

"Mum does the bread," Mason said cautiously.

"We take care of the chickens," Callie burst out. "Me and Maggie. Mason does goats and Charlie."

"See," Dorie said to Rett. "You can teach them anything."

"Not reading and math and science," Rett said. "They have teachers for that."

"Well, whatever," Dorie said. "You're home anyway."

"How's the sanctuary?" Rett said, consciously changing the subject.

"Well, we miss Mason," Dorie said, giving her nephew a fond smile. "The dogs miss him too. He was a big help."

"How's that brindle dog?" Mason asked. "Is she still there?"

"Well, that's a good story," Dorie said. "You remember we weren't sure about who owned her, so we couldn't find her a home?" Mason nodded. Dorie turned to Rett. "You might not have known, but we had this female that landed with us after all that dog-fighting stuff last year, and she's been like part of the family, even though her ownership was unclear."

Mason added, "Even though we love her, we might have to let her go back to her owner. Dorie said so."

"Well, the good thing is that the trial is all over, the dog's owner is in prison, and because she was part of his dog-fighting business, which is entirely illegal, the police could confiscate and dispose of her."

"Dispose!" Mason said. "Like garbage?"

Dorie laughed. "Sounds like it. In this case, it just means find her a good place. We've fostered her for over a year, and she's a great dog. Dad even likes her, you know?" She looked at Rett. "We found a family for her, and she's there right now."

"Oh, Dorie!" Rett said. "That's great."

"Yay!" Mason shouted. The little girls chimed in just for fun.

"Yeah," Dorie said. "We don't do much of that work. Mostly we just get old dogs who are going to die, give them a good home for their last years or months."

Maggie looked horrified. "They're going to die?"

"Everybody dies," Mason said. "They're already old."

"Everybody?" Maggie asked in a whisper.

"Like bugs," Callie said, with an air of authority. "And like that bird we found."

Maggie was frowning, but she licked the jam off her bread.

"It's okay, Mags," Rett said. "Before they die, they get to live at Dorie's barn. You know how fun that is."

"Old people die too," Maggie said then. "Like Grandpa."

"No," Mason shouted. "Not Grandpa." He got up and stomped away from the picnic table.

"Mason," Rett called, then turned back with a sigh. "He's still upset from Dad's hospitalization last spring."

"How did we get on this topic? It's a beautiful September day, your garden is still producing, the sky is blue, it's even warm. Everything's right in the world."

Rett gave her a sidelong glance. There wasn't much to say to that.

"You know Evie's heading out in the morning though, right?" Dorie turned her attention back to the present. "They're off to Cape Breton for five days. Dad must have told you."

Rett shook her head. "Dad didn't mention it," she said.

"Well, she and Stephen are going to be gone, so I though we maybe should be checking in on Dad."

"Dad's a big boy," Rett said shortly. "He can ask for help if he wants it."

"Ohh, what's got you so prickly?" Dorie's eyes were wide.

"I'm not prickly," she retorted. "Dad gave me a lecture about asking for help, so I figure he can ask, too."

"Yeah, but he won't."

Rett fought her rising impatience. "Wasn't that what he promised after his health scare last spring? To keep us in the loop, ask for help, let us know?" She huffed as she stacked up the plates to return to the kitchen.

"He's old, you know," Dorie said. "But don't worry. Chad and I'll check in if you're too busy." She headed toward the goat barn calling for Mason.

Rett shook her head and took her dishes and mugs back to the kitchen. This family was too much. Too much meddling, too much drama, too much work. She dumped the dishes beside the sink and went back outside.

Dorie reappeared as if by magic. "Mason reminded me he's suspended."

Rett scowled. "It's not something to be proud of."

"No, but since he can't go to school, can he work with me tomorrow? I need to get the barn shipshape for a visit from a potential funder. He's a big help."

"He's eight. How much help can he be?"

"Hold up on the salt there. He's a big help. He knows how to feed and water everyone, and that gives me time to clean. Really, Rett. He works hard."

"I don't know. I don't think he should be rewarded for being on suspension."

"Well, I don't think working at the dog sanctuary all day is a lot of fun, but it is probably better than watching videos on repeat."

"Ouch," Rett said, thinking of all the times the kids had been parked in front of screens. Less now with animals, but still a factor. Harry would never have permitted it. "Okay, sure," she said.

Mason, who had been peeking from the side of the goat barn, ran over to give Dorie a big hug.

"This feels more and more like a conspiracy," Rett complained. "What, no hug for your mother who said okay?" He looked at her sideways, but then he slid close so she could hug him. "You know she'll make you work," she whispered to him. He grinned up at her.

Dorie smiled widely. "Thanks for sharing your boy," she said. "I'll pick him up tomorrow." She called Frou-Frou and headed toward the truck.

"Bye, Dorie," Mason called and waved. Rett waved too, a little half-heartedly. She sighed and looked at Mason.

"We still have to talk," she said.

Chapter 23

Despite her protests, Rett soon found herself homeschooling. She couldn't get past the vision of Mason slumped in shame in the office, waiting to be punished more after writing an apology. Maggie didn't want to be in school, and Callie was happy at home as long as there were outings with other children. It seemed like an obvious solution. It was work, sure, but she had never been afraid of work. Only a few days in and it somehow felt like a comfortable new routine.

She paced around the kitchen, phone on her shoulder, while sorting art supplies, getting Mason started on his measurement project, and tripping over KD. "Hey, Dad, when you get this, call me, please," she said to her father's voice mail. "I'm supposed to be checking on you, but you don't answer your cell."

Mason looked up. "Why do you have to check on Grandpa? I thought he was okay now."

She sighed loudly. "He is okay now, Mason, but Evie went away again, and we figured somebody should just check in. Remember?"

"I can check in," he said, lifting his chin. "I can get there really fast."

She softened. "I know you can, right through your secret trail. Checking on grandpa is a grownup job though. Thanks for offering."

As he turned back to his work, she said, "Later you and Charlie could drop over to see him. If you wanted to."

"I always want to," he said stoutly. "Mallow's there too."

"Yeah. Your soulmate, that dog."

"What's a soulmate, Mum?" Callie asked.

"It's an idea that some people are meant to be together," she said lightly. "It's just an idea. But Mallow and Mason have been best friends since Mason was a baby."

"Like you and Daddy?" Mason asked with peculiar intensity.

Rett glanced at him. "Yeah, I guess so," she said. What was he thinking? Before she could ask, a knock sounded at the front door.

"I'll get it!" Maggie and Callie nearly knocked each other down in their rush out of the kitchen. Charlie started barking and followed, while Mason pushed ahead of all of them to get to the door first. Rett sat down. It was probably Jürgen, anyway.

"Hey, Mum! Mum!" Mason's voice held surprise. "It's a lady."

A lady. Rett smoothed her hair back and walked into the living room to find the policewoman Kathryn Gallant patting Charlie on the head.

"Hi, Rett," she said.

"You should have called first," Rett said grimly. "We're busy."

"I'm sure you are," Kathryn said. "I need to talk to you. We can do it here or at my office."

Rett scowled. "I don't have time to go to Saint Jacques. Or a sitter."

"Then I guess it's here, eh?" Kathryn said lightly.

"Okay, kids, you get an early break today. Mason," she suggested, "now might be a good time to visit Grandpa. And girls, can you go collect eggs? Watch out for Frickin Chicken, though."

She turned to Kathryn. "You can sit here," she said shortly. "Let me get them sorted." She ushered the kids to the kitchen and out the door.

Mason whispered, "Mum, who's that lady?"

"Sorry, Mason, I didn't even introduce you. I'll tell you about it later, okay? Call me from Grandpa's please. If he's at home you can stay, but call me either way."

"Okay." He called for Charlie then disappeared into the woods. Rett heard the little girls talking and laughing in the chicken house. She slowly closed the door. The click sounded final; kids outside, herself inside with this policewoman.

"So," she said, returning to the living room. "I invited you to sit down."

Kathryn returned to the couch from the stairway. "Thank you. Yes, let's sit."

"What do you want? Why did you come all the way down here?" Saint Jacques was a good two hours from Stella Mare.

"I need to talk to you, Rett," Kathryn said simply. "We're still looking at the deaths at Streamside, and I'm trying to understand what was going on."

"Nothing was going on," Rett snapped. "Old people go into long term care and die there. That's a fact."

Kathryn blinked and waited.

"Losing a family member is hard on people. It's especially hard when family members feel guilty about using care for an elder. All that guilt floods back when they die, and then blaming starts."

"How long did you work at Streamside?" Kathryn asked mildly.

"Long enough," Rett said. "Really, most of my nursing career. I worked at the River Ridge Psychiatric for a couple of years right after my bachelor's, but psych nursing wasn't for me. Turns out I love older people. Like my Aunt Corinne who's a social worker. I started at Streamside when the Adamson family still owned it. It was a great place to work."

"So how many years were you there?"

"Almost sixteen. I worked part-time while I was doing my master's, and took maternity when the kids came along, but only for a few months. I've been evening supervisor for almost five years."

"How long have you known Angelica Mena?"

"Probably ten years. She started as a teenager, in a high school co-op program."

"You're smiling," Kathryn observed.

"Yeah," Rett agreed. "Our work was hard, is hard. But she made going to work a joy. She's just that kind of person."

"What kind? What do you mean?"

Rett thought. "It's like she's peaceful inside. Full of light, kind of. Hardly ever complains, even when things are hard. She genuinely loves our residents and takes pleasure in caring for them. I wish I had a roster full of Angelicas. It would make being the supervisor much easier."

"Did you know that more than eighty percent of the deaths at Streamside happened when Angelica was working?"

"Eighty percent? That sounds high," Rett objected. "Over how much time?"

Kathryn looked at a paper. "The past three years. You were on shift for over sixty percent of them."

"Are those meaningful statistics? We work in the evening. Evenings and nights are when people are most likely to die. Statistically."

"Rett, can you understand what we're trying to do here?" Kathryn asked, dropping her paper into her lap. "We have to see if there is a pattern, if there is the possibility of criminal activity."

"I don't think you understand our work," Rett said angrily. "We are there to help people live their lives, and sometimes that means help them while they are dying."

"But it doesn't mean helping them to die. Hastening the process."

Rett shook her head. "Nobody was doing that. People die when they are ready and sometimes they decide exactly when that is going to be."

Kathryn gave her a look.

"Don't, Kathryn. I'm telling you from my experience. People wait for their families, sometimes, and sometimes they wait for their families to leave. They hold off until a special date, or die before that date. Sometimes we try to make sense out of what could just be random, but honestly, enough people told Angelica that they felt ready and that they wanted her with them that I believe people truly know."

Kathryn squinted. "They told her they felt ready and then she was with them?"

"Stop it," Rett said. "She wasn't doing anything. She didn't intervene except maybe to put on their favourite music, or to sing to them, or to sit beside them and hold a hand. Don't make something beautiful into something ugly and criminal."

Kathryn's gaze remained intent on Rett's face.

"If I were you," Rett said urgently, "I'd quit wasting my time trying to turn Angelica Mena and me into bad guys. We're the good guys. Instead, look at why Briar Ventures is so insistent on moving dying residents into hospital? There might be some kind of corrupt something going on there."

"You weren't too happy when Briar Ventures took over Streamside, were you?"

Rett shrugged. "It wouldn't have been my choice, but nobody asked my opinion. Mrs. Adamson stayed on as general manager, but I think there's a lot of pressure on her. Not that I'm excusing how she's treated Angelica and me, but I don't think that would have happened in the days before the takeover."

She leaned toward Kathryn. "I really want you to understand what I'm talking about. Have you ever lost someone close to you? By death, I mean?"

Kathryn answered slowly, "I'm a police officer, Rett. I've seen death."

"Yeah, but probably not the good kind. You're probably well-acquainted with accidental death, homicidal ones, stuff like that. Dying isn't always like that. It can be a beautiful transition." She looked hard at the other woman. "You know?"

Kathryn looked away from her gaze. "I do know," she said quietly. "It was my grandfather. He was old, and he did get sick, but he got to say goodbye to everyone. I was with him." Her eyes glistened.

"Yes," Rett said firmly. "This is what we want for our residents. At the time that they are supposed to go though. Not on our timeline but on theirs."

"Okay," Kathryn said. "You've given me things to think about. Thanks."

"If I was dying and my family wasn't there, I would want Angelica Mena with me," Rett said firmly. "She's got the right name, you know. Like an angel."

"Okay. You've made your point."

"If I were investigating, I'd look at the hospital deaths of Streamside residents since the takeover. I bet the death rate isn't any different, but the place is. On evening shift, we supported people's right to die in their own beds, and other staff maybe were not. That's the only difference."

"Thanks for the advice," Kathryn said wryly. "Do people tell you how to do your job?"

"Sorry about that," Rett said, not at all sorry. "It might be worth consideration."

"It might," Kathryn said, heading toward the door. "I'll be in touch."

"Yeah, next time call first," Rett said, but her smile softened the words. "Oh, listen, Kathryn," she said. "Am I under investigation? Because my license has been suspended and I can't work. I've been emailing you every week."

Kathryn frowned. "I didn't get any emails from you. They suspended you without even any charges?"

"Yes. I complained, but it didn't get me anywhere."

"I'll give you a call if I can say anything about your status. And don't email. Text."

Rett closed the door, leaning back against it with a sigh. Maybe Kathryn would be able to clear a few things up.

KD twined around her ankles. She picked up the kitten and buried her face in warm fur. "Well, that was something," she said to nobody in particular. Then she went to check on the children.

When she went outside, Mason and Charlie were playing Frisbee and the girls were in the sandbox. "Did you see Grandpa?" she called to him.

He tossed the disk once more and headed toward her. "Nope. Grandpa wasn't home and neither were the big dogs. I forgot to call you, Mum." He looked shamefaced. "I just came home."

She rubbed his head. "That's okay, bud. Nobody was there, so you came home. That's the right thing."

She checked her watch. Practically lunchtime and hardly any schoolwork had been done. But she couldn't feel bad about it. Her conversation with the detective left her feeling optimistic. Maybe misplaced optimism, she thought, but it felt better than worrying all the time.

"Anybody hungry?" she called and headed back to the kitchen.

Chapter 24

H arry helped pack up field camp, keeping only what he and Marie would need for a few more weeks.

He was surprised by the surge of feelings as he and Marie stood watching a truck drive away carrying Joyce, Denys, and Alpha, along with a lot of the camp equipment. Stabbing loneliness mixed with relief and a little stress. Just a little stress.

Marie immediately refocused on work in the main tent. The morning, though crisp, was bright and clear, so Harry gathered supplies for a day in the field.

"I'm heading out," he said to Marie.

She barely glanced up but gestured to the logbook. "Log your plan and ETA back to camp, please."

"Of course," he said and jotted the information down. What was wrong with her? She'd started out pleasant enough, but over the weeks together at camp, she'd become cold and distant, maybe to everyone a little bit, he thought, but quite a lot toward him.

With a mental shrug, he left the tent and clambered onto an ATV and headed out.

When Thursday came, she agreed to go into town with him. Harry's first stop was the coffee place they all frequented. Not only was there a decent cell signal, the D-Lite had wi-fi.

It was already noon, so he knew the kids would be home from school. It wouldn't be a great time for private conversation with Rett, but at least he'd get to talk to his kids.

Mason answered his mother's phone. "Hi, Daddy. Can we do video?"

"Remember how bad it was last time? We just don't have the signal for it. It gets all messed up and I can't see you properly."

"You need a new phone, Daddy," Mason said. "I want to see you."

Harry chuckled. "Good idea, Mason, but not going to happen. I'll be home before you know it, though."

"Mum! Daddy's coming home!"

"No, no! Mason!" Harry's shout went unheard.

Rett picked up. "Harry?" Her voice was almost tremulous.

"No, he misunderstood me, Rett. I'm so sorry."

She sighed. "What did you tell him? He's off telling the girls you're coming home."

Now it was his turn to sigh. "I was trying to reassure him that it won't be too long. I didn't realize how he'd take it."

She was silent. He could hear the kids in the background, greatly excited. "I'm so sorry, Rett. Now you have to deal with the fallout."

"Yes."

"Nothing's changed, really. Most of the crew left on Sunday. Marie and I are holding down the fort and trying to get a little more work done before winter sets in."

"Marie? What's she like?"

Harry was at a loss to answer. "I don't know. She's busy. Focused. She doesn't like me much."

"Yeah, you said that. I can't quite believe it. Everybody likes you."

"I don't want to talk about her. How are things at home?"

"Okay," she said shortly.

"How was school this week? I missed getting to see the girls go to kindergarten."

"Yes, you did."

"Did they like it? Did Maggie cry? How did you feel, Mum, seeing your babies go to school?"

"You'll have to ask them. Let me get them. Get Mason to tell you about being suspended from school on the second day. And why they're not going any more."

"Wait, Rett!" She had put the phone down or something and was calling the children.

He talked to all three, and when he asked to speak to Rett again, Mason said she was busy.

"What's she doing?" he asked his son.

"She's got her hands all in a bowl of dough," Mason answered.

"You're not in school?" he asked, trying to be gentle.

"Mum's homeschooling. It's better."

Harry couldn't imagine Rett preparing lessons and teaching. "Really, Mason? Does Mum like it?"

"I dunno, Daddy. Hey, Callie's got my truck!" Mason was as distracted as his mother seemed to be.

Harry gave up. "Okay, guys, I'll talk to you next week. I love you. Tell your mum I love her too."

"Bye, Daddy!" He could hear three kid voices shouting the words, Charlie barking, and some other unidentifiable sounds, then the phone went quiet.

By the time he and Marie had gathered supplies, posted packages back to the university, and done a week's worth of email and downloading research papers, it was more than time to return to camp. The trip was long, and the dark arrived earlier now. Soon his days in the field would be getting very short.

The truck was noisy, Harry barely noticed that Marie didn't talk to him, but when they got back to camp and were stowing a week's worth of food in bear-proof containers, it became obvious. It was his night to boil pasta, and he put together the meal and set it on a table in the main tent. When she picked up her bowl to take it away, Harry said, "Please. Sit. We can at least eat together, can't we?"

She looked wary but sat down. With a flourish, he pulled out a cardboard box of wine. "See, all the luxuries." She smiled with effort and held out her mug.

Good start, he thought. He poured his own, and they tucked into the steaming pasta.

"Not too bad," he said.

"It's delicious, really," Marie said.

"That's what I meant. Where I'm from, not too bad is high praise."

"What do you say if it's a gourmet meal?"

"Might go as high as pretty good." Harry smiled.

"You're a Maritimer, right? You guys are not much given to enthusiasm."

"Well, some of us, maybe. I don't think everyone fits that mould."

"No, of course not."

In the silence, she poured herself more wine. "Did you talk to your kids today?" she asked. The question was offhand, but her gaze was intense.

"Yes," he answered. "It's the first week of school. For the twins, the little ones, it's their first time in school." He heard a little wobble in his voice. "I don't like missing those milestones. You know what I mean?"

She gazed at him. "No, I really don't know. Milestones, huh?"

"Yeah, like birthdays and school. All the firsts of your child's life."

"I know I told you I don't have a family," she said. "It's not quite true."

"Oh?"

She looked at him like she was memorizing his face. Then she drained her mug of wine and got up. "I'll clean up," she said. "Thanks for dinner."

Over the next week, the thawing continued. They shared camp duties and were cordial over breakfast and supper. There was no more personal conversation. Harry felt comfortable like this, though. It was a vast improvement over being treated like he didn't exist.

When the weather was clear, he collected data in the forest. When things got damp, he went to see Jeannette, carrying his recorder, his notebook, and a camera. Most days she was happy to talk to him, freely sharing her decades of knowledge. Wisdom, really.

"You never come when the sun shines," she said once.

He was surprised. "I'm getting samples from the woods then."

"We need samples too. How you gonna know what you're using if you don't learn where it grows?"

Well, on reflection, that was obvious. "You are right, of course. What do you want me to do about that?"

She looked up at the sky. "Noon tomorrow, it's going to clear and you're going to go out with me. It's September and we have gathering to do. Come in the morning."

"Yes, I'll come."

They had coffee and some of the cinnamon bread he'd brought her from town. Jeannette wanted to see his children, so he showed her family pictures.

"That's my wife, Rett," he said, holding out a print of Rett with the twins. "She's a nurse."

"Is she now?" Jeannette said, holding the photo close. "She's a handsome woman, too. The girls look like her."

"You think so?" He looked over her shoulder, curious. "Yes, I can see it now. When you're with them every day, it's not so obvious."

She looked up at him sharply. "But you're away so you see differently, no?"

"Yes. I do see differently," he said soberly. "I didn't realize it, but that's true."

"You bring those eyes out in the forest today," Jeannette said. "You'll learn to see."

Chapter 25

R ett bundled the kids into the car, but there were protests.

"Mum, why do I have to wear this tie?" Mason asked.

"My shoe fell off," Maggie said. "Callie, can you reach my shoe?"

"Mum! She took my bracelet!"

Rett put the car in reverse and gently rolled down the driveway. The kids' dress clothes were tight and probably uncomfortable, she thought. It couldn't be helped. She couldn't afford new stuff for one event. They would likely outgrow everything by Christmas anyway.

Her own dressy dress was loose around her hips. She hadn't known until trying it on that she had lost weight. She looked at her reflection in the long mirror after pinning up her heavy hair and, for the first time, she saw her own thinness. Well, there you go, she thought. What I'd never notice because I live in sweatshirts and stretch pants.

They trundled downtown to find a parking place on Water Street near the Fishburne Gallery. Evie's show was opening, and though Rett was not interested in talking to reporters, she wouldn't miss this event for anything.

Parking wasn't too hard. Many of the tourists had left by September, but the downtown was still vibrant in the early evening. The gallery was adjacent to the public dock that also held the Market Square. Rett peered at the square while shepherding her crowd. "Look, kids. This is where the market is on Saturdays. I wonder where our table will be?"

"Down by the water!" Callie shouted. Maggie followed her to look over the edge.

Mason gazed across the expanse, hands in his pockets. "When do we start?"

"Two weeks, I think." She thought of the dried herbs, eggs, peach jam, and bread she hoped to sell. There was so much to do. But right now, the family had another agenda. "Come on, kids. Let's go see Aunt Evie's gallery."

She leaned on the heavy wooden door and the children slipped inside. Fairy lights, fresh flowers, and the conversation of a crowd met her. The building was old, and the brick walls, tall ceiling, and warmly polished wood floors welcomed her. Walls were hung with mixed media displays. The regular offerings had been upstaged by this local show.

At the far end of the long space Evie, elegant in a long dress, stood on a low stage, speaking into a microphone held by a tall man. Rett realized it was her boyfriend Stephen at her side.

"Oh, there's Aunt Evie!" Mason said, and headed toward her, his sisters in his wake. Rett moved to intercept, but her aunt Corinne beat her to it, redirecting the kids to the food table at the back of the gallery.

"Well done!" Rett said to Corinne as she shepherded the youngsters past her.

"Cookies for the win. You can count on me." She smiled as she swept by, following Maggie.

Evie looked vibrant. She looked up at Stephen, then gracefully she reached for his hand. The two of them smiled at the man holding out the microphone. Evie's man was new to the family, and Rett looked at them now, standing together. She thought them well-matched, Evie short, curvy and curly-headed, and Stephen taller, but broad in the shoulders and chest. Their smiles were identical, she thought with a start. How could that be? Or maybe people in love started to resemble one another? She wondered if anyone ever thought she and Harry looked alike but shrugged it off.

Clusters of people were milling around, admiring the carefully hung and lit hand-hooked rugs on the various surfaces. Each one was accompanied by several watercolour renderings of the design, plus a card with information about the original artist and provenance of the rug. That's what Evie called it: provenance. When Rett asked her, she said it basically meant whose attic it came from. Evie had been collecting antique hooked rugs for this display, and many people in town had contributed.

Magda Allen, the realtor, was talking to Jürgen. She turned to Rett with a happy smile. "How is it going at your house?" she asked. "Or maybe, I don't want to know."

Rett smiled at her. "No, actually, it's fine. You should drop by. We're making the most of it."

Jürgen smiled. "Hello, Rett. I was telling Magda about all your improvements. Like goats."

Her gut twisted with anxiety as she wondered suddenly if animals were forbidden by the lease, but she put on her smile and said, "Oh, we're doing a lot of interesting things."

"Well, I am sure you are," Magda said. "I know you get things done."

"Maybe you should come over for a visit," Rett offered. "See how things look now."

"Thank you," Magda said. "I'll do that."

A tap on Rett's shoulder made her turn to see her sister Helen. Rett made a happy noise and they clutched each other. Rett hung on for dear life, feeling her chest nearly burst. "Oh, I have missed you," she said, finally pulling back to look at her sister's face.

Helen was glowing. "I missed you, too. It's so good and so weird to be here."

"Well, it's been forever," Rett said. "It's about time you got here."

"Not you, too," Helen objected. "Everybody's let me know."

"Okay, I'll try to lay off," Rett said, "but it is wonderful to have you here in real life. Not just on some video chat."

"I know." Helen scrunched up her nose. "This is so much better."

Maggie interrupted, grabbing Rett's leg. "Mags, here's Auntie Helen."

Helen bent down to talk to Maggie, James brushed Rett's elbow in greeting, and Mason appeared on her right with a cookie in hand. The crowd was growing, and the door kept creaking open to admit more well-attired villagers.

Rett did another scan of the room and found Callie holding Aunt Corinne's hand, James had his hand on Mason's shoulder, and Helen now held Maggie in her arms.

"Well, I guess the kids are accounted for," she said to nobody, and turned toward the wine and cheese table. Before she could take a sip, though, someone was calling for attention. Evie's friend, Leonard, had stepped up on the little stage, trying to get people to listen.

She couldn't really hear, and she wasn't all that interested anyway, so she slid along the back wall with all the food tables, and found a bit of an alcove to lean in. Turning her face toward Leonard, she gave her attention to the cheese and crackers she'd snared, setting her plastic wine glass by her feet. How did anyone expect to manage all this with only two hands? Distracted, she only looked back up when there was a smattering of applause and Evie started to talk.

Rett tried to pay attention, but she was hungry, and she missed a bunch of the beginning, because Callie was looking for her. "Mum, Mum...where are you?" Corinne spied her in her cozy little alcove and arrived with Callie in tow. She gave Rett a shoulder hug. Rett popped her last cracker in her mouth and smiled around it at Corinne and Callie. She brushed off crumbs and picked up Callie.

"Your dad's so freaking proud," Corinne whispered in Rett's ear. "He's so happy to have you girls here, and proud of Evie on the TV and everything."

Rett smiled and nodded. She still couldn't catch what Evie was saying, something about women's subversive activity in the kitchen and garden, about household tasks being fundamental to human survival, and the power to create sustenance and beauty. It made no sense to Rett, but Evie looked strong and confident, almost like a different woman than she had only last spring.

Time changes things, Rett thought, not for the first time. It certainly had changed things in her life and in her household. Back when the plans were made for this gathering, she'd never have guessed she'd be living in Stella Mare with a bunch of chickens and goats.

After Evie's remarks, the crowd settled down a bit. A lot of people left, presumably to get a real dinner, Rett thought, as she felt her hunger mount. The small crowd left all queued up to talk to Evie and Leonard. Evie's Stephen was always just a few steps away, clearly supportive of Evie's work.

She was leaning on the wall with Corinne, holding a slightly sticky Callie, when Ryan Standish walked up.

"Hi, Rett," he said warmly.

"Oh, Ryan, hi," she said. "Do you know Corinne? Corinne, this is Ryan Standish. He's the principal over at Maple Point Elementary."

They exchanged pleasantries, then Ryan asked, "How's the homeschooling going? I hope you'll let me know if we can support you with resources."

Rett nodded. "It's going fine, thanks. I've got lots to work with right now, but I appreciate the thought. Thank you."

"The kids are always welcome. If you want to take advantage of the library, or to come to programs we have for the whole school, that's good too. Kids need other children."

"Thank you," Rett said firmly. "We're in a homeschool group, so we have other children, but the library is a good idea."

"Good, good." Callie giggled at the funny face he made to her, then he turned away. Corinne looked at Rett, eyebrows up.

"Since when are you homeschooling?"

"Didn't Dad tell you? We've been at it for three weeks now. It's been pretty good. Here, Callie, you're getting heavy. Go find Maggie and Mason." She set down her child.

"He didn't mention it." Corinne was dry. "Like you don't have enough to do."

She shrugged. "I'm used to being busy. I like it better than sitting around and thinking, you know.

Corinne gazed at her. "I bet you miss working."

Rett looked down. "I do. You know it more than anyone. I do miss it. I miss my residents and feeling like I can make a difference. You know."

"I do know. What's kept you from getting work here in town?"

She straightened her back. "I'm busy. The kids, the animals, the gardening, the stuff. You know."

"Is that all? I wondered, and forgive me for this, but I wondered if you've lost your confidence since this nonsense with Streamside."

Lost her confidence? Was that it? "I don't think so. But some things have changed, that's for sure."

"Is that investigation still going on?"

Rett sighed and looked over Corinne's head at the thinning crowd. "I have been doing my best to ignore all of that," she said finally.

"Is it working?" Corinne asked.

Rett gazed down at her aunt, who was just a little shorter, but so much like her mother, Agnes. A slow smile moved across her face. "You sound like Mum. Yes, pretending it's all gone away is working, sort of," she admitted. "All the stuff at the house, the bread, the herbs, the kids, the animals, all of that stuff helps too."

"There are a lot of ways to run away," Corinne observed.

"I've never run away," Rett said firmly. "I stay. I fix things."

"You've always been a problem-solver," Corinne agreed. "That's one reason Streamside was nuts to let you go."

"Thanks. I think they're nuts, too. But like I said, I'm trying not to think about it too much."

Corinne nodded. "I can understand that. I am assuming you've tried everything you can to solve the problem."

"Well, it's not my problem. So yeah, I think so."

"Since you can't solve that problem, you just take on more responsibilities."

"I don't think that's what I'm doing. I'm just doing what needs to be done."

"You don't have to prove yourself to anyone, you know. We all know who you are, what kind of person you are. You can't fix things by just doing more."

"I have no idea what you're talking about," Rett said flatly, jaw tight. She was finished having this conversation. "I think it's time to go. The kids are probably starving."

Corinne glanced at her watch and easily switched gears. "Oh, you're right. It's time to go. James wanted everyone to come for pizza."

Rett's jaw softened as the subject changed. "Yes, that's what he told me. I wonder if I can pick it up?" She peered across the room. "I'm going to find Dad and ask him. I'll see you at the house, right?"

James said no, Chad and Dorie were on pizza pickup, and Rett should just come on over. He had Mason firmly by the hand. "This boy's coming with his grandpa, right, Mase?"

"Okay, then, I just have to corral the girls. I'll see you at the house." She wandered away and landed in front of Evie's pride and joy, the vibrant hooked rug made nearly a hundred years ago by their great-grandmother. Despite her hunger, Rett stood in front of this work of art, gazing on it with pleasure and a little pride.

"Women's work," Rett said, musingly. "What a strange term. Work is just work."

"I probably should always use air quotes when I use that phrase," Evie acknowledged. "We don't think of work in the same way now, thank goodness. Back then, if you were a man who hooked rugs, well, I don't know."

"But men knitted trap heads for lobster traps," Rett said. "They raised the sheep and sheared them for wool."

"Yes, and women also did that. Plus washing, carding, spinning, and weaving or knitting."

"Strange differentiation, I guess."

"Back when our great-grandmother Leonie was making this rug, women and men did a lot of the same work. It was about keeping alive, keeping the family going. That distinction between men's work and women's work showed up after the war, when governments wanted women at home and men at work. Jobs were for men, home work was for women."

"So it was more of a political thing than not?"

Evie nodded vigorously. "Yes! But it was pitched like it was the natural order of things."

Stephen came up behind Evie and slipped his arms around her waist. "Is Evie giving you a lecture? Practising being a professor?" he asked fondly. Evie's face glowed as she turned her head to look up at him.

Rett felt a pang of loneliness as she saw her sister melt into Stephen's embrace. Shaking it off, she said, "What about those Victorian ladies, always fainting at everything?"

"That would be the rich Victorian ladies, of course," Stephen said with a twinkle. "While regular working folk were salting fish, preserving the harvest, taking care of livestock, and herding the kids."

"Sounds like my life," Rett said absently. "Maybe we haven't come very far."

"Oh, we have," Evie said. "You have a choice about whether to live on your urban homestead. You could go back to work as a nurse, a choice that Leonie didn't have."

"Because she was a woman? Or because they were poor?"

"Good question," Evie said with a laugh. "I don't know. Maybe that's a question for a research project. The more work I do on this stuff, the more questions I have."

"Well, you'll be finding out, right? Next year?"

"I hope so," Evie said.

"She will," Stephen said comfortably. "She might not be convinced that she's Ph.D. material, but I am."

Evie gave him a little push. "Yes, but you're not on the admissions committee."

It had the feel of an oft-repeated discussion, so Rett just smiled and changed the subject. "Great show, great speech, and is there pizza in the near future?"

"Pizza and more," Stephen said, waving his arms. "We've got quite a spread laid out at the house."

We do, do we? "Well, Dad sent Dorie and Chad for pizza. I've got to find my girls. See you at home."

It took time to extricate Callie from playing with the gallery kittens, so the street was quiet when Rett buckled the girls into their car seats. Emerging from the backseat, she saw Leonard locking the big front door of the gallery and heading down the sidewalk.

Daylight had not yet fled, and the blue tone of the evening pervaded Rett in some way, making her think about things she didn't want to consider. She drove slowly, cool breeze through her open window, gulls and crows in evening competition, watching the streets of Stella Mare unfold. Evie so happy, Dorie and Chad like a pair of bookends, James proud, Corinne's care...She had never missed Harry so much. Her chest tightened and she swiped at her eyes.

She had to park far down the street from her father's house. When she released the girls, they tore across three lawns to Grandpa's house, leaving her behind. She wrapped her jacket a little tighter, lifted her chin, and headed to the party.

Chapter 26

Rett wondered how long she'd have to wait to hear something from the police detective. Was she still under investigation or wasn't she?

This was as far as her wondering went though. When she thought about getting her license reinstated, her imagination failed her, so she did some necessary task. She punched down bread dough, swept out the chicken coop, practised her feather-light souffle with eggs picked by the twins, and looked up recipes for goat-milk soap, against the day when Nanny Goat's milk might be for her instead of for Baby Goat.

If I am under investigation, I will fight, she thought. That was perfectly clear. I am a good nurse. I did not do anything wrong. She thought about what she'd told Corinne, that she had done everything possible.

She made a note to text Kathryn Gallant again.

Nightfall came earlier in late September. Instead of being out in the field until 9 p.m., Harry was back in camp by seven. He was getting more sleep at least, or he should have been. Instead, he spent a lot of time thinking.

The tasks for Joyce's project were no longer an interminable list. Instead, the list became a race against time. Only a few more days with Marie in camp, then he had only the work he could squeeze in before fall started to close in more tightly and he had to leave.

His ideas about his own work were frustratingly vague.

Instead of prying apart what was known, to find a tiny space to which he could contribute knowledge, he was preoccupied with Jeannette's work. He spent all available time compiling his observations, sketches, pictures, and their conversations. He added samples of the plants and finished medicines along with her stories. He wrote, turning his copious notes from every visit into detailed descriptions and procedures for locating, collecting, and processing the plant medicines she used. He described her kitchen, trying to capture the feeling he had when there, the sense of timelessness.

He wondered what he was really doing.

Maybe he was trying to collect wisdom. But wisdom can't really be collected. Or passed on. Knowledge maybe, and information certainly, but wisdom? Wisdom arrives, he thought.

When he finally lay to rest in his tent, he slept immediately, but often he woke deep in the night. That was when his thoughts would turn to his life before field camp, to Rett and the children. When it happened, sleep was lost.

Rett seemed more and more distant. Each of their not-really-weekly phone calls disturbed him. At times, she was remote. Other times, she was offhand about things he thought were important. He was a little angry at the way she withheld information. Like not telling him anything about the kids' schooling. She was his only conduit to the children's lives, and she wasn't letting him in. He wondered how angry she might be about his absence. She'd never say so, of course. Rett wasn't one to think about stuff too much, but she might be mad, deep inside.

Thinking about Rett's feelings made him sad. Maybe this whole project, this idea of going out to the wilderness to study, following Joyce out to the middle of howling nowhere, maybe it was a bad idea. Maybe it was contributing to the breakdown of his family or something. He knew he didn't like this feeling of being so distant from Rett. Their partnership had sustained him through the hard years. Those were the years when the twins arrived, he had to delay grad school, she was working as much overtime as she could, and her mother was dying. Back then she had felt distant too, but he still felt secure in their partnership. They were in it together.

This time was hard, too. He was tired from short nights in a sleeping bag and long days walking in the forest, plus the internal struggle about his project while trying not to worry about home. Rett might be tired too, but maybe not. Being off work might be a good break for her and getting to spend all that time with the children—well, she'd been saying for years she wanted more time with the kids. She pretty much had things the way she wanted them. He didn't know what she had to complain about.

He thought about his routine with Marie and Jeannette. It was okay as long as it was temporary. Short-term and temporary. He was used to sleeping alone since Rett had been on night shift for years, but he wasn't used to being alone. His own thoughts, interesting though they may be, were insufficient.

He stretched on his cot and repositioned himself. Too much thinking and not enough sleeping. He consciously relaxed his toes, his feet, his legs, slowing his breathing.

When he checked the calendar the next morning, he made an instant decision.

"I'm going to town," he announced to Marie. "Do you want to come?"

She looked startled, then annoyed. "Harry, it's Saturday. We were just there."

"I know. I need to talk to my family."

"Well, if you're going, there are a few things we didn't get on Thursday. Let me make a list."

Jouncing down the track toward town, he tried not to think about the work he wasn't doing today and focused instead on the happy surprise of his wife and kids when he called unexpectedly. This was the big weekend of Evie's local show at the art gallery. His sister-in-law Helen would be at James' house, and the sisters would be all together for the first time in years.

He went straight to the coffee shop. Maybe today he'd try again for video. It had been weeks since they'd had a chance to see each other. The longing to see Rett grew in intensity.

Rett's phone rang but there was no answer.

He called the landline at James' house.

"Hello."

"Hi, James. It's Harry," he said.

"Harry! Where you calling from? You still up there in the woods?" James was jocular.

"Yes. I just remembered it's the big weekend, and I wanted to say hi to everyone. Rett's not answering her phone."

"Oh, well, those girls and the kids are all out for the afternoon. I think they went down to Fundy Park for a hike. No coverage there, you know."

Harry's heart dropped. "I got here as soon as I could," he said. "I have to drive two hours to get to a signal."

"Well, Rett said that. She doesn't get to talk to you much, does she?"

"No. It's not easy."

"How's it going up there? Meet any wildlife?"

"Lots," Harry said. "It's going okay, but I can't say I want to move into a tent permanently. How's it going there? Helen's home, right? Jake too?"

"No, Jakey's got hockey, always the hockey, and his dad stayed in Ottawa to drive him around, I guess. Helen's pretty good. Those girls can talk some though, and drink wine. Evie's opening was last night, you know."

"Yeah, I bet that was great."

"Evie did well," James said. "Funny to see your kids all grown up. Well, you'll know soon enough."

"How's Rett? I talk to her, but she won't say much about how she's doing."

James paused. "Rett likes to think she can handle anything. She's some busy, for sure, with homeschooling, and the chickens and goats, and making stuff for the market. Sometimes I think she likes to be too busy."

"Homeschooling? She's homeschooling? Mason mentioned that."

"She said she was going to tell you," James said. "I might be in trouble."

"Did you say goats?"

"Well, Jürgen, her neighbour, has been helping out a bit," James went on, "but I told her the other day that she's bit off too much. She didn't take to my advice, I have to admit."

Harry had never felt so far away from home. "Do you know when they'll be home?"

"Late, probably. I expect they'll eat out somewheres and just get home in time to put the kids to bed. I'm sorry you missed them, Harry."

"No cell signal in the park, is there?"

"Probably not. But I'll tell them you called, okay?"

"Yes," he said slowly. "Give Evie my congratulations, and a hug for Helen and Dorie, and tell Rett, well, tell her I miss her."

"You coming home for Thanksgiving, son?" James asked.

"I can't. No, I'm here until the weather says I have to be gone, and even then I don't know if I'll be in Winnipeg or in New Brunswick."

"I'm an old man and I get to give advice," James said. "You get to ignore it, just like my daughters do, but I'm going to tell you what I think."

Harry chuckled. "Go ahead. I can take it."

"Come home, Harry. She needs you, but she'll never admit it. She's a pigheaded one, strong and able to get more done in a day than anyone needs to. Doing more is all she knows how to do. She needs you to balance that out."

Harry sighed. "I hear you, James. I wish I could come today, but I'd be throwing away this opportunity. All we've been through so far would be wasted."

"I hear you," James said. "I said my piece. That's all I needed to say. I will tell everyone that they missed a chance to talk to you and that, what, you'll call next week?"

"Right. I'll call on Thursday. Thanks."

"Goodbye, Harry. Take care of yourself."

Chapter 27

They had to take two vehicles to get everyone to Fundy Park, and by the time they'd hiked to a waterfall, pulled Callie shrieking out of the water a couple of times, and hiked back up the hill, the kids were tired, and even the adults needed a break.

"It's so gorgeous here," Helen said, as they rummaged through Rett's van. The kids were whining for snacks, while Rett helped Callie change into dry clothes and gave Mason directions to find food in the cooler.

"It is beautiful, but it must be nice where you live, too," Rett said, emerging from the back of the van. "Near Algonquin Park."

"It's been years since we went there," Helen said. "In New Brunswick, you don't have to travel far to find the great outdoors."

"True," Rett agreed. "You'd be amazed at what Mason's found in our backyard. Or in the woods on the way to Dad's house." She bundled the wet clothing into a plastic bag. "But you're right that it takes a reason to go to the park. We haven't been here for years," she said, looking around. "That's another good thing about you coming for a visit. It gives us a reason for an outing."

"Have I ever been here before?" Mason asked.

"You sure have," Rett said. "You were a little baby, though. Daddy and I decided to bring you camping."

Helen laughed. "There's a story coming, Mason, I can tell."

"Oh, yes," Rett agreed. "Daddy and I liked camping, and we figured a baby was just another person, so why not all camp together?"

"Why not?" Helen grinned at Mason and fluttered her eyes. "What's coming next?" she asked her nephew.

"I don't know," he said. "I was a baby, so I don't remember."

Rett laughed, remembering. "You cried all night, and I was so afraid that the other campers would be upset, I just walked you up and down the camp road in the dark. We hiked the next day with you in the front carrier on my chest. You were sleeping because you had been awake all night, but I didn't get to sleep. I was probably too tired to hike, but we went anyway. I slipped and landed on my butt on a rock."

"Ouch!" Helen said. By now the little girls were rapt, listening to the story. "There I was, sleeping baby on my chest, crashed on my butt on a rock out in the woods, Daddy pretty far behind me on the trail because he'd been taking pictures, and guess what came along?"

A chorus of questions arose. "What? What happened?" Dorie and Evie wandered over to listen in.

"A bear! A great big mama black bear was walking in the woods."

"Oh, no! A mama bear."

"I knew she was a mama because there were two cubs following her."

Dorie scoffed. "This sounds like something in a movie."

"For real, I swear," Rett said solemnly. "There I am on my butt crying, the baby wakes up and he starts crying—that's you, Mason—and this mama bear is coming my way."

"Did you pat her?" Maggie asked.

Evie gasped. "Bears aren't teddy bears. We don't pat the bears," she said. "I bet your mum had to get out of there."

"Well, I couldn't," Rett said, "even though that was what I wanted to do. That, or disappear, me and Mason together."

"What happened?" Helen asked.

"I'm scared," Callie shouted. "Bears!"

"Where?" Maggie wailed.

"Hold on, you guys," Dorie said. "Your mum's right here, so she got away, right? And Mason too." The twins subsided. Dorie shook her head. "You two. Great imaginations."

"Daddy was coming. He was moving fast because he'd heard me yell when I fell, and probably heard me wailing afterwards, but I shouted 'Bear!' and 'Get Away', and he got the cue and came crashing through the woods, yelling and making as much noise as he possibly could. Mama bear turned around and gave those cubs a shove, and they all left. I was never so happy to see anyone as Daddy, and never so happy to see the back side of any animal as that bear. And that's the last time Mason was in Fundy Park."

"Well, that's quite a story," Helen said as they climbed in the car after buckling the kids in. Rett steered along behind Evie out of the parking lot and down the parkway.

"Yeah, only a little more dramatic for the kids," Rett said. "It wasn't a fun trip, that's for sure."

"You and Harry have done some interesting things," Helen said. "I mean, camping a couple of hours away from home isn't that big, but you went to Europe, right? And caving in the U.S. That big trip to

Nunavut, you guys did that. Hey, did Harry know he wanted to work on permafrost back then?"

"What? No, I don't think so. He was still into wildlife then."

"I bet you miss him."

Rett shook her head. "Not really. I mean, yes, sometimes, but mostly I'm busy. We have a lot going on, Helen. You haven't spent any time at our house yet."

"Tonight," Helen suggested. "Maybe we can hang out when the kids are in bed."

"Sure," Rett agreed. "Let's have an early supper on the road, and by the time we get home, they'll be out."

It was almost true, except Maggie had fallen asleep on the way home and was bright-eyed once they reached their house. Rett decided to go with the flow and stuck her in the bathtub while her siblings went to bed and by the time the laundry was churning in the machine, the snack containers rinsed and put away, and Rett's own face washed, Maggie was languishing in the warm water. Rett picked her up, towel-wrapped, slid her pajamas on and tucked her into bed.

Helen was in the living room sipping a glass of wine, listening to music. "That's nice," Rett commented. "How'd you do that?"

"Bluetooth speaker," Helen said. "You don't have one? Makes music possible anywhere."

"Not where Harry is," Rett said darkly. "He doesn't have cell service or internet at all except when he goes into town."

"Really? That seems so, I don't know, old-fashioned. I'm surprised that a university isn't better set up."

"The university is fine. It's the field camp. There are places in the world without connectivity."

"That reminds me. Dad said to tell you Harry called today. No cell coverage in Fundy Park apparently, so he called Dad."

"Today? He usually only calls on Thursday. Did he say why?"

Helen shrugged. "Dad said it was because of Evie's show and every-one being home. He just missed out on the timing."

"Oh, well," Rett said, raising her glass. "That's how it goes."

"You don't seem too bothered," Helen said, narrowing her eyes.

"I'm not," Rett said. It was quiet, with only soft pop music playing. "Hear that?" She stretched out. "Peace and quiet."

"It's nice," Helen said. "Dad said Harry didn't know you are home-schooling the kids." Rett's jaw tightened despite her relaxed posture. "He said Harry didn't know about the animals, either."

"Of course he did," she retorted. "The kids tell him everything."

"But you don't?"

"Thin ice, Helen."

"This is serious. You can't leave your husband out of all these deci-sions."

"Oh, yes, I can. He's not here, they don't have anything to do with him, and I can handle it."

"That's unreasonable."

"I am always reasonable. Harry is thousands of kilometres away, busy with his life. He can't help me here, and I don't need to worry him there. I've got this."

"That sounds scary to me," Helen said. "Like you're living your life without your husband."

"Well, he's not here, is he?"

After a soft knock on the front door, Jürgen let himself in. "Good evening, ladies," he said smoothly, pouring himself a glass of wine. He sat in the chair opposite Helen and Rett on the couch. "How are you finding your visit, Helen?" he asked.

"Nice to see you again, Jürgen," Helen said. "It's fine, thank you."

"I'll get some crackers," Rett said, abruptly getting to her feet. In the kitchen, she leaned on the sink to look out into the dark garden. The solar-powered lanterns hung around the yard giving a little light, but otherwise there was a moonless dark.

The conversation from the living room receded as she gave in to the flow of memories; Harry, shouting and chasing the bear in Fundy Park, carrying infant twins in back and front packs, with Mason stuck to his leg. Then his welcoming arms as she slipped into bed late after her shift. The unbidden recollection of his warm, sleepy body and her own, stretched against his length took her breath away. The memory of their goodbye at the airport sent her into imagining; Harry living in a tent, driving a truck in the middle of the wilderness, hurt and being cared for by somebody's grandmother, all without her. With people she'd never met. Rett felt small and tired.

"Rett?" Helen came into the kitchen. "Were you getting crackers?"

"What?" She turned from the window and her thoughts. "Yes, here they are."

"He's nice," Helen whispered in her ear.

"Who?" Rett whispered back. Helen jerked her head toward the living room. "Jürgen? Yes, I guess so. He's helped me out a lot," she added.

"Well, I like him," Helen said. "It's good for you to have some help."

"I really don't need it," Rett reiterated. "But he seems to like to do it."

"Listen, sorry if I was out of line before," Helen continued quickly. "I just don't want to see anything disturb what you and Harry have. You guys have things just right, you know?" Helen's eyes glistened, for some reason.

"Us?" Rett scoffed. "We have our troubles. You and Reggie have things right. I've always thought that you two had the perfect arrangement. Friends, partners, lovers, spouses."

Helen picked up the cracker plate. "I need another glass of wine."

Chapter 28

Rett was glad Helen planned to stay a week. Evie and Stephen were travelling again, which meant James was on his own at the house. Rett was glad to know Helen would be there. Besides, she needed legal advice.

After getting the kids started on a project for Monday's home-school, she called Helen. "I need your lawyer brain."

"I don't know, kiddo. I charge a lot," Helen said.

"Very funny," Rett answered. "I just need to talk to you about a legal issue."

"You're not thinking about leaving Harry..."

"No, no! Good heavens, where did you get that idea? No, it's about the work stuff."

"When will there be quiet time to talk?"

Rett looked around her kitchen. The girls were making designs to dye cloth for curtains and Mason was calculating how much feed he would need to increase the size of their flock of laying hens. "Maybe

Dad will hang out with them this afternoon for a while. Will you ask him?"

James arrived after lunch, bearing a canvas bag full of wood scraps. "We've got projects," he announced. Seeing the kids fully engaged, Rett took Charlie through the woods to meet Helen.

Helen looked relaxed and pulled together. Rett brushed regretfully at her sweatpants. "You're even wearing makeup," she said accusingly.

"It's nothing," Helen said. "Now what do you want to talk about?"

Rett took the proffered cup of coffee. "The association has suspended my nursing license. Temporarily, I hope, but apparently it's a thing they do when there's a criminal investigation."

"The police have confirmed that you are under investigation?"

"Well, nobody there will deny it. I've seen a detective twice, but that's all. They didn't even recommend a lawyer, so it's not like there are any charges or anything."

"What have you done about this?"

"Nothing," Rett answered flatly. "Well, almost nothing. I've been clear with my association that it's bogus, but they insist they need confirmation that I'm not under investigation."

"How hard can that be? Either you are or you're not."

"You'd think. Detective Gallant said she'd look into it, but nothing has happened."

Helen said nothing. Rett sighed.

"Well, in the meantime, I've been lying to Dad about it. He thinks I'm wilfully ignoring my responsibility to have a job."

"Why not tell him? You're not responsible for what happened."

She looked away. "When you say it that way, I wonder about myself. I didn't do anything wrong, but I still feel ashamed of losing my job and my license. I don't want Dad to see me like a loser."

"I'm sure that would never happen."

"It's a risk," she said wanly. Her shoulders felt heavy.

Helen was energized. "Let's figure this out. If you're not the target of investigation, you can pursue getting your license reinstated. If your association pulled your license based on rumour, you may have a case against them."

Rett sank in her chair. "It's all too much, you know? I've got the kids and the animals, and I have contracts now to deliver homemade bread and eggs and I..." She put her hands over her eyes.

"You're making excuses," Helen said critically. "This doesn't sound like you at all. I can't believe you'd let yourself be treated this way."

Rett pushed up from the table, carrying her mug. At the kitchen sink, she leaned against the counter and stared out the window.

Helen went on. "You've got to get your priorities straight. Get this cleared up."

Still staring outside, Rett said, "The thing is, there might be a pattern."

"What?"

"There might be. I worked nights with Angelica, almost always. She was on my shift, most nights, for maybe the last three years." She turned back toward her sister. "There were a lot of deaths. A lot of people died when Angelica was working."

"You were working when Angelica was working."

"Right."

Silence filled the kitchen. The big clock ticked on the wall by the stairs.

"Do you think Angelica was doing something to hasten death?"

Rett shook her head slowly. "No. I don't think so. But we did have a lot more people die when we were working."

"Do you feel responsible?"

"No. Well, maybe. I feel something. Maybe I should have been supervising her more closely. Maybe I wasn't entirely aware of everything going on. Maybe I should have done something." Her throat was tight, and she could barely breathe.

"I see." Helen watched her for a moment. "You haven't done anything about this because you're wondering if you're responsible."

"You don't mince words, do you?" Rett said sharply. "I've been busy."

"You've made yourself busy," Helen corrected. "Nobody required you to homeschool. Or grow your own food."

"Harry left," Rett said bitterly. "Right when I needed him the most. I had to take charge."

Helen leaned back in her chair. "Have you talked to anybody about this? You're really angry."

Rett scowled. "Like a shrink?" She thought briefly of Ryan Standish suggesting the school counsellor for Mason. "Nobody here needs that kind of help, Helen."

"I didn't mean..."

"I am talking to someone. I'm talking to you," she said loudly. "My big sister, the big-shot lawyer who is supposed to help me."

"Are we fighting? Do you really want to fight with me?" Helen's clear-eyed gaze pierced her. Rett stared, then sighed and turned away.

"No, of course not. I don't want to fight with anybody. This is just so hard to talk about."

"I'll help you," Helen promised. "I'm here until Friday. Do you want me to call the police detective for you?"

"Yes, please. Maybe she'll respond to you. But please, can we do this without anybody else knowing?" Rett asked in a small voice. "I just can't bear it if Dad finds out."

"Finds out what? He already knows that you're being unfairly targeted."

"He doesn't know about my license. He already gave me a lecture about my career. Please, Helen. This has to be between us. Client-attorney privilege, or something."

Helen scoffed. "First, understand that you are not my client. You're my sister. Yes, of course I'll be quiet about it. I don't think it should be a secret, but it's your story, not mine."

"Maybe there is something I can do," Rett thought aloud. "I'll talk to Angelica again. See where she's at."

"Good. The start of a plan," Helen said with a smile. "You'll get through this, you know. When does Harry come back?"

Rett's heart squeezed a little more. "I don't know."

"You told him about your projects, right?"

"Just because you tell me to do something doesn't mean I have to do it," Rett snapped.

"It's not good, you know," Helen said. "If you shove him away, he might stay there."

Chapter 29

Helen called Detective Kathryn Gallant early Monday morning, but the woman had nothing to report. Tuesday, Rett finally made time to call Angelica, feeling her stomach buzzing with nerves and her mind full of "what if?"

"Why don't you come out here for a visit?" she asked. "Bring your son. We've got animals and, of course, the kids are here."

"He's in school," Angelica replied. "Don't your kids have school?"

"I'm homeschooling," Rett announced. "I keep forgetting that everyone isn't this flexible."

"It sounds like the opposite of flexibility to me," Angelica said with a laugh. "Kids and lessons and stuff all the time. No, I'm pretty happy when Ricky goes to school."

"Can you come then? Or I'll come to you. I want to talk with you."

"Could you come here? You know what I drive. It's not trustworthy."

"Sure. I'll come. My sister will take the kids."

"See, that's what's different. You've got family there."

"You're right. How's Thursday? We can go out for coffee."

On Thursday, back in Saint Jacques, Rett looked over as Angelica climbed into her van.

"It is so good to see you," Rett said. She reached awkwardly across the center console to give her a hug, then she held her friend by the shoulders for a moment as they gazed at each other. Smiling, Rett found her eyes moist.

"You, too," Angelica agreed. "Thanks for coming to get me."

"My pleasure," she said, turning back to the steering wheel. "Looks like nothing has changed here at the Daily Grind," Rett noted as they found a table at the café near Streamside Residence.

"We mostly got takeout," Angelica reminded her. "I'm not sure I ever sat down here for coffee."

"Or sat anywhere," Rett said with a laugh. "My feet like being off, even if the rest of me doesn't." She gazed across the table. "You still look like you."

"Weird, isn't it? So much has happened that I expected you to be, I don't know, different."

"Still me. Still looking for my next hit of caffeine." She waved to the server, and they ordered. "So."

"Yeah," Angelica said. "I miss being at work. This mess has taken too long."

"What do you know about the investigation? They ask a lot of questions, but they don't share much information. The police detective came to my house a couple of weeks ago, even though she interviewed me in July. What's happened on your end?"

"They brought me in three times. The issue is those three deaths at Streamside," she said abruptly. "I would never.... I can't believe anybody thinks I would ever harm a resident." She dabbed her eyes with a paper napkin.

Rett's nervousness subsided. This was Angelica. Of course, she would never hurt anyone. "Who is the idiot that thinks you did?"

"The police. The boss. The corporate whatevers."

"Have you been accused? Like, are there charges?"

Angelica looked horrified. "No, I don't think so. They would say so, right?"

"My sister the lawyer says we would definitely know if there were charges. I guess I just can't understand how they can keep us from working, if we're not being accused," Rett fretted.

"You, too?" Angelica was surprised. "I thought you decided to move to Stella Mare because Harry was away."

"Well, sort of. But mostly, because without my salary I couldn't afford to stay in my house. Things have been tight."

"Yeah, I know about tight. We're getting by, but barely. Ricky got a job after school, and I'm doing some babysitting for cash."

"I'm sorry."

"Yeah. Me too. At least you've got Harry. He's working out west, isn't he?"

Rett scoffed. "Harry's working on his Ph.D. It's not like a job, exactly. He barely makes enough to feed himself. Right now, he's up north in some field camp, and believe it or not, that's better for us, because he's not paying rent and his food is supplied."

"Winter's coming," Angelica said with a shiver. "He's up north?"

"Yeah." Rett thought about Harry. "He's doing some research. I don't know much because he's out of touch. He probably will be back in December. Or something."

"You're not sure?"

Rett scowled while thinking. "Yeah, I guess I'm not. It's kind of like we've each moved into our own universe. There's no internet or phone service, so we only talk when he goes into town. Then it's mostly him and the kids."

Angelica looked at her curiously. "Does he know about all this work stuff? I'd be lost if I didn't have my mama to talk to about this. Even though she worries, at least she listens."

"I've got Dad," Rett said quickly. It wasn't the same, of course, especially since she wouldn't tell him much. No point in worrying him. "Besides, you and me, we've got this. We'll get it figured out."

"I wish I was as certain as you are," Angelica said. "I just keep thinking about Mr. Martin, and then Eloise Friedman before him, and Ricky Stubbs."

Rett smiled. "You loved Eloise, didn't you?"

"I sure did. I still miss her. She was so alone, you know?"

"At one point, I was sure she thought you were her daughter," Rett reminisced. "Even without dementia!"

Angelica laughed. "I know. I think she wished I was. The night she died was so sweet. I remember you came in, too. Lit a candle."

Rett's voice was soft. "You had that tape playing, the one Paula made." Their guitar-playing chaplain had recorded some of Eloise's favourite folk songs. "It was a peaceful passing, for sure."

"Yes." Angelica wiped at the corner of her eye. "I hate to see them go, but it is such a privilege to be with them at the time."

"Especially people whose family can't be there," Rett agreed. "I know you've always felt like that."

"Not always," Angelica said. "It really started after Ricky was born. Something about being so close to the edge myself, seeing a calm and peaceful place, it made me stop being afraid of death, and dying people. Then I could just be myself with them."

"Hmm," Rett said. "Well, you made a difference for a lot of folks. You often seemed to know, too, when their time was coming."

Angelica nodded. "Yes. It's kind of a feeling, not really a knowing."

They sat in quiet for a moment.

Then Angelica said, "I think that's the problem. People used to wait for me to be on shift."

"They did, yeah," Rett said. "Why is that a problem? Except you're not there now, obviously."

"It might look like I was, you know, doing something to them."

"Absolutely not."

"Well, you know that, and I know that, but how does it look? More people die on my shift than any other time. The police said so."

"More people die at night, Angelica. You know that. We work nights."

"Yes, but apparently Briar Ventures doesn't know. That's why we're both unemployed right now."

"That's one more reason why investment firms shouldn't own healthcare facilities," Rett said bitterly. "They don't know how things work, and they don't have any reason to care. Just worried about the bottom line, and public opinion."

"I'm worried about my bottom line," Angelica said. "Worse, I'm afraid I'm going to be thrown in prison, and then what will my mother and Ricky do? It's bad enough being out of work, but at least there's hope for another job."

Prison.

Fear chewed at her gut again. Angelica had named it. "We're not going to prison. That can't happen. We did our jobs and did them well. I'm not going to let this ruin either of us."

Angelica gave her a wan smile. "I know you're good at solving problems and fixing things, but honestly, I don't know if this thing can be fixed."

The shorter the days became, the more time Harry had to spend on the activities of basic survival. As October closed in, the nights grew longer and colder.

Marie prepared to leave before Thanksgiving, in the first weekend in October. She gathered her work materials from the large tent. Harry sat on a folding stool and watched her pile notebooks and stray electrical cords into a box.

"Are you sure you don't want to stay?" he asked, hearing his plaintive tone.

She tossed a quick smile over her shoulder. "Not a chance," she said. "You could come back, too, you know."

"Yeah, well," he said, shrugging. "Joyce wants me to stay. I'm not really finished here."

Marie scowled. "Joyce does indeed. You might have to decide if it's good for you, though, Harry."

"What did you do, back when you first started working for her?"

She scoffed. "Yeah. Anything she wanted me to. I get it." She gazed intently at him. "But Harry, I was a twenty-four-year-old grad student. No ties back home. Your situation is different."

He sighed. It was different, of course. "I hate to think I missed my chance," he said to her.

"Chance for what? Overwork, frostbite, dragging your degree on for another dozen years?"

He spluttered. "Are you talking about me or about yourself?"

"You're right. Sorry. I'm just realizing how resentful I am, have been. You're afraid you missed out on grad student suffering. I'm afraid I missed out on making a home, having a family. Having a life in addition to my research. I expect that's not a popular thing to say, but that's what I've been thinking lately. I might not even finish," she said, looking down at her box.

"Really? You'd quit now, at this point? How far along are you, anyway?"

She laughed. "Isn't that what people ask about a pregnancy?"

Harry reddened. "Probably. Sorry. No offence."

She shook her head. "None taken. Sometimes I feel like my only baby is going to be this dissertation. I collected my data, finished collecting, last season. The analysis was done in April. I've been trying to write an acceptable version of the results for six months. That's what I've been doing at five a.m., because otherwise, this time has been Joyce's. I mean, it's my work, too, don't get me wrong. I'm her project manager. But my research for my degree...just waiting for me to write a decent draft."

"What's stopping you? You've written a pile of published papers; I've read them. Obviously, you can write a results section."

She leaned back against the table, folding her arms. "I keep asking myself that. Maybe I'm just scared of change? Maybe it's easier to blame Joyce and her demands than to notice that I am my own biggest obstacle. I can't figure it out. What I do know, very clearly, is that I have one more semester to get this wrapped up or I'm out, no degree."

"You've been at it a long time then," Harry said. It put his own slow start into a different perspective.

"Don't do what I did," she advised. "Get in, get your data, write your paper, get out."

He nodded. "That is what I had in mind. Things haven't started off the way I expected, though. I don't even know if I want to be a scientist."

"Now's a funny time to notice."

"No kidding. It's part of what I'm hoping to figure out."

"Staying in field camp is a hard way to make life decisions," she said.

"On the contrary. Having to focus on fundamentals should make life decisions clear. I'm not quite there yet."

"Harry," she said, walking close to him. "You've got a big life back home. I'd love to have what you have. For weeks, I could barely look at you for my jealousy. You're a good man, and you're probably a good father and a good husband. Get done here and go."

He looked at her dark eyes welling up a bit. He nodded tightly. "Sounds like good advice," he said.

She gave a brief smile and turned away. "It is. My last night here, maybe my last night here forever," she said. "Let's have a drink." She slid a bottle of scotch out of her oversized backpack. "My treat."

The fall morning was still dark when he drove her the two hours to town where she had arranged her ride. Her friend was there with a van. Harry helped her load her stuff, then he stood awkwardly while she prepared to leave.

"Bye, Harry," she said, poised to clamber into the van. "Let me know how things are going."

He nodded. "I'll email on Thursdays," he said over an unexpected lump in his throat.

She smiled. "Or whenever. Weather will be your wildcard. You don't have to have everything figured out to come back to Winnipeg. It's okay to call it when you think the time is right."

"Thanks. I'll tell Joyce you said so," he said with a grin, and she laughed. A moment later, the van pulled out and left Harry in the parking lot. What a strange relationship, he thought. First she hates me, then she gives me advice that she can't seem to take on her own.

Chapter 30

After hours disturbed by messy, complicated dreams, Rett rose in the full dark of an early October morning. She silently hauled on her sweats and pinned up her hair. Maybe the children would sleep a few more hours. After all, it was only four-fifteen.

She headed down to stoke the fire, let Charlie outside, and start the coffee. Shivering slightly, she pulled a blanket off the couch and wrapped it around her shoulders while she stood near the stove in the living room. Kindling crackled, coffee dripped, refrigerator hummed, and Charlie scratched at the kitchen door. She met him with a treat, then poured her coffee and sat. The blanket slipped off her shoulders as she sipped, cupping her mug in both hands. The kitten leaped gracefully into her lap.

Gazing up at the big wipe-off calendar on the wall, she noted the activities for the day, colour-coded by category. Homeschool, blue, included a library visit this morning. Homestead, green, included a scheduled egg drop-off in the village. Family, gold, included a call with Harry. Maybe. If he managed to call.

Her list didn't include her regular text to Kathryn Gallant, her perusal of the help wanted files, or addressing the big knot of uncertainty that had taken up residence in her belly. She sighed and slumped in the chair. This was not how things were supposed to go. She was supposed to be at her usual job, they were supposed to be living in their own house in Saint Jacques, the kids in their old school, and she was supposed to be able to talk to Harry any time.

She hadn't signed on for this. Ire rose and tears formed. She sniffed and thought about her mother, Agnes. Not Agnes as she last saw her, frail and sick, but the mother she had known growing up.

She glanced at the photo of the four girls with Agnes where it sat on the sideboard. Well, Mum, she thought, did you ever have it this hard? Did your life ever go off the rails so completely that you couldn't manage? You always had Dad. It's tough doing this all alone.

A rap at the back door made her jump, scaring the kitten off her lap. Jürgen. What was he doing here?

"Good morning, Rett," he said easily. "Coffee?"

"Barely morning. Yes, there's coffee," she said, letting him in. She wrapped the blanket around herself again and sat down. He opened cupboards until he found a mug, filled his cup, and came to sit beside her.

"I saw your lights," he said. "Figured you were up."

"Did you also figure I wanted company?" she asked rudely.

He shrugged. "If you're up at 4 a.m., you're either working on a problem I can help with, or you're struggling with demons. I can also help with them."

She frowned at him. "I don't know about demons."

"Oh, sure you do," he said. "Those nasty thoughts that keep you up at night."

She looked into her mug. "I sleep well."

He chuckled. "Yes, of course. That's why you're drinking coffee at this hour."

She glanced up. "Why are you up and out?"

"Demons of my own," he said. "Sleep isn't high on my list. I mean, I like sleep, but I don't get a lot."

A moment passed. "I'm not working on anything," she said.

"Hmmm. You must be thinking," he offered.

"Maybe."

"What are you thinking about?" he asked, but his voice was gentle, not probing. She glanced at him again.

"Stuff I have to do," she said. A log dropped in the woodstove, and a crackle of sparks went up the chimney. Charlie shifted and sighed. The refrigerator cycled off.

"You've got it tough all alone," Jürgen said. She startled, hearing her thoughts reflected to her. She said nothing.

"I have a lot of respect for what you're doing," he went on. "It's a big sacrifice to give your husband his chance. You're the one making a home for your kids, taking on this old house, the farmstead stuff. Homeschooling."

She gazed at the table, the rubbed pine glowing in lamplight. His voice washed over her.

"You're a strong and beautiful woman, Rett. But I know it's hard. Even a strong woman gets lonely sometimes."

His voice was hypnotic, gentle. She felt almost like she could sleep.

"Being strong doesn't protect you from being lonely. Lonely happens when you've been left to do too much for too long. Without any breaks, without anyone to love you and tell you that you're doing a good job."

While he paused, she heard her own breath, in and out, in and out.

"I see you, Rett," he said. "I see how hard you're working and how lonely you are. I can't believe he would leave you with all this responsibility. If you were mine, I'd never leave you like this. It's not good for people to be so alone."

She shook her head to try to clear it. This sleepy feeling, this wasn't good. Abruptly she got up from the table. "I'm getting more coffee," she said. Turning her back on him, she went to the counter with her mug. What was happening? This was Jürgen, her nosy neighbour. Was he coming on to her? She turned back, mug in hand, and leaned against the counter. She pulled the blanket tighter with her free hand.

She cleared her throat. "You know, Harry did all the family stuff for years. He hasn't left me."

"Oh, I know," Jürgen said. "But did you leave the province while he was taking care of the kids? Did he have to do everything all alone?"

"They were babies," she said. "It was different."

"Of course," he agreed. "I'm not criticizing. Just noticing. Please don't take my interest the wrong way."

What would be the right way? He was her neighbour and probably the most helpful person on their street. "Okay. Thanks for your interest," she said.

"Well," he said. "I guess I'll get going. It'll really be morning soon. Lots to do."

"Right," she said, ushering him to the door. "Bye." She gazed at his receding form. Tall, taller than Harry. Lean, too, jeans hanging nicely off his hips. But it's Jürgen, she told herself. The neighbour. Just getting a little more weird than usual early in the morning. She locked the kitchen door.

Back at the table, she was restless. Bread. She could always make bread.

Chapter 31

Maggie's bed-wetting had become a nightly event. Rett washed sheets daily. The laundry line was never empty and a rainy day became a disaster requiring the laundromat. Rett could not seem to stop Mason from teasing his sister in a most uncharacteristic way.

"Baby Maggie," he muttered while they were doing math problems at the kitchen table.

"Mum!" Maggie wailed immediately.

Rett gave them the side-eye from the stove. "Mason, enough."

"She's a baby really, Mum." He got louder over Maggie's shrieks. "Babies wet the bed."

Rett glared and waved her wooden spoon. "Knock it off, Mason. Maggie, hush. You have work to do, both of you."

Callie looked at her mother. "I'm being good, aren't I, Mum?"

Rett rolled her eyes. "Come on, guys. Get those pages done and we can go do something. No more fighting."

She turned away, but not before she saw Callie stick her tongue out at Mason. Rett tightened her shoulders, but no wail or complaint arose, and in a few minutes, she'd dumped her cranberry bread out to cool and the kids were getting jackets and backpacks for their walk to the library.

Mason and Callie ran ahead to meet their friends, the Smithson kids, whose mother Kyra was homeschooling too. Maggie held Rett's hand and dragged her feet a bit.

"What's up?" Rett asked. "You like going to the library, don't you?"

Maggie hung her head. "Yes, but..."

"But what?"

"I lost my book." The little girl sniffled. "The library lady will be so mad at me."

"What do you mean, you lost it? I put the library books in your backpacks last night," Rett stopped to rummage in Maggie's pack, leaning over the child.

"No, Mum, it's not there. I looked."

"Hmmm." Rett zipped the pack up again. "It must be at the house, Maggie. Don't worry."

"Mason said she would put me in jail." Maggie wailed.

"Oh, for Pete's sake," Rett said, grabbing her hand again. "Mason's trying to get you upset. There's no such thing as library jail. The worst thing is you have to pay a fine."

Maggie looked horrified. "A fine!"

"Come on," Rett said. "A fine. A few cents. Don't sweat it." They climbed up the granite steps to the heavy library doors. Just inside, Callie, Mason, and the Smithson family waited. Mason leaned over to Maggie. "Lost your book, eh?" he asked nastily.

Rett narrowed her eyes. "Kyra, can the girls go with you?" she asked the other woman. The cluster of children followed Kyra away, but Rett kept hold of the shoulder of Mason's jacket. She squatted down to his level.

"Just exactly how did you know Maggie's book was missing?"

He tried to pull away, but she held on. "Mason, look at me."

"She's such a baby, she can't keep track of her stuff," he said, looking anywhere but Rett's face.

"Mason. Where's her book?"

"I don't know, Mum," he snapped, and twisted away from her. In a moment, he was in the children's room, parking himself beside Jericho Smithson, his back decidedly toward Rett.

She sighed gustily, then headed toward Kyra.

"Bad morning?" Kyra asked softly.

Rett shrugged. "Not really. I think we're all having some adjustment issues. My mother used to call this sort of thing growing pains."

"It took us a good year of homeschool before we had things running fairly smoothly," Kyra said, "and some days you'd still think we were brand new at it. But maybe that's just life with kids."

"Yeah, maybe," Rett agreed absently. She hoped it really was growing pains. Between Mason being mean, which he had never been, and Maggie's persistent dependency, Rett wondered if homeschooling was good for her kids. Then, maybe it wasn't homeschooling so much as all the other things that had changed. She sighed again and tried to listen to Ms. Jordyn, the storyteller.

When the kids went to return their books, Rett made Mason explain Maggie's missing book to the librarian. He spluttered and was red in the face when he finished, but Rett gave him a hug as they left the library. "Good job. I'll help you bring it down tomorrow. Now you just have to apologize to your sister," she reminded him.

His hangdog expression told her plenty, but he agreed. "Hey, Maggie, I took your library book, and I'm sorry."

"And what else are you going to tell her?" Rett prompted.

"There's no library jail."

Maggie scowled at him. "Why did you take my book?"

He shrugged. "I fixed it, okay?" He stomped ahead, muttering.

"Hey, Mum, can I carry the eggs?" Callie asked.

"Nope," Rett said. "I promised these eggs to customers and I'm responsible."

"We collected them," Maggie reminded her.

"You did," Rett agreed. "I'm guaranteeing delivery, so I'll carry them. They're already safe in my backpack."

"Are we going to Auntie Corinne's house?" Callie asked.

"Not this time. Just the gallery and the real estate office."

Their walk with egg deliveries took an hour. By the time the crew was back home, it was near time to start dinner. Rett sent them outside to play, pulled vegetables out to chop, and opened her ancient laptop. She could probably get her whole soup prepped before the thing booted up.

Mason stuck his head in the kitchen door. "Mum, it's Thursday, right?"

"Right."

"Dad?"

She shrugged. "I'll let you know if we hear from him. Don't get your hopes up." He dragged outside, leaving the door open. Her heart clenched at his sagging shoulders. I know just how you feel, buddy, she thought. You can't count on Harry. She leaned out the door to grab the handle.

"Hi," said Callie brightly, and she heard a man's voice. Could that be? Her heart sped up and she stepped outside.

Jürgen was holding something out to Callie and Maggie. "Hi, Rett," he said, looking up at her. "I brought the children some special gummy bears from Germany."

The twins were making appreciative noises as they stuffed their mouths.

"It's almost dinnertime," Rett pointed out.

"They're little," Jürgen said good-naturedly. "They won't spoil their dinner. Where's Mason?"

"Mason," Callie called, turning around. "Come get some gummies. Jürgen brought some."

A crash and a shout came from behind the chicken coop, but no crying.

"Mason?" Rett called.

"No," Mason shouted.

"Guess he doesn't want any," Rett said, shrugging. "What can I do for you, Jürgen?"

"I was hoping for a dinner invitation," he said smoothly. There was a shout from behind the chicken coop. Rett cringed. Mason was being so difficult.

"Tonight's probably not a good night," Rett said. "Besides, we're just having vegetable soup. Maybe some other time."

Jürgen smiled at her, and for some reason, her stomach contracted. "That's lovely, my dear. I'd love to have dinner with you another time."

Confused, she said, "What?" Another noise grabbed her attention. "I better see to that," she said, gesturing.

He smiled. "I'll go. Have a nice evening, Rett. Let me know if you want some company."

Another yell came from behind the coop. Rett stomped in that direction, noting Jürgen saying goodbye to the girls. Her mind was on Mason, though. She came around the corner to find him with a big rock in his hands, getting ready to throw it.

"Whoa, whoa!" she said, putting up her hands. "Watch out!"

He dropped the rock and looked at her sullenly. "Did he go?"

She sighed and sat down on a stump, putting her at his eye level. "Yes. He's gone."

Mason picked up a long stick and swished it through a pile of leaves.

"You don't like Jürgen much, do you?" she observed.

He ignored the question and kept poking at the leaves.

"He's just a neighbour, you know," she said. "Like we had neighbours in Saint Jacques. You liked our neighbours there."

He looked at her from under his hoodie and nodded slightly.

"It's the same thing. Neighbours."

"Daddy was home in Saint Jacques."

"He was, yes."

Mason sighed. "I miss him."

"Oh, come here, baby," Rett said, pulling him close. "I know you do. I miss him, too."

Mason sagged against her. "I want that guy to go away."

"He's gone," she told him. "He's our neighbour and you're going to have to be polite. We're not mean to people in our family. Even if we don't like them."

"Do you like him, Mum?"

Her heart beat a little faster. What was he seeing? "He's our neighbour, Mason. I like him okay." She squeezed his shoulders. "I'm going to go finish dinner, and I'll call you in a few minutes, okay?" She tugged on the point of his hood. "Okay?" He looked up from where he'd been gazing at the ground and nodded.

She left him behind the coop and headed back to the house. "Ten minutes until dinner!"

Back at the stove, her soup had boiled down to a stew. She ground her teeth and refilled the pot. Kids. Her mind briefly skated over the image of Jürgen leaving the yard, his height, so different from Harry, his long legs. She caught her breath and frowned. The neighbour, she thought. He's just the neighbour. But maybe she shouldn't have him in the house anymore.

Chapter 32

It was getting cold, and not just at night. The July day he'd packed for field camp was a long time ago. Just keeping warm and fed was taking up a lot of his time. Gathering wood for the stove and making sure he had enough calories to both stay warm and work made his data-gathering time limited.

He also found himself spending a lot of time in contemplation. Besides dropping in on Jeannette, he rarely talked to anyone. The long evenings were spent by the stove, thinking and writing.

He'd never kept a diary. He had kept field notes, a journal of findings, but never personal reflections. He'd also never spent this much time alone. He tapped his pen on the notebook, then began to write.

It's cold here. Not in the tent; I make sure there's enough firewood and I keep it pretty toasty in here. I closed up my sleeping tent and moved my cot here, in the big tent. Privacy is hardly an issue, under the circumstances. So I eat, sleep, dress and work right here. Except when I'm out there, obviously.

Today I spent almost two hours getting firewood. I hope it lasts a couple of days but it'll depend on how cold it gets and whether I got the good stuff. I have maybe only ten more working days here; I'm reaching a point where the time I can spend outside working is less than I need to spend gathering wood, hauling water, feeding myself and staying warm. I didn't know that cooking takes longer when everything is so cold. Duh, as Mason might say.

The landscape is incredible. As things dry out, the browns and greys and pale yellows all blend into some mosaic of colour I've never noticed before. The light slants through the trees, so there are shadows all day long. Everything has a mysterious feel. Part of me wants to stay, become a part of the mystery. Another part of me wants to turn my back, run away. This is not for me. But then I go back into the woods, back to the hills, back to Jeannette's house to find out what new nuggets I can take. No, not take. Borrow. Learn. She is generous with her wisdom and experience. She sees the land as generous, too, but right now, I experience it as, well, almost dangerous. This cold, oncoming winter, these things are not compatible with human life. At least not without said humans making a lot of accommodation. No wonder we moved south, where there was a longer growing season, where the light lasts more than a few hours, all of that. I am captivated by the beauty of this place, but I am also afraid of what can happen here. I really am a Nova Scotia boy. I wasn't made for this kind of wilderness.

Marie. Marie, what to make of her. She is a fine scientist, at least I think that when I've read her papers, but she seems to be a troubled person. She's been kind to me, then cruel, then cold, then warm, and finally she's gone. Joyce isn't to blame for her inability to finish her project. Just like Joyce isn't to blame for my struggle. Joyce is demanding and she also wants us to succeed.

Why haven't I done what I set out to do?

He pulled off his glasses to rub his eyes. His weeks in the field were coming to an end, and what would he take away? Joyce introducing him to Paul. The vertiginous feeling of tumbling down that ravine. The relief of hearing Paul's voice. Lying on a cot, Jeannette offering her medicine tea. Her face as she went about her work in the forest. The forest itself, and the vastness of the land. That feeling of being tiny, microscopic against the hugeness of the wilderness. Tiny and yet huge, expanded against a horizonless sky. Aware of his own irrelevance–Nature didn't care about him–and also powerfully aware of his place in the system. Systems. If I died out here, he thought, my parts would feed the animals and the soil and the microscopic fungi. I'd return as something else, a million somethings. This planet birthed me and will take me back.

All true. But not the entire truth. There is more.

He let his mind wander, recalling his arrival in Winnipeg, the evening out with the team before field camp, the hope he'd felt at the beginning of the summer. His desire to keep working at something that once compelled his interest. To make something of himself, to become the scientist his former supervisor said he could be. A desire he could not find in himself, no matter how he searched.

I don't belong here, he wrote, then looked at the words, then continued.

For sure, I don't belong here. This landscape isn't mine. The cliffs, the rocky drop to the Bay of Fundy, the broad stretches of agricultural land, the remnants of old forest, what bits are left after heavy industrial forestry, that's my landscape. Maybe I need to find my ancestral lands, too, like Paul said. I love this place, but it isn't mine.

I love this place, but I don't love the work. Don't love the research, digging into minute bits of data to try to draw out some kind of small conclusion that might possibly be read by a dozen other researchers.

His stomach hurt as he wrote the words, but they felt true.

What I love is capturing images of the places I've been. Listening to Jeannette and watching how she gathers plants. Seeing the light slanting over the landscape. Hearing the migratory birds. Watching myself fall down that damn hill and knowing, knowing that it was going to be bad. Even that, I loved. It was as real as it could be. I can love my experiences here and know I don't belong in the research world.

He had belonged, he thought, back when he finished his master's degree. That was when his thesis supervisor had been painfully disappointed Harry wasn't continuing his studies. He had agreed to be the parent-at-home and he never looked back.

Until now. What did he see?

He recalled Mason's first steps, heard his first word. Helping him to navigate the big feelings that came up at two and then, again, at three when the baby sisters arrived. Nothing seemed more important than teaching the kids about the world. He recalled Mason showing Maggie a worm, listening to his son's careful explanation of worm life, words he'd used a year before to explain to his son. Climate change was personal, once he was a parent. It wasn't about saving the planet, but about keeping a safe place for his children to live. He'd loved teaching the kids composting, recycling, and using less. He thought about Jeannette and Paul, living here on their ancestral lands. Jeanette finding medicines growing in the forest. Paul and the other hunters respectfully harvesting animals for food, leather, and their fat. He shook his head. Too many thoughts. Too many images. But still, none of them had him painted as a scientist.

He flipped the pages of his notebook back to the front. There were his notes from his first days, early in July. He'd written up little stories to tell the children, one about their field camp, that he called a village made of tents. Another story spoke of his first trip into deep forest.

He flipped faster. Were there no clues, no hints, that he was misplaced here? Why did it take until now, after a long separation from the people he cared most about, for him to realize he was chasing a failed dream?

There. September, after his conversation with James.

Rett, homeschooling. She's doing what I didn't have the courage to suggest. I can't imagine it for her, really, but part of me wishes I were there, doing it with her.

Below he'd scribbled another story for the kids, this one about being cared for in Jeannette's kitchen.

He sighed deeply. He now knew he didn't belong in field camp, but he had no idea where he did belong. Other than at home with his children. And Rett.

Chapter 33

Despite Rett's plan to avoid Jürgen, he kept showing up. Well, she thought, he's being neighbourly. At the same time, she wondered why she didn't just tell him to stay home. He'd been helpful, for sure, but Mason's obvious distress made her reconsider her position.

She was in the front yard stabbing at the leaves with her rake late Wednesday morning. Starting in the middle, she pulled some leaves together, then wandered to the perennial border where she yanked on dried out flower heads, and then poked with her rake at a pile of weeds. The twins barrelled from the back yard and leapt into the small pile of leaves she'd managed to pile up, spreading them around.

"Mum!" Callie shouted. "Make another pile!"

Looking over her shoulder, she scowled. "Come on. How can I get anything done if you keep undoing it?" She stomped back to her leaf pile and scraped at the edges of it. "Go on. Get out of here." She nudged Maggie with her toe.

"Owww!" Maggie shrieked. "You hurt me!"

Mason flew from the front door, Charlie leaping behind him. "Mum! What are you doing?" He ran to Maggie and helped her up, then glared at Rett. "She's just little." Maggie wailed.

Rett stuck out her jaw. "That's about enough, Mason."

Mason narrowed his eyes at Maggie. "You're just a baby, Maggie. Stop it. Get out of here!"

The shock of hearing her own words reflected to her felt like a blow to the chest. Rett was trying to catch her breath when a car pulled into the driveway and a strange woman got out. This silenced them all, so when the woman said, "Loretta Madison?" she nodded. The woman handed her an envelope, got into her car, and took off. After a quick glance, Rett stuffed it into a pocket.

"Mason Brown," Rett said firmly. "Come over here."

Mason stomped over, reluctance in every step. "What?" The twins sat in the leaves, watching.

"I did not hurt your sister, and you are not to be mean to her." *Or to me.* "Do you understand?"

"She said you hurt her."

"That is not your business. You don't need to be the grown-up here. Now go inside and take a break. We'll all be in for snack in a few minutes."

He sighed dramatically and dragged his feet, but he headed to the front door, Charlie on his heels. Rett turned to the twins, who were angelically quiet and gazing at her face.

"You two, up and out back," she directed. "Check on the chickens and then go in to wash up for snack. I'll be right in. Got it?"

They nodded and left. Rett made a few more ineffectual swipes with the rake, then leaned on it to pull out the envelope. Probably another bill gone to collection, she thought, and tore it open.

She scanned the document, pressure increasing in her chest. Gasping, sobs overtook her. Hand over mouth, she tried to stuff them back down, but tears dripped through her fingers, and her throat closed up. "Oh, no, oh, no," she said, dropping the letter, hands over her face, rocking back and forth. What next? She felt her legs start to buckle. Suddenly, strong arms held her, and she leaned into the warmth of another person.

Get a grip, she told herself, but it just felt so good to finally let down and cry. It was probably only fifteen seconds, when she raised her head and realized it was Jürgen, now holding her by the shoulders.

"Oh, dear Rett," he said with great tenderness. "My dear."

Before she realized what was happening, he leaned in and kissed her. She pulled away, rigid. "Don't do that."

"Sorry," he said swiftly. "I was out of line. But what's wrong? Are you hurt?"

She shook her head and nodded at the paper on the ground. As he bent over to pick it up, she glanced toward the house. Mason's pale face was at the living room window.

Could this get any worse? She reached to take the paper from Jürgen, but he turned away, reading.

"This is a subpoena," he said.

"Yes," she replied, grabbing it from him. "It's not really your business."

"Are you getting a divorce?" he asked. "I can help."

"Divorce? No! Good heavens. I don't need any help." Your help has caused all sorts of trouble, she thought. "I'm going in now. Thank you for your...Thank you." She nodded to him, wiped her face with her hand, and walked swiftly to the front door. Too damn polite, that's what she was.

Entering, she looked into the living room. Mason was no longer at the window. She could hear the girls in the kitchen. She tucked the subpoena back into her pocket and headed to the kitchen to make snacks, more distracted than she'd ever been.

Chapter 34

Two sleepless, fretful days later, she put the kids to bed without stories and called her sister. "Helen?"

"Hi, Rett," her sister said. "Rett?"

Rett swallowed. "I need legal counsel."

Helen giggled. "That's what you always say. How are you?"

"I'm not kidding," Rett said. "I need you to take this seriously."

Helen sighed. "I wish my sisters would call me because they love me, not because they need a lawyer."

"Well, sorry," Rett said sharply. "Does that mean you won't help me?"

"No, just me being petty," Helen said. "What's the problem?"

"I want a divorce."

"Come on, Rett, the man's only been gone a few months and he's coming back. It can't be that bad."

"You don't know," Rett said. "You have no idea."

"It's not like anybody's cheating or anything," Helen went on, voice tight.

There was silence. "Rett?"

"What?"

"Is there cheating? What happened?"

Rett plunked herself on the squishy couch. "It's been awful," she confided. "Mason's turned into some kind of monster, the bills are piling up, and Jürgen, remember him? He's been hanging around. I hardly ever hear from Harry, and I just hate what I got myself into here."

"What about Jürgen?" Helen was the best listener Rett knew. She could hear things that nobody actually said.

"Yeah. Mason hates his guts. And a couple days ago, he kissed me. Like right on my front lawn."

Helen was silent.

"I don't even really like him, but I did like having somebody there, you know," Rett went on. "I was almost thinking, like, maybe Dad would take the kids and I could invite him over..." she choked.

"Did you do that?" Helen's voice was calm and even.

Rett scoffed. "No, of course not. He's a little bit creepy, actually, though he's been unfailingly helpful. Remember, he kind of hit on you when you were here?"

"I remember all right," Helen said. "It made me think for a minute, too."

"Well, all of that. I have no idea if or when Harry is coming, and he's not part of this life here in Stella Mare. Our life was in Saint Jacques."

"You made a lot of changes when he left to study."

Rett sighed. "Yes. Probably too many. I didn't think I had any choices."

"What about now?"

Rett started pacing. "Now? Now I can't sleep. I'm up all night but afraid to put the light on because when I did that a few weeks ago,

Jürgen came over at four in the morning. The kids are driving me nuts, and I feel so terrible when I am impatient with them. Maggie wets the bed, Callie whines, and Mason is bullying Maggie and me. Nobody is functioning."

"Rett, take a breath," Helen said evenly.

"Oh, for heaven's sake, I can't," she shouted into the phone. "I got this subpoena too, you know. The police are accusing me of murdering my patients. I might be a murderer and a cheating wife and a terrible mother. I yelled at the kids. I can't bear it. It's all going to shit. Everything's falling apart including me. I can't, I just can't do this anymore. Thanks for nothing, Helen."

She clicked off and dropped back onto the couch. Her phone buzzed immediately but she turned it off.

"Stupid Helen. Stupid, stupid, stupid."

She was buzzing with anger. Flipping open her laptop, she wrote an email to Harry.

"I know you won't get this email until you bother to try to find out how we're doing, but I can't wait to say this. It's over. Our marriage has broken down. I'm done. It's over. I can't see a way forward, so I think we have to end it. That's the only way to solve this problem."

She read it over, read it again, and paused over the send button. Should she?

Yes, of course. Problems must be solved. No Harry, no unmet expectations. No Harry, no guilt. No Harry, then maybe things wouldn't hurt so much. Before she could think further, she tapped send. Then she snapped her laptop closed and got up.

Pacing the downstairs, she entered the kitchen and opened all the cupboard doors. "No food in this place," she muttered. The full pantry mocked her. "Nothing I want to eat, anyway." She picked up a nearly empty bottle of cooking sherry, sniffed it, and put it back.

No wine, no chips, no ice cream. Not even hidden chocolate. For a Madison sister, she was ill equipped to eat her feelings.

The kitten padded down the stairs and wound around her ankles. Rett absently picked her up and scratched under her chin. Carrying her, she returned to the living room couch and tucked herself into a corner, legs under her, kitten on lap. The purring softness under her hands slowed her heart. She sighed and tears slipped down her face.

I just told Harry I want a divorce. Did I really do that?

She gulped at the thought. It's the only way, she thought. Look at me. Screaming at Helen on the phone. Mean to my own children. A murderer and an adulterer. Having lustful thoughts about the neighbour I don't even like. Her face heated.

Where was that paper? Sliding the kitten off her lap, she rummaged through the piles on the coffee table to find the subpoena. She smoothed it out and tried to read it.

The words wavered on the page. She was so tired. She could almost make out the words. You, Loretta Madison, are required to attend a deposition to discuss how you murdered three old people at your last job?

She shook her head. The words didn't say that. Even squinting, she couldn't find the word "murder" anywhere on the page. But it's all she could think of. She really needed Helen, but maybe she'd burned that bridge. She imagined her sister walking away from her, shrugging. "Do it your way," Helen said in her mind.

Just like she'd burned her bridge back to nursing by losing her license. Burned the bridge back to Saint Jacques by letting people take over her house. Burned her bridge back to a normal life. A normal life with Harry.

Enough with the stupid metaphors.

Suddenly sick to her stomach, she leaped to grab her laptop. She flipped it open again, but her email program wouldn't load. Aghast, she paced in a circle, tears sliding down her face, wringing her hands. Life without Harry. Going to prison. The children...She was so tired she thought she might fall asleep standing up, if only she could stop crying and worrying. She had no idea how long she paced.

The sound of a vehicle in the driveway pulled her out of her thoughts, and she went to the door. She leaned out to see Chad's big truck, Dorie looking dwarfed in the driver's seat. Dorie jumped down, pulling out a tote bag with her.

"Hey," she said, approaching the front door. "You going to let me in?"

"I don't know," Rett said, holding the door half closed. "What are you doing here? It's midnight."

"Helen sent me," Dorie said. "Baby sister to the rescue. Open up."

Rett scowled, but she opened the door. "I don't need a rescue."

Before Dorie could respond, another vehicle pulled in. "What now?" Rett asked.

Dorie chuckled. "Looks like Dad." She elbowed past Rett to go into the house.

"You knew. You're not even surprised," Rett accused Dorie, who headed toward the kitchen, patting Charlie on the head.

James strode up to the front door. "Come on. I'm taking you home."

She shook her head. "What are you doing here, Dad? It's the middle of the night." She stepped back to let him in. "I think there's a conspiracy."

"You could be right," James agreed. "Get your stuff, Loretta. You're coming over to the house."

"No, I can't," she protested. "I'm fine. I don't know what you heard, but I'm really fine."

"I know you're fine," James said. "But humour an old man. Come over to the house and sleep. Dorie can manage here."

Dorie came back into the living room, mug in hand. "Yep. You go. I can hold down the fort."

"That Helen," Rett spluttered. "Spreading my business all around. I shouldn't have trusted her. And her a lawyer!"

James stood close to Rett. Now that he was shrinking a little with age, they met at eye level. "Loretta Madison, you listen to your father. I've learned from experience that we have to help each other."

"I don't need help," Rett hissed. "Everything is fine."

James pulled back. "Okay. Everything can be fine. But I'm not leaving without you. Your sister Dorie came all the way into town at midnight to take care of the kids, so you can't leave her hanging. We're here and that's that."

"Well, that can be that. I didn't ask you to be here," Rett said, a little loudly. James lifted his chin. Oh, she knew that look. He was immovable when he got that look. When she decided at twenty she was going out west as a roadie with her boyfriend's band, Dad had that look. When she'd taken Helen's bike and crashed it and blamed Dorie, he had that look.

A sound on the stairs gave her a chance to look away.

"Callie! What are you doing up?" A sleepy, weepy little girl sat on the top step.

"Mum? What's going on?"

"Everything's fine, Callie," James said. "Mum's going to come over to my house for a sleepover."

"Mum?" Her voice was tiny, unsure.

Dorie gave Rett a sharp glance. "I've got this," she said, and headed up the stairs. Rett sighed prodigiously.

"It's okay, Callie. Auntie Dorie's going to babysit you," she said, while turning a steely gaze on her father.

"Get your coat," James said to Rett. "Time to go home."

The inside of the pickup was quiet as James drove her around the long block to his house. Even Rett's mind was quiet as they crossed the back porch to the kitchen door. The big dogs got up to greet them, but the house was warm, dimly lit, and peaceful. She hung her coat on a hook at the back door and headed to the living room. James put on the kettle.

When she sat on the couch, Mallow came over and put his big head in her lap. She absently stroked his silky ears, feeling her own breathing slow. It was so quiet.

She heard a quiet conversation between her father and Evie, then Evie padded into the living room and sat beside her.

"Hi."

Rett nodded. She didn't want to speak. Evie held out her hand. "These pills helped me sleep last summer," she offered diffidently. "If you want them. It might be worth a try."

Rett nodded and took the proffered box. For some reason, her eyes filled. "Thanks," she managed, and Evie offered a hug. Rett held up her hands to keep her away; a hug would be her undoing. "Thanks," she said again when Evie smiled kindly and dropped her arms.

"Your bed's all ready, and I put some pajamas on it." Evie said. "Good night."

Rett nodded again. Evie headed toward the kitchen as James leaned into the living room. "I made chamomile tea. It's in the pot."

He came closer. "I'm going up now, and I'd like you to try to sleep. Do you think you can try?"

She closed her eyes and sighed. "Yeah, I think so. I'm going to stay down here and have a cup of your tea first."

He put his hand on her shoulder. "It's all going to get sorted. But you don't have to sort it out tonight."

"Yeah, I know. Thanks."

With a pat, he left too, and Rett followed to the kitchen. While James went up the stairs, she found a mug and poured tea, then returned to the living room. The big dogs were settled back into their beds in the sun porch, and the single lamp cast a warm glow. She sat and sipped, fingering Evie's box of sleeping pills.

Her father's words stayed with her. *I don't have to sort it all tonight.* She sighed and headed up the stairs to her childhood bedroom.

Chapter 35

Rett woke in full daylight, yawning and stretching luxuriously. Sleep never meant more than when you'd been missing it, she thought. She could probably sleep for a week, but right now, coffee sounded good.

She pulled her clothes back on and headed downstairs. It was peculiarly quiet, not even doggie sounds to keep her company, but the silence was comforting. She moved gently around the kitchen, noticing even her mind was quiet. No racing thoughts, no list of things to do. Just noticing this was enough to get the monologue started, but she stopped herself. Not right now. Now was for coffee, and this note from Dad on the kitchen table.

Rett, I hope you had a good sleep. Take the day. The kids are getting Grampa-school today. No worries on this side. You take care of you. Dad.

Below was another scrawl.

I baked sunshine muffins. I'm working at the gallery until late afternoon but call if you need me. Evie.

Rett sighed. They meant well, of course, but she was responsible. For those kids getting schooling, for keeping the homestead businesses going. For getting stuff done. She stood up, mug in hand. Dad didn't need a houseful of kids. She grabbed for the house phone and called his cell.

"Morning, Rett," he said cheerfully. She could hear music, giggling, and Charlie barking.

"How's it going?" she asked, wary.

"Oh, it's good, it's good," he said. "We're having a good time here. Did you sleep good?"

She settled a little. "Pretty well, thanks. I hate to admit it, but I really needed to sleep."

"Even you, eh?"

"Even me. I'll be right over and you can come home."

"No, but thanks. We've got plans. Maybe you could get a nap or something."

She paused. A nap. What a lovely word.

"Well, can I talk to the kids at least?"

"You can talk to the girls. Mason went to work with Dorie. She'll drop him off at lunchtime." He called to the twins. "Want to talk to Mum?"

The two of them apparently shared the phone. "Hi, Mum. Grandpa's playing with us," Maggie said.

"Yes, and Custard's being silly," Callie said, giggling. Rett could imagine the big dog headbutting her child, and Callie encouraging it.

"Sounds like fun," she said. "Listen, I'm going to stay at Grandpa's house today."

Callie stopped giggling long enough to say, "Grandpa said you needed to sleep at his house to feel better. Do you feel better?"

Rett softened. "Yes, baby, I feel better. Thank you. I might even take a nap today."

Now Maggie was giggling. "Ooh, Mum, like a baby."

"You bet. Just like a sleepy baby," Rett went along. "Be good, okay?"

James came back on. "There you go."

"They're supposed to be doing social studies stuff today," Rett fretted. "It's also egg delivery for Leonard and Magda."

"We'll handle it, Rett," James said sturdily. "I saw your calendar. You're pretty organized, you know that?"

She scoffed. "It's essential. Especially when you think you might be losing your mind."

He laughed. "That's a temporary thing though. We'll be over later. Supper at my house."

"Okay," she agreed. "I'll cook."

"No you won't." He was firm. "We have it managed. You rest. Today is for rest."

It probably was a good idea, but her worried brain disagreed. Too many things to do. Too many balls to juggle, problems to solve. The things she had said to Helen. And to Harry.

Her breath caught as she imagined Harry reading that email. The pang of feeling got bigger as she remembered Jürgen. How could she ever admit to Harry that she'd betrayed him with another man? Wanton woman, she thought harshly. Can't be trusted. Can't even be trusted to take care of patients.

Kitchen walls were closing in around her and she had to get out. Grabbing her jacket, she headed across the back porch and jumped down onto the dormant lawn. Clouds hid the sun, and a hint of winter brushed her cheeks. The cold air felt good, and as she pulled it into her lungs, her racing mind settled.

Putting her hands in her pockets, she felt her phone and heard the crackle of crunched-up paper. A text notification glared red: Helen. When she unfurled the balled-up paper, she recognized the subpoena. She sighed, stuffing them both back into her pockets.

The shed sat squat at the far end of the driveway. Rattling the padlocked door proved useless, so she walked around to peer through the window. This was where her father had collapsed last summer. Right there, the scene of the crime, she thought. But it wasn't a crime, not at all, just poor health. Evie found him and he got treatment. Everyone pitched in to help, and he was fine. Or as well as anybody his age could be, her nurse voice added.

She rolled her eyes at herself. Yes, Dad was okay, but he needed help. I don't need help, her inner voice pointed out. I'm just fine on my own. Her eyes suddenly overflowed.

She sniffled and knuckled away tears. She hated feeling at odds with everybody, even herself. Walking back to the house, she considered what to do. Maybe she would call Helen. That might be a good place to start.

Chapter 36

Rett spread the subpoena on her father's kitchen table. She left it there while she turned on the kettle, then she leaned back against the counter. Her glance grazed the sideboard across the room and Evie's watercolour painting on the wall above. That old sideboard held a lot of memories. The kettle hummed away, and Rett crossed the room as if in a dream.

Framed pictures of the family sat atop ancient doilies. Rett picked up a photo from her wedding; she and Harry were impossibly young, surrounded by her sisters in bridesmaid dresses, even Dorie, only a child at the time. She and Harry looked so optimistic. Looking at Harry's young face brought tears. She set the photo down gently as if it might shatter.

Next to it was the last formal photo of her parents together, big smiles on the occasion of their fortieth anniversary. Agnes was in good health then, and her smile, just like Helen's, was infectious. When she held the photo in her hands, Rett could imagine her mother looking directly at her.

"Bet you never thought you'd see a subpoena on your kitchen table," Rett whispered. "Or that one of your daughters would get a divorce." She sniffed and laid it face down.

The kettle called, so she filled her mug and sat at the table. She might as well get on with it.

Can you talk? She texted to Helen. *I'm such an idiot.*

She had to wait for Helen to call back. It was a workday after all. She took her tea to the couch and sank into the soft cushions. She remembered taking two deep breaths, and the next thing her phone rang in the kitchen.

"Helen, thank you."

"You're welcome."

"I was pretty well out of my mind last night. I wasn't too happy that you called in the cavalry, either."

Helen snickered. "Who showed up first? Let me guess: Dorie."

"Dad was right behind. I'm surprised I haven't seen Corinne yet."

"No worries. I think she's bringing dinner."

"I knew she'd show up. Uh, Helen..."

"Yes?"

"Acknowledging I'm wrong isn't my best thing, so listen good. I'm really sorry."

"Ha! You're even bossy when you're apologizing." Helen's laugh softened the criticism, but Rett felt the sting.

"I deserve that. I am in a mess though. Can you help me sort it?"

"Of course. I have to ask though...you said murder? You're accused of murder?"

"Well, maybe not," she said. "Let's see what this document says." She pulled the subpoena closer. "Let me read it to you."

Helen listened. "This is a request for you to give information and bring any evidence that relates to the question of this Angelica person committing manslaughter. Nothing about murder, and not implicating you."

"This Angelica person, as you say, is a close colleague of mine." Her voice was loud. "Angelica is a wonderful human. The person I would want with me if I were dying. How can they think Angelica would harm a patient?"

"Don't yell at me. I'm trying to help."

"Right." She exhaled hard. "I'm sorry, Helen. It just makes me so mad."

"I can hear that," Helen said. "You have to stay cool about this though."

"Yeah," Rett agreed. "Okay, I'm better now."

"You sure?"

"Yeah. Go ahead."

"First off, they're not accusing you of anything. They simply want you to give evidence. It's a deposition. They'll ask questions, you'll make a statement."

"I get to make a statement?" For some reason that lifted her a bit. "I've been waiting for months to tell them what I think. They're barking up the wrong tree. Or there really isn't even a tree. Old people die in care. It's not criminal."

"Well, maybe you can educate somebody about that. Lydia will help you. You have talked to her, right?"

"Lydia?"

"The lawyer I recommended. Back when this started?"

"I think I talked to someone," Rett said vaguely. "Do I need a lawyer?"

"It would be smart. You've never given evidence before, and you have things you want to communicate. She can help."

"Okay. Lydia. Got it."

"What else is a problem right now?"

"Well, because of this nonsense with work, I'm trying to survive financially selling eggs, bread and preserves in Stella Mare instead of being a nurse, like I always wanted to do."

"Your license is still suspended? I thought you had that fixed."

"Nobody would say for sure that I'm not under investigation."

"Obviously you're not the target."

"Because they're focused on Angelica," Rett said bitterly.

"Hold on. This deposition process also makes it clear you're not being investigated. Maybe you can use it as evidence your license should be reinstated."

"That would be good."

"What I meant when I asked about other problems was Harry."

"Oh, Harry." Rett slumped. "I'm a terrible person. I sent him an email last night telling him I was going to divorce him."

Helen was silent. "Oh."

"Yeah, I know. It was such a mistake, and I tried to get it back, you know, unsend it, but I had already closed the program, so it went. He hasn't gotten it yet though, I don't think," she added hopefully. "I still feel really bad about, you know, about the neighbour."

"Ah, yes, another man all too eager to help the damsel in distress," Helen said.

"Damsel! Not me," Rett objected. "No way."

"Really? It sounds like that was how he saw it," Helen said. "It doesn't matter anyway. He was out of line, or he wasn't, but you're not a cheater. No matter what your sleep-deprived brain tells you, you didn't kiss him, you sent him home. You did not cheat on Harry."

"But in my mind..." Rett protested again.

"Listen, sister," Helen said firmly. "You've been married a long time. What happens in your mind is only in your mind. It isn't real and it isn't cheating. Do you think Harry's never had thoughts?"

Rett was sure Harry had never had those kinds of thoughts, but she wasn't going to convince Helen. "I'm not sure I buy it because I feel so guilty. Why do I feel this bad if I didn't do something wrong?"

"Listen hard. Feelings aren't facts."

"Right, but I feel really, really guilty."

"You feel bad about the investigation too, but you didn't do anything wrong there either. Don't trust your feelings when you haven't slept in days."

She settled. "I guess you have a point. I'm willing to take your word on it. Now I have to tell Harry I'm not really divorcing him."

Helen chuckled. "You can't divorce him without him knowing anyway, so no worries there. Send another email, let him know you were slightly out of your mind."

"I can do that. He'll get them at the same time anyway," she said. "He's sensitive though. Just the thought of it is going to hit hard." Her chest tightened at the thought of Harry feeling hurt by her. "Oh, my goodness, what did I do? It's going to kill him." Tears started again. "Helen," she choked out.

"Wait, wait, wait," Helen said. "Don't go down that road. You can't fix everything right now. It doesn't help to beat yourself up."

"Right," Rett said with a mighty sniff. "I guess I'm still sleep-deprived."

"Have you eaten yet today?" Helen asked.

Rett shrugged and looked in her mug. "Coffee."

"I can't believe Evie didn't bake anything. No muffins?"

Rett looked at the counter where the plate of muffins sat. "Yeah, there's muffins. I'll have one."

"Good. Anything else on your list?"

Rett considered. "Those are the biggest, once we take murder off. Not being able to work and Harry being away. There's not really an end to either one," she said, sniffling again.

"There certainly is," Helen said firmly. "Call Lydia. I'll pay the retainer. She needs to write a letter to your credentialing organization and demand reinstatement. She'll help you with your deposition statement too."

"Are you sure I need a lawyer?" Rett felt a little sick. "Helen, really?"

"You probably wouldn't under normal circumstances," Helen said. "You're not feeling like yourself though, are you?"

"I've never felt so many different feelings in a single phone call," Rett admitted. "You're right, not like me. More like I'm barely here."

"Since you're not feeling great, getting support for this process is a good idea. I'll call her and have her get in touch, okay? That way you don't have to reach out."

Rett sighed. Not having to do something sounded much better than another task. "Sure. Okay. I appreciate that."

"That's how you get your license and your job back," Helen continued. "Harry being gone, well, that's something you two will have to sort out. Not today."

"Right," Rett said. She sighed.

"It's really going to be okay," Helen said. "I know it probably doesn't feel possible right now, but this is all manageable."

"Okay," Rett agreed, suddenly feeling incredibly sleepy. "Thank you, Helen. I think I'm going to have a nap."

Helen chuckled. "You do that. I'll call you tomorrow."

Rett was nearly staggering with fatigue when she headed back toward the living room couch, but she tapped out a brief, apologetic email to Harry on her phone.

She recalled pulling the afghan over her legs before dropping off.

After Marie left field camp, Harry still had samples to collect and process, so the short daylight hours were full. By the end of October, he was waking in the dark and had to move fast to complete his outside work. At the same time there was the business of staying alive. He had to carry water daily, find firewood to keep the stove alight during the cold evening and overnight, and his appetite grew as the cold weather advanced, so feeding himself took more resources.

He assessed his situation to decide what he could complete before survival activities took over his time. Picking a date to leave, he worked backward from there. Prioritizing Joyce's tasks, he set aside his goal of figuring himself out. Marie was right; he could do that elsewhere.

His food would hold out, he calculated, and even if he was running short, he knew where to find a warm meal. Jeannette had been clear about his welcome. Tapping his pencil against the table, he pondered. Leaving field camp was one thing. It was something else to leave the university, his assistantship, his plan for the Ph.D. He knew it was important to end well with Joyce. It would be better if she were not surprised by his plan.

Looming larger was telling Rett and the kids he'd failed in his goal, but he pressed that down. There was no time to wallow in feeling guilty. He had too much to do. Instead, he focused on getting himself back home. His personal journal reflected his preoccupation and his uncertainty.

Steps to get back home. 1) finish work and pack up field camp 2) return to university 3) ?

He wrote the leave date in large letters. Getting back to Winnipeg was only a step, but it was a big one. At the university, he could talk to Rett and the kids every day.

Isolated and lonely, he wrestled with shame, guilt, and his longing for his family. When he'd arrived, his research was the most important thing. Now, getting reconnected with Rett was more important. Even more important than how Joyce received his decision.

Since number 3 was still blank, he focused on getting field work completed. The long evenings were spent checking over the cataloguing of his samples, making sure everything was logged in, labelled appropriately, and packaged securely. Between keeping himself alive and getting as much done as possible, he was exhausted, but he still took pictures and kept notes. Maybe he'd write a book someday.

Chapter 37

Rett woke from her second nap on her father's couch to angled sunlight glimmering through the living room windows and children's voices outdoors. She got up quickly to greet them in the backyard. A crowd crashed through the woods, two massive dogs, one medium yellow Labrador, three children, and her father. Maggie, unaccountably, was in front.

"Mum!" she shouted, waving at Rett who waited on the back porch. "Mum! Here we are!"

Charlie and Mason sprinted to beat Maggie to the house, but Rett picked the little girl up and gave her a squeeze. "Hiya, Mags," she said, burying her face in the child's neck and blowing raspberries. The little body against hers felt so good it was hard to let her go, but she set her down full of giggles and more hugs. Mason leaned in for a hug. Callie was holding James' hand and the two were in deep conversation, walking across the lawn. Mallow scratched at the back door and gave Rett a baleful look.

"Suppertime for these lugs," James said when he and Callie arrived at the porch. "They have a pretty good built-in clock."

"Yeah, Mum, Grandpa says he knows when it's time to get up and time to eat because of the dogs," Callie said. "Aren't they smart?"

"Very smart," Rett said, bending down for another hug. She couldn't understand why she was crying again, with her arms full of kids and dogs licking her face. She felt like she'd been away for a year, had returned a different person, but everyone was still here, still hers.

She stood, coming face to face with her father. He smiled.

"Dad," she started. "I want to apologize."

He nodded. "It's okay, Rett. I hope you got some sleep."

"Yes. Thank you. Thank you so much."

Mallow let out a mighty woof that made Maggie jump and Mason laugh. "Let's go in," James said. "Mason wants his supper."

"Not me!" Mason said. "Mallow."

"Oh, right," said James. "Sometimes I get you two confused."

"Oh, Grandpa!" Callie scoffed while Mason giggled. "Mason's a boy and Mallow is a dog."

"Are you sure about that?" James queried.

Rett held the door open, her heart feeling like it might burst. As they flowed into the house, a truck roared into the driveway, disgorging Dorie and Chad and their white poodle, Frou-Frou. Chad carried a cooler.

"Hey, did we miss the party?" Dorie called.

Rett shook her head and held out her arms to her baby sister. "Thanks so much," she whispered in her ear. "I hope you got some sleep."

Dorie pulled away, smiling. "Yeah, everyone was great. Mason worked hard all morning. I figure that's as good as homeschool. He calculated how much our dog food bill should be, then matched it to the invoices. Pretty clever of Auntie Dorie, don't you think?"

Rett could only nod. "Impressive."

"Yep. That's me. Just don't give me anything hard to do," she said. "I'm going in. You okay, Chad?"

"Fine," Chad said, putting the cooler on the porch. "Hi, Rett."

She followed him into the unexpectedly empty kitchen. "Hey, where'd everybody go?" She heard kids' feet above her head and voices in the living room. The sole occupant of the kitchen was Mallow, who whined at the cupboard. "Guess you're out of luck, buddy," she told him, and they went into the living room.

James was opening the sun porch, while Dorie chatted to him from the couch. Rett sank down beside her sister. "Mallow's complaining, Dad," she said.

"I can do it," Chad said quickly. He headed back to the kitchen, followed by the rest of the canine pack.

"Canine mental telepathy?" Rett asked.

Dorie snickered. "Something like that."

James returned to sit in his usual chair. "Who are we thanking for our meal?" he asked.

"We brought pie," Dorie said smugly. "Alice's pie."

"I took a nap," Rett said apologetically. "I can make pasta, I guess."

"Corinne's cooking," Evie said from the doorway.

"Evie!" Dorie jumped up to give her a hug. The two returned to the couch.

"Are you okay?" Evie asked Rett.

"A lot better," Rett assured her. "Thanks. Was I a total jerk last night? I wasn't very nice to Helen or Dorie, or Dad."

Evie shrugged. "You were fine."

"I've seen worse," Dorie said. "Heck, I've been worse."

"But not me," Rett said. "I'm not usually the focus of these family discussions."

Dorie laughed. "Right. You're usually the one with the answers."

"Ahoy, the house!" Corinne's voice trilled from the kitchen. The door slammed and she and Chad murmured. Rett felt suddenly exhausted and sank against the couch. Exhausted and totally supported. Her head lolled while she closed her eyes for just a moment.

She opened her eyes to Dad patting her shoulder. "Come on and have some dinner."

"What? Right," she said, struggling to rouse. "Coming."

She rubbed her face with both hands, then got up to follow him to the dining room. Taking her place at the old table, she looked around. Yes, all there. The kids, the sisters, Chad. Aunt Corinne, smiling over her shoulder, potholder in hand. Maggie and Callie. Mason next to his grandpa, of course. Everyone in their place. Just missing Helen, of course. And Harry. Her eyes stung, thinking of his warm smile and funny laugh. What if he never sat at this table again? What had she done?

Corinne brought a platter of baked salmon to the table. "Check this out," she said. "I happen to know it was caught this morning."

"Right," said James. "Caught down there at the salmon farm, you mean."

"Well, fresh anyway," Corinne amended, smiling. "Broccoli? Mashed potatoes?"

"Nice spread," James said appreciatively. "Thanks, Corinne."

"It was my turn," she said modestly. "You and Evie have been feeding me for months. Plus this way I get to see Rett and the kids."

Rett felt fragile under Corinne's smiling gaze, like she might dissolve into tears at any minute. Maybe she'd been better off sleep-deprived and angry. But no. Tears were just water, anyway. She smiled at her aunt. "Thanks," she mumbled.

By the time everyone had filled up and had Alice's apple pie with ice cream Evie scrounged from the freezer, she felt much better. The kids were dismissed to cartoons after taking their dishes to the sink, and the adults settled back with tea.

"Dad, did you have pie?" she asked. James had been managing diabetes for a few months.

"I did," he said. "Did you see what a sliver Dorie cut for me? No ice cream though. I'm doing good."

"You don't have to give up your life to live with diabetes," Evie sing-songed. "We've all been learning that, right, Dad?"

"Once I got you to stop policing every bite," he said with a grin. "Evie and I have been doing a lot better the last few months."

"Good," said Rett. She felt a stab of shame. "I've been so, I don't know, preoccupied, I guess, I haven't been paying attention."

"Not your job," James said. "Mine."

She scoffed.

"But," he went on, "I have been a dite worried about you."

Dorie snickered. "A dite."

"Then when Helen called last night," he went on, "that was it."

Rett sighed. "What, exactly, did Helen tell you?"

"She called me first," Dorie said importantly. "Woke me up and said to get over to your house. Then Dad called while I was on the way."

Rett turned to her father. "What did she tell you?"

"It doesn't matter what she said. Just that you were exhausted, needed sleep, and could we figure out some way to take care of stuff, so you could have time to rest."

"I don't believe you," Rett said slowly. "That's not a very compelling story at midnight, is it?"

"She said you were irrational, thought you were being accused of murder, and that you wanted to divorce Harry immediately," Dorie said rapidly. "Is that what you want to know?"

Rett sighed and looked around the table. "All of you heard that?" Evie and Corinne nodded gently. Chad was looking at the table but glanced up to meet her eyes.

"Well, that's mortifying," she said.

"Is it true?" Dorie pressed.

She looked over at the sideboard at her mother's picture. "Yeah, that's what I was thinking last night." Bringing her gaze back to her father, she added, "But not today. I slept until eleven, then took a nap, then took another one right before dinner. My brain is working a little better now."

"What is really happening?" Corinne asked.

"I did get a subpoena, but I'm not the accused. They think my colleague was to blame for those resident deaths," she said with a trace of anger.

Corinne was ever the social worker. "People don't like to think about dying."

"But long-term care homes are places for the end of life."

"Of course," Corinne agreed. "That doesn't make grieving family members any less sorrowful. Who thinks your colleague was to blame?"

"I guess the police. This deposition is to gather evidence for a trial. I over-interpreted it. Helen's helping me with that."

"No murder charge," James said, twinkling.

"Well not for me," she said. She would have to check in with Angelica. "I really felt accused," she insisted. "It's a terrible feeling. You know I lost my job and my license over this."

"You lost your license?" Corinne said, aghast. "How?"

"Suspended, anyway," Rett said. "That's why I've been trying to sell eggs and bread. I can't work as a nurse."

"I thought you were into urban homesteading," Dorie said. "That you were living according to your principles. Yours and Harry's."

"Well, yeah, sort of. I'd like to be paying the bills on time though."

"So that's why you're not working at the Downtown Clinic. I didn't know that part," James said. "Why didn't you tell me you were having financial trouble? I told you I'd help you out." He looked hurt and disappointed.

"Dad! That's not your job."

"My goodness, Rett," he said. "What are parents for?" He gazed into the distance.

She felt terrible. "Dad, your adult kids aren't supposed to be leaning on you," she explained. "You're supposed to be able to lean on us."

Anger flashed in his eyes. "The one who needs support gets to lean."

Chastened, she looked down. "I'm sorry. I don't like admitting that I'm struggling, I guess."

Corinne was still stuck on the license issue. "How can they suspend your license when you're not being accused of anything? That's terrible."

"Helen says we'll work on that."

"You're still a nurse," Corinne went on.

Rett pondered. "I am. I'm not so sure about going back to my job though. The fact that Angelica is under suspicion is outrageous. That has to be stopped."

"Hold on," James said. "That's not your responsibility, is it?"

"Well, I don't know. I'm responsible to tell them my point of view through this deposition thing."

"You don't have to go back to Streamside. There's plenty of work for nurses right here in the village," Corinne said. "If you want to stay here."

"I can't decide anything," Rett said. "I'm here now. I don't even know what to expect tomorrow or next week."

"What's this about divorcing Harry?" Evie asked in a small voice. "When is he coming back?"

Rett's eyes overflowed again. "I don't know," she choked out. "I don't know anything about Harry anymore." She dropped her head into her hands. Somebody slid a box of tissues her way, and Corinne patted her shoulder.

"Divorce?" Evie pressed.

She shook her head. "I was temporarily insane, I think. No, I don't want a divorce. I just want Harry to come home. I want this whole thing to never have happened."

She wiped her face and said, "Do you guys know how much it stinks to be crying in front of your whole family? Ugh."

"Yeah," said Dorie. "Especially when you're the bossy one."

"Ha ha," Rett said, but Evie snickered, and even James had a smile. "Have your fun, guys. I'm coming back."

"I have no doubt of that," James said. "I think maybe I'll sleep over to your house with the kids tonight, and you have another sleep-in."

"No, that's okay, Dad. I could probably use a month of sleeping in, but you can sleep in your own bed. Thanks."

"You stay right there," he insisted. "Dorie, help me corral the younger generation and get them over to their house."

"No prob, Dad," Dorie said, jumping up. She leaned over to say to Rett, "Listen to your father."

Chapter 38

H arry scheduled a visit to Jeannette and Paul into his second
to last day on site. The truck creaked into frozen ruts outside
Jeannette's little house. He swung out of the cab, absently patted the
dogs on the head, and called out as he climbed the porch steps.

"Hey, you," Jeannette said, leaning out the door. "Nice to see you."

"Nice to see you, too," he said. He couldn't have stopped his smile.
Her face was as dear to him as his own mother's might have been. He
stopped, hat in his hand.

"You coming in or what?" she snapped, but her eyes were smiling.
"I've got coffee."

He followed her into the familiar kitchen, sat at her table. She set
the brimming mugs on the table and sat across from him.

"I'm leaving tomorrow," he said, a little diffidently. "It's earlier than
I planned."

She nodded. "Good. You need to go home."

"How do you know these things?"

She gazed at him. "Anybody could see it."

"I miss my family," he admitted, feeling misty.

"That's good. It's good to miss them when you're away."

He scoffed. "Well, missing them makes it hard to get work done, but I think you're right."

"There is always more work."

"Yes," he said, and they shared a smile.

"Thank you so much for helping me," he said. "For letting me go into the woods with you. For tolerating my questions and helping me to see the medicines under my feet. I can't wait to find out what we've got growing in New Brunswick."

"It's no secret. Find an elder who knows," she advised. "If you don't ask, you don't find out. Sometimes white people don't ask."

"I've been one of them."

"Maybe. It's hard to know what you don't know."

"I'm trying to keep an open mind about that," he said with a grin. "I changed my thinking about a lot of things." He drank. "Can I write to you?"

"Sure. Where are you going?"

"Winnipeg, this week. After that, I don't know." He looked at the floor. "I think I'm going home. I realize now I'm not meant to be a scientist. It's not who I am anymore."

"Who are you, then?"

"I don't know. I don't have whatever drive I used to have."

"People change."

"I'm kind of ashamed of it. I don't know how to tell Joyce."

Jeannette laughed. "Joyce will have something to say about that, won't she?"

Harry nodded. "I owe her a lot, and I don't think she's going to be happy with me."

"Joyce doesn't have to be happy with you. You have to be happy with you."

"I hate disappointing people." He gave a heavy sigh. "It's not just Joyce. My wife too. My family sacrificed a lot for me to come out here, and now I'm saying I don't want it. The situation isn't great."

She looked at him. "You didn't know until you came. That's all."

"Can it be that simple?"

She shrugged. "Is it true? If it's true, it doesn't matter how simple."

He was oddly comforted. "It is true. It's been a hard lesson, and expensive." He stretched and stood up. "I'm going to go now. Thank you for listening. For the coffee. For putting me back together a few weeks ago. For everything."

She looked up at him. "I'm glad you came here, Harry Brown."

"I'm glad too. Do you know where Paul is? I need to tell him goodbye."

Harry caught Paul when he was home for lunch. They agreed Paul would visit next time he was in the Maritimes, and Harry agreed to the same should he ever return. He doubted he'd be back, but the idea of leaving forever this land and these people brought a pang of longing. Once he imagined bringing his family to meet Jeannette, his doubt evaporated. Of course he would be back.

Packing up for the university wasn't difficult because he'd been planning ahead, but preparing the field camp for the upcoming winter was a bigger job than he realized. Harry underestimated the time it would take, and when he finally left camp, it was late afternoon.

Two hours on the forest road brought him into town, where he'd have to stay overnight, since November days were short and the weather unpredictable. Before heading to the only motel, he stopped at the cafe where he could finally check his messages.

Scrolling down brought him to a series of emails from Rett. Excited to finally get caught up, he checked dates to read them in proper chronology.

Finding the first one, he felt a pleasant anticipation, and clicked.

Reading, his stomach dropped. "...Our marriage has broken down... I can't see a way forward, so I think we have to end it. That's the only way to solve this problem."

Now he felt frankly ill.

The server arrived carrying a menu. His appetite had evaporated, but he knew he had to eat, so he ordered something and returned to the screen. He re-read her words. "We have to end it."

It felt shocking, extreme. He'd been absent, sure. They hadn't talked in so long he could hardly remember the last time. He'd left his responsibilities. He'd left her when she needed him the most, with the stuff going on at her job. Then moving and even – he gulped – homeschooling. Was it the children? He'd abandoned all of them. Was that enough to make her want to end their marriage?

Things would only get worse when she found out he had nothing to show for what he'd put her through. If she already wanted a divorce, she'd be only more certain when she found out about his failure.

His hand shook as he clicked on the next note.

"I'm so sorry, Harry. Helen says it was temporary insanity and she's a lawyer, you know. I don't want a divorce. Things have been a little harder than I expected, that's all. It's all under control though. You just keep on getting your project going. I can't wait until we are able to celebrate Harry Brown, Ph.D. Love you. Rett."

He shook his head. Too much to take in, so he read it again. "It's all under control." That sounded more like Rett, but he still felt shocked.

Emotional whiplash, that was what it was.

First a divorce. Then no divorce. Things were so hard she was finished with him, and then she had everything under control.

It was a little hard to know how to feel, but one thing was perfectly clear. Her unrelenting support for his Ph.D. stabbed him in the chest. Divorce might be an option if she knew the whole truth.

He steeled himself to click on the next email. "Helen says to tell you I am going to give evidence in the case about the deaths at the care home. She is getting me a lawyer. They think Angelica is responsible, which of course is ridiculous. It's a mess, but it is all going to be okay. You don't have to worry about it."

How could he not worry? The server brought his food. With effort, he turned to his meal, but the sandwich tasted like ashes.

Divorce, then no divorce. Now she needs a lawyer, but don't worry. Guilt formed around his own tenuous hold on his future. He sighed. He'd never felt so alone and so far from home.

His mind raced. Rett couldn't be safe from prosecution if her supervisee was being accused. It was only a matter of time before Rett was also accused.

Why wasn't he there to help? But he imagined her throwing him out when she learned of his failure.

Guilt intensified. This situation was his fault. If only he'd been available, they would have talked regularly, and he wouldn't be catching up on his life by email. A wave of regret was followed by anger. If only she hadn't moved the family, got a new house, started that homeschooling stuff, maybe it wouldn't have been overwhelming. He might be to blame, but he wasn't the only one. If only.

He looked at the date of the last email: she had sent it over a week ago. He gazed out the window at the sere landscape, sorrow squeezing his heart. While he'd been in field camp, struggling to figure himself out, Rett, too, had suffered.

Something had to be more recent. He scrolled through the flood of university emails and, finally, he located a note dated yesterday.

"Everything's okay, Harry. The kids are doing well."

Had they been struggling, too? He pressed down a new layer of guilt.

"Dad is spending a lot of time with them. I have a good lawyer, who is communicating about my license and helping me with the deposition, which is on Friday. It's been a difficult time, but the Madison crew has jumped into the breach, as they do, and things are okay. Don't worry about a thing, just enjoy the work you are finally getting to do. I love you and miss you, and I am glad you are there. Dad took some pictures for you."

She included shots of the children dressed in pirate costumes, hanging out on the fishing docks, and painting pictures on an old kitchen table. His throat tightened and he checked his watch.

He sent a text. *Are you still up? Can you talk?* He waited, ten minutes, twenty. It was late in the Maritimes, he knew, but he had a Rett-shaped hole in his heart.

Before he slept, he sent another text. *I'm heading to Winnipeg tomorrow, starting early, so no coverage all day. I love you so much. Every little thing is going to be alright.*

He only hoped it was the truth.

Chapter 39

Rett woke in her childhood room once again. Luxuriously late, she relaxed over coffee and breakfast, then hiked through the woods to her house. She was a new human, bright-eyed and ready to do something.

Charlie tore across the yard to meet her, wagging and whining. Nanny Goat bleated a welcome. Frickin Chicken wandered over to peck at her sneakered feet, while the rest of the flock scratched at the fall-worn garden. The house, despite still being dilapidated, looked lived-in and cosy. It was funny what getting enough sleep could do. The roof was still falling apart, but it was okay.

She pushed open the kitchen door to music and giggles. Her father looked over Mason's shoulder, and the twins messed with paste, scissors, and coloured paper.

"Mum!" Maggie shouted, seeing her first. "Look at what I'm making!"

"Oh, my," she said, pulling off her coat and slipping into a chair. "Look at what you guys have going on!" She gave her father a grateful glance.

"Good stuff here," he said. "You're looking perky."

"I'm feeling a lot more perky," she said with a grin. The kids were eager to show her their work. When she looked up from that, James had vanished. She got up to find him in the living room, sitting on her big sofa. She sat across from him.

"Hey, flowers!" she said, noticing the bouquet on a side table. "Where'd those come from?"

"Your neighbour," James said, eyebrows raised. "What's going on there?"

She frowned and shrugged. "Is there a card?" Getting up, she found the little envelope and opened it. "Hmm."

"Well?"

"An apology," she said, looking up. "He got a little too friendly the other day."

"Out of line, eh?"

She sat back down. "Yeah. I've leaned on him for help around this place, maybe too much."

"A misunderstanding, then."

She sighed, gazing away. "Yeah. I could have been...sometimes I just don't know myself. It's been a hard fall, Dad."

James got up to put another log in the woodstove. "You've made a pretty nice little place here."

"Thanks."

Returning to his seat, he added, "I like helping the kids with projects for their schooling. That thing Mason's doing, he's doing math, and map reading, and even a little human biology, right there, planning out his camping trip. You've got Callie and Mags keeping records of the eggs they gather and sell. Arithmetic. Handwriting."

She nodded. What was he getting at?

"I'd like to help out," James said. "Maybe a couple mornings a week, be the teacher. Or the learning guide or whatever."

She was touched.

"I don't want to be in charge of anything," he added quickly. "But a few mornings would give you some time to work on, well, whatever you like. Your own stuff."

"That's great," she said soberly. "For the next couple of weeks, I'm going to have a lot of stuff to work on. Thank you."

He nodded. "It's my pleasure, really."

Later, Helen texted Rett with a list of action steps. Calling that local lawyer was first. Rett had something on her own list that came ahead of that.

"Angelica."

"Hi, Rett," Angelica said. "I guess you heard."

"I didn't hear anything," Rett said, "but I got a subpoena. What's going on?"

Angelica sniffed. "They arrested me, Rett. Right in front of Ricardo and Mama. Police car, handcuffs, my boy watching, Mama crying."

She caught her breath. "I'm so sorry," Rett said. "When did that happen?"

"It was so awful." Angelica was crying now. "It was so humiliating, and to have your family see that, it was just terrible."

Rett could feel it in her own body. She thought briefly of Mason's white face in the window as Jürgen kissed her. Her stomach clenched.

"Are you at home now?"

"Yes. But I can't stop thinking about it. Those people coming to get me, riding in the back of the police car, all my neighbours watching…" She dissolved in sobs.

Rett made a sympathetic sound. "This is a travesty," she said tightly. "Makes no sense whatsoever."

"They think I did something, maybe by accident," Angelica choked out. "I had to tell them, over and over, and now I keep going over and over in my mind. Maybe I did? Maybe I did do something to make those people die. But then I just can't imagine it."

"Listen, you have a lawyer, right?"

"Yes. I don't know how I'm going to pay, but yes, and she's good."

"Well, I have to give a deposition next week," Rett said. "I'll be telling them what I think."

"Yeah? What do you think?" Angelica's voice held a trace of hope.

"This whole thing is ridiculous. We both know it."

"Innocent people go to prison all the time." Angelica's tone was bleak. "There's a lot of people involved in this. The company looks better if they blame someone."

"We just have to convince them," Rett said sturdily. "Try not to worry, okay?"

Angelica gave a shaky laugh. "Easy to say," she said. "You're not the first person to say that to me."

"Sorry. I'm sure it's not helpful. What has helped?"

"Mama's church. They've been fundraising and my lawyer's a member, too. We're okay. I keep telling myself that."

"This whole thing stinks."

"No question about that," her friend agreed.

"Let's keep in touch, okay? Call me if you need me."

She sat on the couch after hanging up, thinking about Angelica. Why accuse her? Rett wondered. Why not both of us? She was ashamed of the relief she'd felt when she finally read the subpoena, not even considering Angelica. She was going to give the best damned deposition anyone ever heard.

Pulling up Helen's list again, she called the local lawyer.

Chapter 40

James took charge of her house and kids in the mornings. Rett used the time well. Sitting in her father's kitchen, she created a timeline of her last six months at work, referencing her personal calendar, her work shifts, her shifts with Angelica, and the dates there had been resident deaths. She collected information from Angelica, consulted with her lawyer, and wrote and rewrote her ideas.

Her lawyer, Lydia, warned, "They're going to ask you questions. You can prepare a statement, but you might not get to deliver it. Really this is about the Crown prosecutor getting to ask you all the things they've been thinking about."

"What might that be?"

"I don't know, obviously, but we can make some good guesses. Let's consider, and you can practice."

In the evening, she video-chatted with Helen, who listened to her statement and made suggestions. "How're you feeling about all this?" she asked.

"I'm good. It's so much better than months of not knowing. Now I have something to do."

"Some people need action."

"That's right. I feel like I was muzzled, but now I can tell everyone how bogus this entire investigation is. Angelica and I have been caught in the fall-out from a public relations campaign to divert attention from a fact of life. Hedge funds shouldn't be in the long-term care business," she stated firmly.

Helen laughed. "Well, you have your energy back."

"I do, at least about this," she said. "It sure helped to get some sleep. Dad's been watching the kids so I can meet with Lydia and do my own thinking. I haven't had this much time to think since I was in school, you know?"

"You sound a lot better than when I saw you in September. How are things with Lydia, by the way?"

"Great," Rett said with enthusiasm. "She really understands what I'm trying to communicate, and she's helping me put it into legal language. She's excellent."

"What do you think she'll be like to work with?" Helen's question caught Rett by surprise.

"I just told you. She's good."

"No, I mean as a colleague, not as a client."

Rett paused, then said, "Is there something you want to tell me?"

"I'm just thinking," Helen said quickly. "That's all."

"You're being mysterious," Rett said. "I'm willing to let it go though, because you've been so helpful."

"Thanks," Helen said. "What else do you need for Friday?"

"Your opinion. I want to tell Angelica what I'm planning to say. Would that be okay?"

"No." Helen was firm. "Not now. You don't want it to look like you're matching your stories."

"I wanted to support her," Rett said. "Tell her not to worry."

"I'm sure she'll worry no matter what you say, but talking to her now won't help and could harm. Call her afterwards."

Rett sighed. "Okay. I feel good about what I'm going to say, you know?"

"That's good, but it'll help her more if you deliver it in the right place."

Harry left town before dawn for the long drive to Winnipeg. Many hours down the road, his pinging phone informed him he was within range of a cell tower. He stopped on the side of the road to look at the texts that dropped.

Marie, offering him a place to stay. *Yes, please,* he tapped back, and gave an ETA.

Rett: *Call me, whenever you can, please just call me. The time doesn't matter.*

Sitting on the side of the road wherever he was, no real place except for a cell tower, he listened, tense, for the call to go through. He hoped she really meant it about the time.

"Harry?"

He softened on hearing her voice, releasing a fear he'd never hear her say his name again. "Yes, it's me," he said, eyes wet. "Hi."

"It's so good to hear you," she said shakily. "Where are you?"

"I don't know," he said. "Somewhere south of Thompson by the side of the road. I don't know how good the coverage is, but it is so good to hear your voice."

"You, too," she said fervently. "Things have been, well, complicated."

"I understand," he said. He was soaking in her voice, listening for every nuance. "Are you okay?"

She laughed. "Better than I was. Yes, I am okay."

"I'm so sorry," he said. There was so much to atone for.

"No, I'm sorry. Those emails. It must have been hard to read them. I felt bad, thinking about you reading all that mess."

"I should have been there."

"You should not!" she said. "You are doing exactly what you should be doing. It was just circumstances, really. All under control now."

He didn't believe her. "That sounds good. Friday's the day, right?"

"The deposition. Yes. Two p.m."

"Are you ready?"

She laughed. "Yes. I am totally ready. Lydia's been helping me, and I've got a nice statement, plus we've practised the questions she thinks they might ask."

"That sounds good," he said. "I wonder..."

"What?"

"I don't know the right way to say this. If Angelica is being accused, and you were her supervisor, why aren't they also looking at you?"

She was silent. "Rett?"

"I don't know," she said. "It's an obvious question. Great, now I won't sleep tonight, either."

"I'm sorry," he said. "I shouldn't have mentioned it."

"Probably not," she agreed. "It's an obvious and reasonable question. Your timing is off, though."

Harry felt lousy. "Yep, bad all around. I am so sorry."

"Well, either I am implicated or I'm not. On Friday, I'll make the point that neither Angelica nor I have any culpability. My lawyer would have warned me, I think, if I was at risk." Her words sounded more certain than her tone.

"I wish I could be there," Harry said.

"It's okay, really. Lydia is the only one who could come in anyway. You do your stuff, I'll do this, and when we get back together, we'll get everything sorted."

"The complications?"

"Yes, those. I have to get some sleep, but I am so glad you called."

"Me, too. I'll call you tomorrow, okay?"

"Yes, please. Good night, Harry."

He clicked off with a sinking feeling. Why couldn't he keep his worries to himself? He certainly didn't tell Rett anything about his failure as a grad student. Before he could start the truck again, a text came through. Rett.

Every little thing...

With a slow smile, he tapped back. *....gonna be alright.*

When he pulled back onto the road, he smiled, just a bit, as the truck picked up speed.

"You're leaving." Joyce sighed. "Have you considered the ramifications? I think you're making a mistake."

Harry gazed out her office window. He had arrived late last night and crashed on Marie's couch. Though tired, he still woke early. He had walked to the university, picking up coffee while he pondered how to tell Joyce he was leaving. He hadn't arrived at an answer before his appointment time, so there was no nuance in his delivery.

"I might be," he said, facing her. "It wouldn't be my first mistake."

She rose and paced the room. "We trained you," she said sharply. "You're finally turning into a decent assistant." She stopped walking and sighed.

"I'm sorry about that part," he said. "I appreciate everything I've learned, and especially the chance to live in field camp."

"I should have known when I sent you off to work with Paul you'd come back with some different ideas. And that Jeannette."

A laugh bubbled out of him. Clearly Jeannette meant something different to him than to Joyce. "That was a big experience."

She shook her head. "I didn't see it when we interviewed you, you know, online, but I could tell, once you got to camp, you weren't driven. Not like Marie. Not like Denys." She looked at him critically. "There is something burning in you, but it's different. Something else."

Surprised, he nodded. "I know that now, but I thought I was supposed to be a scientist."

She sat back down, folding her arms.

"It's hard to admit," he said, "especially when you've done so much for me. Getting a place on your team was a dream come true. I couldn't imagine failing. But here I am."

"Failing? You think you've failed?" She got up, pacing again.

Of course he'd failed. He failed Joyce and, worse, he failed Rett and the children. They sacrificed to let him go away to study, to become a research scientist. Here he was with a notebook full of scribbles, a camera full of pictures, and no idea what to do with his life.

"It will be a failure if you don't turn it into something. You only fail if you don't learn anything. You don't have to let this be a failure."

With a start, he remembered Joyce was a teacher as well as a researcher. "I don't know how to salvage it," he admitted, opening his hands.

"I guess that's your job, isn't it? You don't have to leave. We have your funding, and we have to spend it on you. Even though you don't have a project, there is lots of work. Have you ever taught? I'm short a teaching assistant now, and for next semester, too. We need someone in the undergraduate lab, too."

Harry felt torn. Teaching assistant sounded good, funding was a happy word, but he was also desperately missing his family. Rett. "You're making me think," he said. "Maybe I don't have it all figured out."

"Obviously. You only got as far as quitting." She sounded scornful. "You still have work to do, inside work." She thumped her chest. Her eyes bore into him. Maybe there were some similarities between Joyce and Jeannette. Something about seeing deeper than the surface. Or simply older and wiser. Older, wiser women.

"I can't fill your position mid-year," she said, sitting abruptly. "Even if you're sure about your degree – and I think you might be overreacting a bit – you can stay, teach, work in the lab, get your feet under you. Don't decide today. There are only three more weeks in the semester."

"I have to think."

"Let me know later today. I'd like to be able to count on you for a few more weeks."

"Thanks for your time," he said. "I'll let you know. I appreciate everything."

"Right," she said, but her attention was already gone elsewhere. He got up with a little smile. Similarities in age aside, Joyce was not Jeannette. But she'd been helpful. Maybe he could salvage something from these months away from home.

Despite Rett's misgivings, she decided to be direct and walked up Jürgen's front walk. Nobody answered the door though, much to her relief. For a moment, she thought she could avoid talking to him, but then she remembered Mason's pale face at the window and her own desperate email to Harry. For herself and maybe for Jürgen, she had to set limits. Flowers and apologies were nice, but she needed to make her point.

She was headed back home when his car pulled into his driveway. She saw his delighted look with some discomfort.

"Rett! So nice to see you." The car door slammed. "Do you want to come in?"

"No, thank you," she said. "I just wanted to talk to you for a minute."

"Of course," he said. Smiling, he walked close to her. He reached for her hand. She pulled away and backed up.

"See, that's what I want to talk to you about," she said.

"What?" he asked, taking a step toward her.

"Could you please just back up a little?" she asked, feeling her face flame.

"Of course," he said smoothly, stepping back. "I'd never want to make you uncomfortable."

Well, you've failed at that, she thought. "I am uncomfortable. Last week you kissed me, and that's just not okay."

His brow wrinkled and he leaned toward her. "I didn't mean to upset you. I just wanted to comfort you."

Now her brow was wrinkled. "Well, it didn't. I appreciate all the help this year. The chicken coop, the repairs, the rides now and then. I even appreciate the flowers."

"I know you do," he said. "I thought you appreciated me."

She sighed. "I do like having a good neighbour," she said with emphasis. "I don't need a boyfriend."

"Of course not," he said with a laugh. "That's not what I intended. Heavens. Not at all."

She felt slightly better. "Good."

"I just know that a woman, a vibrant, beautiful woman like you, Rett, a woman has needs," he said. "That's all."

"I'm married," she pointed out.

"He's away," Jürgen said pointedly back.

"Not relevant," she snapped. "Just to be clear, any needs I have are not your concern. Okay?"

"Okay, okay," he said, palms facing her. "That's very clear."

She softened a little. "Thanks for the good neighbour part."

"You're welcome."

"I'm going now," she said, and walked down the driveway toward her house. She heard him enter his house. As soon as she was safely past the big cedar hedge, she grinned.

Chapter 41

On Friday, Rett dug around in her dresser. She knew there had to be something suitable to wear, but so far she'd only found aged dress pants and a wrinkled white blouse. They would have to do. She stomped down the stairs, swearing under her breath, and grateful that the kids were at her father's house. Swinging into the kitchen, she gasped.

"Helen! What are you doing here? You're supposed to be in Ottawa."

Her sister sat placidly at the table, a mug in front of her. "Having coffee," she said. "Is that okay?"

Rett blew out a sigh. "Of course." She poured herself a mug. "I didn't even know you were in town."

"I had some business," she said mysteriously, "and it coincided with your deposition date."

"It happened to coincide, did it?" Rett said. "I'm not complaining. I'm stuck in the wardrobe department." She waved at the handful of fabric. "Hey, can you come with me today?"

"Sure," Helen said. "I can't come in the room with you, but I'll drive you into Saint Jacques."

"Thanks," she said. "I can do it, of course."

Helen smiled. "I know you can, but you can also let me help."

"Is it normal for me to be so nervous? I'm sweating just thinking about it, and I just got out of the shower."

"Perfectly normal. You have big hopes for today, don't you?"

"I need to clear Angelica of blame, make the police understand the nature of working in long-term care, and make sure I'm not implicated. That's all."

"The stakes are high. Let me see what you're wearing."

Rett held out the pants and blouse. "This is what I've got."

"You're kidding, right?"

"Don't be annoying. Maybe I should show up in scrubs."

Helen leaned back in her chair. "Well, you could do that. I guess it depends on the kind of impression you want to make."

Rett narrowed her eyes. "You look and sound a lot like Dad right now."

She laughed. "Thanks."

"I wasn't being complimentary."

"I know. I've got a suit you can wear, if you want to look like a reliable, professional person."

"Yeah, okay." A smile crept through her annoyance. "Thank you."

Waiting to be called in, Rett sat with Lydia, Helen sitting beside them. Harry called. Rett walked down the hallway to talk with him.

"Hey."

"Are you there already?"

"Yes. We're up in about fifteen minutes. If they're on time."

"How are you feeling?"

"Good enough. Helen dressed me up in a fancy suit, so I look like an Ottawa lawyer." She smiled though, looking down at the dark skirt and heels. "Pretty impressive, I must say."

"You'll be great," he said. She could hear his smile. "I know you've got things on your mind, so I won't keep you long. I wish I could be there."

Her eyes filled. "I wish you could, too," she said with a sniff. "I miss you."

"I miss you," he said huskily. "I'm counting the days, but I still have stuff to get sorted here."

"I know. You've got to get that project all worked out and keeping Joyce happy."

"A lot has been happening," he said. "I'll tell you all about it later."

"Good," she said. Lydia called to her. "Oh, I have to go. I'm up!"

"Good luck. I love you."

"Bye, Harry."

Harry gazed at his phone after she clicked off, staring at his children's faces on the home screen. Something in Mason's gaze disturbed him. He wondered how much damage he'd done by leaving them for so long. Failed as a graduate student, as a husband, and maybe even as a father. Shoulders bowed, he leaned over the library table.

He was torn between wanting desperately to get home, to hold his children, look into his wife's eyes, and his worry about how they'd receive his news. Shame lay heavy. He pulled off his glasses and rubbed his eyes.

A text popped up. Marie, inviting him for coffee. Oh, why not? Really nothing else he could do. He packed up his things and met her across the street.

"Joyce said you could stay, even though you told her you're not going to continue for your degree?" Marie was incredulous.

"I know. She was incredibly pleasant about the whole issue. Pleasant for Joyce, I mean."

Marie laughed. "She's not known for social graces."

"She invited me to finish the semester as a teaching assistant."

"She's been swamped with that undergrad course," Marie said. "She's been looking for help since September."

"Maybe I could rescue my reputation with her by helping," Harry thought aloud.

"You might like it. I can see you teaching."

He shrugged. "I never thought about it."

"Stay," Marie said. "It's only three more weeks, you can camp on my couch—it's no worse than field camp—and help Joyce while you figure yourself out."

"I've been trying to figure myself out for weeks. Why do you think it's going to happen now?"

"I'm optimistic. Besides, I need your help with the dissertation. I'm in the last throes of writing. I need someone to listen and critique."

"Good for you," he said. "You are going to finish this year, after all."

"I am," she said. "I'm still surprised about the progress. Beyond that, I'm looking for a professorship for next year, which is terrifying."

"You're moving, though. Momentum."

"Yes. Maybe that's why I can be optimistic for you, too." She smiled at him.

"Well, I guess I could stay through the end of the semester. It was part of the original plan." He swallowed. "I don't know how I'm going to tell Rett that I've failed at this project though. She's gone through a lot so I could follow this dream."

"The dream didn't fit you," Marie said practically. "You weren't deceitful. You just didn't know."

"It wasn't my dream after all, I guess," he said. "I wish I had known that before I put my family through so much."

She shrugged. "What's done is done, my father used to say. Now make the best of it."

"Good advice," he said. "Easy to give."

"You got in so late and left so early, I haven't told you my other news," Marie said, smirking.

"What news?" he asked, smiling back. "That's quite an expression. What's the big secret?"

"I met someone," she said. "Right when I got back to Winnipeg. He's a hydrologist, works as a consultant, and he's wonderful."

"You look happy," he said. "That's great."

"His wife died a couple of years ago, and he's got a little girl, Nell, who's three. Here, want to see some pictures?" She pulled out her phone.

"Look at that," Harry said. "You're finishing your project, you met someone, and now you've even got a child. I don't see you for a few weeks, and all that happens."

She was glowing. "Amazing, isn't it? A lot can happen in a short time."

He nodded. A lot can happen, good and not so good. He hoped his next few weeks would be about the good kind of changes.

Chapter 42

Rett emerged from the boardroom where she'd given her deposition as if emerging from under water. She looked around the hallway like she'd never seen it before. Lydia followed her to where Helen waited.

"Well?" her sister asked.

"I don't know. What do you think, Lydia?" Rett glanced behind her.

"It went well. You didn't hesitate on the questions, you were clear and concise, and they gave you enough time to make your statement. It could not have been better."

"Let's go celebrate!" Helen slipped her laptop into her bag. "Time for a late lunch."

"You two go ahead. I've got to get back to the office. Well done, Rett." Lydia smiled, then she turned to Helen. "I'll be hearing from you, yes?"

Helen shook her hand. "Soon."

The sisters settled into the cafe across the street, and the young
server poured coffee. Rett looked around appreciatively. "I haven't
been in Saint Jacques for a while. Not since I had coffee with Angelica.
It's nice to be in the city."

"It's such a little city compared to Ottawa, but maybe it feels cos-
mopolitan compared to Stella Mare."

Rett laughed. "Larger, anyway. When do you think I'll hear anything?"

Helen shook her head. "You won't unless something changes. The
court date is in three weeks. The Crown prosecutor must think there's
a case, or she'd drop it."

Rett sighed. "Poor Angelica. I'll call her tonight. No, actually, wait
a sec." She grabbed her phone and started texting. "Sorry, Helen. Just
a quick note to her and to Harry, telling them I'm done."

Helen sipped coffee until Rett put her phone down. "Helen, thanks
so much for all your help."

Helen smiled. "It has been my pleasure, truly."

"You even dressed me," Rett pointed out.

"It looks good on you." Helen eyed her critically. "You might have
gotten too thin, though."

Rett sighed. "Before you comment on my weight, tell me what
you're doing here. I can't buy that you showed up for my deposition."

"Why not?"

"Because you can't fool me," Rett said. "I'm happy you're here, for
sure, but you came in September, too, and before that we hadn't seen
you since Mum died. Like years, Helen. Dad was sick last summer, and
you didn't even come then."

"You told me not to come!"

"I don't remember saying that. I do know that Dad and everyone
has forgiven you for years because you live so far away, because your

life is so busy. But somehow you've managed to get here twice in three months. What's going on?"

Helen looked down. "You're right, this is different. I'm not ready to talk about it though, okay?"

"You're worse than me about needing anything. You've always been the got-it-together big sister, and I understand that pressure, but still. Two visits to Stella Mare must mean something."

"Please don't pry, Rett. You're right, but I can't talk about it. Not right now."

Rett's phone buzzed. "You're saved," she said, and picked it up. The text from Harry made her smile all over.

When she looked back at Helen, her sister said, "I can see you sorted that out."

"What? What do you see?" Rett put her hands on her flaming cheeks.

"Divorce is not imminent."

"No. Hopefully homecoming is imminent. Like in a few weeks. He's going to be teaching."

"Teaching? Starting in November?"

Rett shrugged. "Yeah, I don't get it either. As long as he's happy, it's fine with me." Her phone rang. "It's Lydia," she announced, and answered. "Hi."

"Hey, Rett. When I got back to the office, there was a letter here from your association. They have reinstated your license and will be issuing a formal apology. Congratulations!"

"Wonderful! Thank you so much!" She clicked off. "My license is back! I can work again."

"Great," Helen said. "Good news."

"Oh, such good news. I don't really want lunch. Can we get some champagne and a cake and go home? To Stella Mare? This is news to share with the family."

"You bet. What's your favourite bakery?"

That evening, the family gathered at James' for celebratory pizza. When even Mason had eaten enough, Corinne took the leftovers to the kitchen.

"Don't clean up," Dorie called to her. "We're having cake."

Evie served the cake on their mother's china dessert plates, and Rett poured tiny sips of champagne for everyone. Callie spat out hers and Mason surreptitiously poured his into a plant, but the adults seemed to enjoy it.

"To getting my license back!" Rett said, lifting her glass.

"To a great day in Saint Jacques," Helen added.

"To Mum," Maggie said, and then hid her face in Rett's lap.

"What kind of cake is it?" Callie asked.

Evie, busy serving, said, "It's pink. What do you think it could be?"

"Unicorn cake?"

"Maybe," Evie said. "What does a unicorn taste like, anyway?"

"Eeewww," Callie said.

"It's strawberry," Mason said, butting in. "Pink is strawberry."

Rett's phone rang, so she went into Evie's den to take the call.

"Angelica."

"Rett." She was crying.

"What? What's wrong? What is it?"

"I just wanted to thank you," Angelica choked out. "I just heard."

"Heard?"

"My lawyer. They're dropping the charges." A burst of sobbing made Rett's eyes water, even as her shoulders loosened.

"Wonderful. That's wonderful. Thank goodness. You scared me, there, with that crying." A burble of laughter escaped her.

Angelica laughed too, through sniffles. "Yes, happy crying this time. It can be hard to tell. But Rett, listen, thank you. My lawyer said it was you who did it. You convinced them there's no case."

"Me? Really?" Her chest was about to burst. Angelica was free. She was free. "It's over, really over. Finally."

"Yes, finally. I feel lighter, and Mama is laughing, for the first time since last summer. Oh, Rett, I am so grateful."

Rett straightened her back. "No need to be grateful. I just told them what they needed to know. The truth. People want you to be with them when they die, and you would never hurt anyone. It was simple."

"It was simple, but it sure got complicated."

"It did." Rett thought about the last months, moving to Stella Mare, chickens and goats, and baking bread, hanging up on Helen, Jürgen in the driveway, Mason in the principal's office. Harry far away, getting her email about divorce. "Yes, it got complicated. But now..."

"Now we can both go back to work," Angelica said with a sigh. "Streamside will have to take us back."

"Yeah." Suddenly Rett felt unsure. "At least we have options. I've got another call. Let's talk tomorrow, okay?"

"Sure. Rett, you're the best."

Smiling, she took the waiting call. "Hi, Lydia. We're having cake to celebrate my license."

"That's a great way to celebrate. Here's another bit of good news. The Crown dropped the charges against Angelica."

Rett laughed out loud. "Isn't it great? She just called me to tell me."

"You already know? News travels fast," Lydia said. "Her attorney let me know so I could tell you. You were persuasive today."

"I had a good team. Do you want to come to my father's house for cake?"

"Another time," Lydia promised. "Enjoy your celebration. It's been a long haul."

"Thanks. Good night."

The clatter and chatter in the dining room was the soundtrack of home, but Rett knew her face would get attention. "Well?" Helen asked. "Was that news?"

"Yes."

"What news?" Dorie asked, and the chatter quieted, except for Maggie asking for ice cream.

"They dropped the charges," Rett said, grinning widely.

Helen beamed, Evie exclaimed, and Dorie jumped up to give her a hug. "That's good news," James said with a wide smile. "Good news for sure."

"It's over. This nightmare is over." She thumped into her chair. "Where's my cake?"

Chapter 43

The best part about being in Winnipeg, Harry decided, was daily contact with Rett and the children. He checked in every evening before the kids' bedtime.

"Guess what we did, Daddy?" Maggie shouted, bouncing on her bed. "We made Christmas bread for the market."

"Christmas bread! It's not Christmas," he said, just to get her going.

"It's almost," Callie shouted. "We have to get ready."

Mason was single-minded. "When are you coming?"

"You know already," Harry reminded him. "Look at your calendar." Mason carried Rett's phone down the hall, sisters following. He turned it to the big calendar on his bedroom wall. "Right there," he said. "The blue square."

"That's right. In one more week."

"Mum says we're going to pick you up at the airport and take you out to lunch," Mason said.

"I'm going to hug you so hard," Maggie shouted. "Charlie too."

"I don't think dogs give hugs," Harry said. "It's the arm thing."

"Well, we'll hug you a lot then, Daddy," Callie chimed in.

"Are you kids about finished with your father? I want to talk, too," Rett called sounding far away.

"He's going to read us a story," Mason said. "Then you can talk."

"A short story," Harry warned. "You guys need to get to bed."

The three kids piled on Rett's bed while he read a story he'd written about a white wolf in the north. When he finished, they said good night and Mason handed the phone back to Rett. She carried it while they went to their respective beds and each one said goodnight to Harry. He waited while Rett handed out kisses, clicked off the lights, and carried the phone downstairs.

"Whew," she said, sinking onto the couch. "Thanks for helping with bedtime."

"My pleasure, in so many ways," he said. "What's with Mason? He asks me every day when I'm coming home."

"He misses you," she said simply. "So do I."

"Not for much longer. I'll be home soon. We do have to talk about next semester."

"I've been trying not to think about it," she admitted. "I'd rather talk about your time here at home."

"I need to tell you something," he said, his chest feeling tight.

"That sounds ominous," she said lightly.

"It might be."

"Well, hurry up then. Don't make me wait."

He gazed away, looking at the dusty, small-paned windows high in the wall of Joyce's lab. "I'm not going to do a Ph.D. project."

"What?"

He took a quick look at her face. "I'm not Ph.D. material. I found that out."

"I don't know what to say." Her face registered surprise and something else. Maybe it was disappointment. Harry's shoulders sank.

"I've failed at becoming a scientist," he said. "I've failed you and the kids."

She was uncharacteristically quiet.

He went on. "Joyce says this doesn't have to be a failure though. She thinks there is still something here to take home."

Rett shook her head. "Like what? You went out there to finish the training you started before Mason was born. It's been part of our whole plan forever."

"You think I'm not aware of that?" He was sharp. "I don't feel good about it, you know."

She sighed. "Listen, what's happened here went far off the plan too. I never thought we'd be homesteading in Stella Mare. I expected to work at Streamside until I retired."

He relaxed slightly. "Do you want to go back there?"

"I don't know. Probably not, but then what?"

"That's where I am too," he offered. "If I don't do the Ph.D., then what?"

"The big question," she said. "Then what?"

They were quiet for a moment. Then she said, "I recently discovered the negative consequences of trying to solve a problem too quickly."

"Was that when you said you wanted a divorce?"

She visibly tensed.

"I know that was my fault. I'm sorry you felt so alone," he said. "I wish I had been there for you."

She wasn't looking at him.

"Rett? Forgive me?"

"It's not what you think," she said flatly. "Something happened."

"Happened? What?"

"Maybe nothing happened," she backpedalled, "but it felt bad to me. The neighbour, Jürgen, you know him?"

Harry nodded. "You've mentioned him."

"He spent a lot of time here this fall. He makes himself at home, shows up any time of day, pours his own coffee, you know. He's been very helpful with the chicken house and other things."

Harry didn't like this guy making himself at home with his family. "So? Where's this going?" His heart rate was up and not in a good way.

"That terrible day the subpoena came, that day, he kissed me." She gulped. "I stopped it right away, but it happened, and I don't know if I was leading him on. I didn't think I was but..."

The world stopped. As if from a long distance, Harry heard himself ask, "What else?"

"Nothing else."

"Nothing else?"

"No. Nothing happened, but I realized I liked the attention. Which I hated. It made me feel so guilty, I couldn't think straight. I felt like a terrible person, like I had betrayed our marriage. All I could think of was to break up because I was such a bad wife. That was the night I screamed at Helen, and wrote you that awful email, and Dad and Dorie had to rescue me."

"Did something happen with that guy?" Harry needed to dig into this. His thoughts raced uncontrollably.

"Well, after I got some sleep, I went over to his house and told him he was out of line and he should leave me alone."

Harry's breath eased. "I bet you did."

"It was complicated because he was genuinely helpful. I didn't know there were strings attached. I'm so sorry, Harry."

"What are you apologizing for? It sounds like he was out of line."

"I sent you that email. I just wanted to fix how bad I was feeling, and if we weren't together, I didn't have to feel so terrible. I was trying to solve a problem that wasn't even a problem."

"Now I know what you meant about trying to fix things before you know what the problem is."

"I don't want a divorce. Ever." She shook her head.

"I don't either. Let's not try to solve everything right now. Some things take time, but we need time together," he said. "Not time apart."

She reached toward the screen with a finger; he could swear he felt her touch on his cheek. "You're right. Time together. Soon."

After their talk, Harry stayed late in the lab creating a learning activity for his undergraduates. It reminded him of doing things with the kids. Decide what you want them to learn, figure out what they need to play with, manipulate, construct, or reorganize, in order to learn it, and then make or find the materials. He hummed to himself as he thought about his students working through the lab early next week. Two more weeks until final exams, then he would be going home. This was not too bad. Not too bad at all.

Rett rose early on baking day. The hens had slowed production, so she ramped up her bread sales to make up for lost revenue. Maggie was right about Christmas bread; it was a good seller, and she'd streamlined the process, so production was smooth.

It was still a lot of work. She thought about her conversation with Harry as she kneaded the dough. Maybe it shouldn't have been such a surprise he was changing directions. She would never have imagined herself earning a living with her hands in sticky dough. She pushed and pulled, sprinkling flour on the pine table. He didn't know what he wanted any more. But did she? It was hard to be too angry with him when she found herself in a similar situation.

She formed the dough into a ball, dropped it into the buttered bread bowl, and flipped it over. As she tucked it into its warm place to rise, she looked at her organizing calendar. One of the kids had drawn yellow stars all around next Thursday, the day Harry was coming home. It would be okay.

The Wednesday night before Harry was coming home, the kids were difficult to put to bed. "You guys, you have to go to sleep," she warned them. "I'm not coming back up here, so just close your eyes. That will make morning come faster."

"Not really," Callie contradicted. "It takes the same time, no matter if you're asleep."

Rett sighed. "Just go to sleep."

Downstairs, she heated water for chai, refusing to respond to noises from upstairs. After about ten minutes, everything got quiet. She took her cup into the living room and settled on the couch.

Somebody rapped on the front door. She'd been keeping it locked against overly friendly neighbours, so she got up to answer it.

"Jürgen."

"Hello, Rett," he said with a smile. "May I come in?"

Frowning, she held the door open for him. "What do you want?"

"Is it time for wine?" He wandered over to the sideboard and picked up a glass.

"I'm not entertaining tonight," she said.

"Really?" He turned to look at her. "It's our last chance, isn't it?"

"Last chance?"

"Harry's coming tomorrow, you said. This is our last chance for a quiet drink together."

She snapped her jaw shut, then said, "You need to go."

"Don't misunderstand me," he said, still smiling. "I'm looking forward to meeting Harry."

She thought about Jürgen and Harry in the same room. "You need to go," she repeated, still holding the door.

He examined the glass. "You're letting the cold air in."

"I want you to go."

He put the glass back on the sideboard. "Maybe this isn't a good time. I'll see you tomorrow, and get to meet the famous Harry, who leaves his wife and children all alone."

"You don't know anything about Harry and me," she said. "Please go."

"I hear you," he said. "I'm going."

She closed the door behind him and turned the deadbolt with a satisfying click. How had she ever had any thoughts of being attracted to that man? She was revolted by his presumption.

Sinking back on the couch, she sipped her cooling chai. Her longing for Harry was a palpable lump, right in her midsection. It made her get up and wander the house, looking at the preparations they'd made for his arrival.

He'd never been here in this house, she reminded herself. How would he see the place? Her gaze became critical, seeing the age and wear of the house, but on balance, they'd made a pretty good home here.

She looked around the living room, at the crayoned welcome banner the kids had made. KD purred on the couch, and Charlie lay in the comforting warmth of the woodstove. Wandering around, she admired the little Christmas lights in all the oddly placed windows of the dining area. The kitchen's dim light came from the dining room and the moon just visible over the backyard trees.

It was a good house. She hoped Harry could see it that way. She and the kids had planned a big homecoming day for him, starting at the airport, and finishing with the necessary dinner at her father's house. Maybe she should take her own advice and go to sleep. It might make tomorrow come sooner.

Another rap at the front door made her jump. "That idiot!" She stomped into the living room but stilled when she heard a key in the lock. Who had a key? She was dimly aware of moving headlights as a vehicle left her driveway, but she was riveted by the door opening.

Chapter 44

"She's going to be some surprised," James said as he pulled into the driveway, moonlight spilling over the pavement.

Harry looked up at the house. Old, dark, overhung with trees in the front. Rett's van was parked in the driveway.

"It's quite a place. Is that a turret?"

"Yeah, it is. The kids have their playroom up there."

"I never saw the outside, except pictures of the kids on the front porch," Harry said. "It's not quite how I imagined it."

"Now you don't have to imagine," James said. "I'm going to drop you off, but I'll expect you all for dinner tomorrow night."

"You bet. Thanks for picking me up, and for keeping it a secret."

"Best fun I've had all week," James said. "Take care now."

Harry hauled his gear up to the front porch. Lights were still on in the downstairs, though he was sure the children would be in bed. He rapped once on the door, then used James' key to unlock the door.

He pushed it open with his shoulder and looked in.

She was the most beautiful woman he had ever seen. Beautiful in her sweats and hair a messy pile on her head. But she looked annoyed. Angry, even.

Then her face changed. "Harry? For real, it's you?"

He pushed through the doorway, leaving his gear behind, and reached for her. She stumbled a little but landed in his arms anyway. He clutched her, holding on as if he could make up for all the months of separation. Inhaling her, he felt her warmth right through his winter coat. She clung to his neck.

He kicked the door closed with the heel of his boot. No point in letting all this warm air out.

She giggled and pulled her head back to look at him. "You have totally ruined our plans."

He wasn't letting go. "So sorry."

"No airport trip, no lunch out, no big Daddy homecoming song."

"My bad."

"Nobody says that anymore. But here you are. Don't let go, by the way."

"I might like to take off my boots and parka," he said diffidently. "I'm getting warm."

"I thought that was just us."

He chuckled. "Could be. It also could be that I'm a bit overdressed for the living room."

"I can help you with that. I can help you with all of that."

Having crossed several time zones meant Harry was still sleeping when Rett got up, but she'd been literally getting up with the chickens for months now. She carefully closed her bedroom door and went downstairs. The morning routine came easily, though she still hated waiting for the downstairs to warm up after stoking the fire.

When Charlie came downstairs, she knew Mason wouldn't be far behind, so she poured two cups of coffee and put them on a tray. She carried it gingerly up the stairs. Leaving it on the floor near her room, she went to find Mason dressing quickly in the frigid temperature.

"I have a surprise," she said quietly. He looked up, intrigued. "Let's go get your sisters."

He followed her without complaint, and the girls roused easily too. "What's the surprise?" he asked.

"There's a surprise?" Maggie asked.

"Not Christmas," Callie said. "Not yet."

Rett laughed. "No, not Christmas. The surprise is in my room. Go ahead, you can go look."

Waiting in the twins' room she heard Mason whisper, "I'll open the door, I'm the oldest."

Squeals from the girls erupted . She followed them down the hall, picking up her tray.

Harry was in the bed, surrounded by kids. He was in fair danger of being hugged to death. Maggie ran back down the hall to get her latest stuffie to show him. Charlie thundered up the stairs and took a giant leap into the middle of the bed. Rett put the coffee tray on the dresser.

"Daddy is the surprise!" Callie shouted at her mother.

"Be gentle," Mason warned Charlie.

"Coffee?" Rett asked Harry. He pushed himself to sitting, kids all over him. "I don't have a free hand yet, but thanks for the thought," he said, smiling at her. "Hi, everybody."

"Daddy, we're going to the airport today," Maggie said, but then she stopped. "Except..."

"Except he's already home!" Mason was jubilant.

"I sure am," Harry agreed. "Right where I want to be." He looked up at Rett. "Come on in."

She shook her head. "Nah, I've got stuff to do," she said.

"What could be more important than this?" He raised his eyebrows over his armfuls of kids.

"You're right. Move over, Charlie. Make room for me." She climbed under the covers. Mason moved to let her snuggle with Harry, but then he sat on her lap. Harry leaned into her side, Mason against her chest, Maggie on her legs and Callie, who was leaning against Harry's other side, reached over for her hand.

"This is cosy," she said.

"This is us," Harry said.

"Can we stay like this forever?" Callie asked.

"No," Mason decided. "Somebody will get hungry." Charlie barked obligingly.

"Not me," Harry said. "I'm not breaking this up."

Rett giggled. "Well, it does feel pretty nice to be all squished up together."

"But I can't stay here forever," Maggie wailed. "I have to pee."

Mason scoffed. "Maggie, you're such a ..."

Rett laughed. "That's fine, Maggie. Let's all have a big squeeze and then we can let go. Ready? Squeeze...one, two, three!"

Charlie leaped down and Maggie trailed him down the stairs. The other kids got out of the bed. "The coffee offer still stands," Rett said to Harry.

"It was a pretty short night," he said, sliding down in the now-spacious bed. "I think you kept me awake."

"Oh, ho," she laughed. "Funny how those stories change, depending on who is telling them."

He pulled her down under the duvet with him. "Let them eat cake," he said.

"You mean junk food and watch cartoons."

"Whatever," he said sleepily. "Stay here with me."

"Oh, you are a mess."

"Time zones. I'll be better in a couple of hours."

She slid her arms around him. "Okay. I'll grace you a couple of hours, but then you're Daddy on call."

"Right where I want to be." He was nearly snoring as she slipped out of the bed and headed back downstairs.

Chapter 45

Harry was introduced to the animals, homeschooling, home-stead work, and living in Stella Mare. Three weeks together wasn't nearly enough. However, it was what they had.

The January morning Rett took him to the airport was cold. It was so early, the complimentary hotel breakfast wasn't open, but they made coffee in the room for the trip. Rett took a grateful swallow as Harry pulled the van into short-term parking.

"Are you sure you want to come in? You could just drop me off."

"No way. I'm losing you for twelve weeks. I'm going to get every last drop before you go."

"Sounds more like coffee than a relationship," he observed.

"You know how I feel about coffee."

"Maybe I should be happy to be in second place."

They entered the departures level. Harry reflexively checked the screen. "Looks to be on time. We have a little while before I have to go through security. Want to sit?"

"Sure."

Side by side, they stared at the people walking by.

"I really don't want you to go," she finally said. "I mean, I know you're going, and I'm glad you're going, but I really don't want to be apart from you."

"Same."

She looked at him, surprised. "Really? I thought you were looking forward to getting back there."

"I am. But that's not all. I wish you were coming. You and the kids."

She sighed. "It's only twelve weeks."

"Right. You're starting that new job, too."

She perked up. "I figured the Downtown Clinic was a good place. It just took longer than I thought."

"Your dad is very excited about being with the kids."

"I know. It's weird. He loves this homeschooling thing."

"Teaching feels good. That's what I'm looking forward to in Winnipeg."

"Yeah. One semester, and then..."

"That's the question, isn't it?"

"You know what? We will figure it out. We don't have to do it right now."

"We don't even know the right questions yet, do we?"

"Like what?"

"Like what is my career? Or, maybe, will we stay in Stella Mare?"

"Those questions," she said. She started humming.

"Everything really will be all right. We'll make sure." He chuckled, then added, "We do know some things. We know you're not going back to Streamside."

"We do know that much." She nodded her agreement.

"How about this one? Don't try to protect each other from worry. Worry shared is cut in half."

"Oh, I like that," she said. "Do you think you can do it? Tell me your worries?"

"I'm willing to try." He put his hand on her cheek. "I have another one. The most important thing is us, you and me."

"You and me." She gazed at him.

"We might be apart temporarily, but we're never alone. Partners in it all."

"The full catastrophe."

"The whole thing. No matter what." He stood, pulling her up by the hand.

"I'm going to miss you, and this time I'm letting myself know it," she said as they walked slowly to the security gate. "I tried to hide from it by staying busy, but we know how that turned out."

"No field camp this winter," he said. "We'll be in touch, so you don't have to feel alone."

"That goes both ways, doesn't it?"

"You bet. When we have each other, we're not alone."

"I'm going to try to be better with my family, too," she said. "They've all called me on trying to do everything on my own." she said. "Dad was especially annoyed with me, and Helen lectured me about you."

He laughed. "Nothing like family to show you yourself."

"Never the image you hope to see."

He stopped and turned to her, taking both of her hands. "Okay, this is it."

She looked at him, tears blurring her vision. "How do I keep this?" she asked. "This feeling of being us?"

"We need a selfie," he said suddenly. "Here, turn around." He wrapped his arm around her and lifted his phone.

"It's not a selfie, it's an us-ie. Two-of-us-ie," she said. "Besides, your arm is too short. You can't do it without me."

He held onto her as she reached up to click the button. "You're darn right I can't. And neither can you."

"Partners. All the time."

"Better together. Always." He held her close to his chest and gazed up at the phone. Her smile was there, though her eyes were full. He leaned his face into her hair as she clicked the button.

The End

Did you enjoy Rett and Harry's story?
Read more about the Madison sisters,
Dorie, Evie and Helen here. https://books2read.com/ap/8vMG-Gl/Annie-M-Ballard

About Annie

I write under the name Annie M. Ballard, and my women's fiction is set in the Canadian Maritimes, where I have settled after growing up in New England and living all along the East Coast of the US, plus Louisiana. The history of each place I've lived has been a part of what fuels and inspires my writing. I'm interested in how the geography and culture of places influence the people and the stories they tell about themselves.

My first book was about an American who came to the Maritimes to find the father she never knew. It's an exploration of place and the meaning of family. The Sisters of Stella Mare series is about four sisters from the same small fishing and tourist village, based on a real New Brunswick place. I capture realistic life experiences with an emphasis on how strong communities support us even in our most dire moments, and a focus on how everyday experience can be transcendent. Most of us live large lives within our own frame and that's what I want to share.

Want to know more?

Check out my website at https://anniemballar d.com.

Newsletter: https://www.subscribepage.com/newsfromannie

Made in the USA
Middletown, DE
03 July 2023

34514857R00205